THE GOVERNOR'S WITCH

VOLUME ONE OF THE BOOKS OF WITCHERY

KEVAN DALE

KEVAN **DALE** FICTION

GET SORCERY OF THE STONY HEART
FOR FREE

To instantly receive the free novella *Sorcery of the Stony Heart* and the exclusive novelette *A Spark of Will* (unavailable anywhere else) sign up for Kevan's free Readers Club at kevandale.com

1

THE GOVERNOR'S WITCH

It was no accident that the rich morning sunlight of Boston fell most spectacularly across my wide table. The intricate window at the high end of the hall—round, immense, and shot through with bright colors—illuminated me. Behind me, beams of black oak, shouldering the ceilings of whitewashed plaster, framed me. Waxed floorboards gleamed beneath rows of windows along the sides.

My stage, if you will. And I the featured performer: the Governor's Witch.

"And with the curve of the river, so near the forest as it be, Minister—" The man glanced up and found me looking him in the eye. His words caught in his throat, as happened. I suspected the patch I wore over my missing eye gave people pause. Striking. Dramatic. Iconic, even? My advisers flattered me it was the piercing quality of my good eye that unsettled people.

Straightening one of the trio of embossed seals before me, I offered the man a brief—but encouraging—smile. "Near the forest. Go on." I'd already decided to give him what he needed once I'd heard the tremor in his voice and watched his fingers crumple the edges of his hat: a floppy, threadbare affair that had caught the attention of more than one of the other council members.

He blinked. "And what with that little, narrow stretch, dropping over the rocks as it does, it'd be just right for a wheel, ma'am. Water wheel."

"For a mill of some kind."

"Yes, ma'am. Sawmill. Only it's—"

"Too near the boundary of the forest adjacent to Salem and thus, as with all acreage abutting the forests of that region, under the purview of the Lands Decree Act of 1738, specifically the decree's Provisions of Tenancy and Trespass, requires explicit dispensation from the province's Minister of Magickal Sciences. No?"

"I—I'm sure—yes, ma'am. I believe so. Yes. Minister."

"And the lumber you'll craft will be straight and true?"

"Ma'am? Ah, yes. That's the idea. Ma'am."

"See to it, then—I'll take that as a promise. Dispensation granted."

He stood there. Twisted his hat. I bequeathed him another smile: *Run along.* He turned, then remembered and bowed, thanking me.

Mary Whitelocke, pearl strands wrapping her neck and draping the front of her gold-embroidered vest and jacket, motioned for him to step to the side, where an aide escorted him back through the hall and out into the rest of his life.

"Straight and true," Mary said to me. "Your concerns over joinery are an inspiration to us all, Minister."

WITH NO MORE PLEAS TO ATTEND TO, the drama around the high table shifted to a minuet of paperwork. A busy minister was a worthy minister, clearly. Papers ascended and descended. A word or two, a signature or two. A letter might merit a brief look. The seals, a brass cup of wax kept warm, inkwell, quills—I might wield any or all. More often, an aide would handle the details at my nod. A claim. A report. A charge.

"It was the hat, wasn't it?" Mary offered.

My tea had gone lukewarm. A glance was enough to bring forth a server. As he lifted it away, I suggested that water in tea ought to be boiling, not simply hot.

"The way they looked at him," Mary continued. "Like wolves watching a newborn lamb stagger across the green grass of a meadow."

She wasn't wrong. The other council members were altogether too pleased with themselves. As though their finery set them apart. As though they weren't themselves beholden to the threads of power running through our ranks. One only had to observe their own choices of embroidered coatees, silken breeches, polished shoes, elaborately tied cravats. All bound by the flattery of fabric. The obeisance of hue. The curtsy of collar height. In Boston, such distinctions mattered.

"Well, we can't all be ready to thrill the portraitist at a moment's notice, poor fellow." Mary leaned against the far edge of the high table, one hand on her hip, the other at her chin. In the light from the window, she looked magnificent as ever. Graceful hands. Dark hair gleaming, tied back with a black ribbon, no strand out of place. Silken breeches above pale stockings. Delicate shoes.

The head of my guard strode from the side doorway, thin saber hanging from her white buff leather belt, hair in a tight braid, boots polished to a regimental sheen. Lieutenant Colonel Henrietta Brookshire—six inches shorter than me with a pleasingly rotund figure—intimidated most of the city. Skin the color of walnut set off the blue of her uniform and the pale insignia traced around her collar. Her eyes missed nothing, and the jut of her chin announced she had little patience for obstacles. She whispered to Mary.

Mary swept up the papers from the table and said to me, "She's arrived, Minister."

Was I the finest actor in Massachusetts? In all the Colonies?

In that moment, I believe I was.

Nary a hint of my incandescent rage showed. I likewise refrained from flinging my arms wide and setting the entire hall and everyone in it ablaze, curtains of searing flame leaping from my palms.

Though that would have made for a spectacular exit.

2

A SINGULAR SITUATION

The carved doors along the southern wall were opened for me. I passed into the long hallway beyond. Cream-colored wainscoting and green silk wallpaper glowed where sunlight hit them. A fine-legged table held an alabaster bust of the late Doctor Ephraim Rush, my predecessor in the office of Minister of Magickal Sciences. I let the sight of him calm me.

By a stairwell descending from the balcony level of the hall stood a woman with brunette hair loose upon her shoulders. Skirts of plain muslin, good needlework around the waist. Small flourishes of lace decorated the shoulders and cuffs of her dress. No more than five years my senior, she looked me over with obvious disappointment. Perhaps if I'd appeared in a burst of lightning and brimstone?

Though I was tempted to have her removed in just such a fashion.

"Mrs. James Spenser, Minister," Henrietta announced, stepping off to the side.

"Mrs. Spenser," I said. "I hope you haven't been waiting long?

My staff has a terrible habit of keeping important guests standing around while the all-important paperwork they worship is attended to."

"Not terribly long," she said.

I gave her a tight smile and set off by the tall windows lining the hallway. Perhaps she'd expected my full and immediate attention? By some accounts the most influential woman in the province, she might well have imagined Ten Gables fully at her disposal. As my staff fell in after me, Spenser hurried along to catch up. I didn't slow for an instant until we reached my private audience chamber. A musket inlaid with elaborate golden fleur-de-lis hung above the mantelpiece; I'd yet to fire it, tempted as I was when a meeting dragged on too long.

"And how might we assist you, Mrs. Spenser? I confess to being rather curious as to how you should find yourself in need of a '*doe-eyed chimney sweep playing dress-up, gifted with an inherited library, intimations of magic, and little else.*' If I recall your words properly. Which I think I do."

My rise from a penniless apprentice to the office I held was an endless source of rumor in Boston. The money I'd had bequeathed to me, the bookshop I'd run for the better part of a year before selling upon my appointment, my influence over the curious design of Ten Gables itself: each step along the way questioned, loaded down with ridiculous assertions, freighted with hidden meaning. No one had done more to keep such talk alive as Spenser herself.

"Perhaps my coming here was a mistake." Spenser didn't look away, and her words didn't falter. My eye patch—or my piercing good eye—didn't have the same effect on her as on others.

Maybe if I reached for the musket?

"Yet here you are," I said. "I don't imagine you a frivolous woman. And I'm willing to listen." I adjusted the cuff of my jacket. "For the moment."

With a glance at Henrietta and Mary, she said, "My situation is of a sensitive nature."

"Secretary Whitelocke and Lieutenant Colonel Brookshire are well aware of the confidentiality this office demands. Fully versed in the details of every situation I involve myself with. You may speak freely in their presence."

She treated them to the same quick, discounting appraisal I'd received outside the hall. "Very well. But I must count upon your discretion."

"Says the one with the endlessly prattling printing press." Mary sniffed. She folded her hands behind her back.

"This isn't easy for me, Secretary Whitelocke."

"Whyever might that be?" Mary asked.

"I take nothing lightly, Mrs. Spenser," I said. "I'm charged with protecting the citizenry. Whoever they may be."

Or whatever they may have written.

She said nothing further, regarding me. I wondered if she hoped for me to quote from another of her broadsides. I settled for holding her gaze until she blinked.

"It's my brother. Gerald Phipps Jr.," she said. "I believe he's done something—dreadful. No. I *know* he has."

"Go on," I said.

"Involving—well, a woman. Who is now a corpse."

"Are you saying your brother murdered someone?" I studied her expression, my curiosity piqued. I'd long thought of Mrs. James Spenser as sharp-witted, opinionated, incisive, and troublesome—not as someone willing to swallow her pride to protect a sibling.

"Not exactly," she said. "Though maybe in a narrow sense. Possibly."

Henrietta arched an eyebrow. "I don't think murder generally involves so many qualifiers."

"No? Well I don't believe a dead woman generally speaks, sits up, or thrashes relentlessly. Amongst other *qualifiers*," Mrs. Spenser said. "A singular situation which seemingly places it within Minister Finch's...area of expertise."

The remnants of the fire shifted in the hearth, sending a twist of embers into the flue.

3

NOT AS STILL AS A CORPSE SHOULD BE

I placed another quartered piece of maple in the hearth, reviving the fire. Behind me, the door opened, and a servant entered, bearing a tray with a teapot and four fine-handled cups. He placed the tray on a hutch next to one of the eastern windows.

"We'll serve ourselves, thank you," I told him.

He left. I poured four cups—the tea steaming satisfyingly—and brought one to Mrs. Spenser.

She'd taken a seat. "Grace Susanna Stoughton," she said. "Age seventeen. Her father is one of the richest sea captains in the city."

"And you say she's dead?" I said.

"Oddly enough, I ran into her just this morning in Cambridge. Making her way to the schoolhouse where she helps the teacher with the younger children."

"So she's *not* dead?"

"She seemed hale as ever."

"Then I'm afraid I don't understand."

"I also saw her corpse last night. Without question dead. But soon enough, not quite as...*still* as a corpse should be."

"And how do you account for this change in condition?" I asked.

"It's not a change," Spenser said. "Forgive me, I've been unclear. There are—seemingly—two Grace Susanna Stoughtons at the moment. The Grace I saw this morning: one. The more or less deceased version I saw last night: two."

"Then you're mistaken," Henrietta said.

"I would very much like to be mistaken, Lieutenant Colonel Brookshire. I'm not. Nor am I given to flights of fancy, or easily confused. I run the most accurate news gazette in the colony and have rightly earned the reputation of being a fair, concise, and truthful purveyor of information. Whether that leaves people happy or not."

"No one is impugning your reputation, Mrs. Spenser," I said. "We're just trying to understand."

She half closed her eyes and shook her head. "After seeing Miss Stoughton this morning, I went back to where we'd left her, thinking I'd been mistaken as to the extent or nature of her condition. But, no. While she walks the streets of Cambridge as though without a care in the world, she also claws and pries relentlessly at the door of the root cellar we locked her in."

"We?" I said.

"Gerald and me. It's his fault, naturally. And I'm left trying to clean up his mess, as ever. Why, look where it's brought me, of all places."

I ignored the urge to make the fire flare to life dramatically. "Perhaps if you start at the beginning."

"Last night," she said, "I was setting type in the print shop of the gazette, somewhat after eight o'clock. The weather, if you recall, was abysmal. Rain lashing the windows, thunderstorms shaking the beams. Gerald banged on the door. He looked like a madman. Soaked, muddied, desperate. I could barely get a coherent word out of him as he pleaded for me to help him, that he'd done something terrible, did I have any whiskey to steady his nerves. When I finally got him to focus, he wiped the hair from his eyes and stared at me. 'I've killed her,' he said. 'They'll hang me.'"

"Not words one wants to hear from one's brother," Mary offered.

"No. Though I can't say I was surprised," Spenser said. "Not that Gerald is violent, or ill-tempered. Quite the opposite. It's just that he's selfish beyond all accounting, incompetent beyond any familial explanation, and frequently in the grip of an impulsiveness of the poorest sort. Calamity, inevitable."

"Remind me to not have you write up my obituary," Mary said.

"What had he done?" I said.

"He didn't say, not then. He only pleaded for me to help him. And of course I did. Not for his own sake, mind you. I did it for our father." She paused. Put her tea down. "My father is deep in the twilight of his days. Failing alarmingly. I only relay this to underscore my contention that the slightest whisper of controversy reaching his ears will do him in."

Judge Gerald Phipps—renowned throughout the province as a learned minister, onetime vaunted captain at the Maine frontier, lieutenant governor for five years, respected magistrate in the decades since—was a political institution in his own right. His influence could make or break most governing endeavors. Or governors. Or their ministers.

"So I wrapped a shawl around myself and followed Gerald out into the night," Spenser continued. "I felt like the wind would blow me from my horse. My brother rode behind me as we made our way to a thin strip of forest against the fens. My family owns a small boat shack there, though I don't think anyone's used it in a decade."

"Did you notice anything unusual as you neared the shack?" I asked. The infernal might make itself known through senses, impressions, or harder to define instincts.

"Only how fierce the storm had gotten," Spenser said. "And how stepping into the shack gave me little relief, given that it was dripping and musty and dank. Rather dreadful—yet about to get worse. Gerald fumbled for some time with bringing a lantern to flame. The light soon revealed Miss Stoughton splayed out on a knitted blanket on the dank floor: pale, still, and lifeless.."

"You're certain?" I asked.

"Her skin was cold. She wasn't breathing, and I couldn't find a pulse on her throat, chest, or wrist. The tissues beneath the backs of her feet had grown dark. She was dead."

"Take me back for a moment," I said. "They knew each other how?"

"Apparently, Miss Stoughton had struck up an interest in Gerald. Whether it was romantic or of some more charitable, innocent nature, well, Gerald certainly took it as the former. In his telling, they conversed regularly, discovering a shared fondness for tales of ghosts. They alighted on the idea of communicating with the spirit realm." She looked at her fingers, twisting her gold wedding band. "They'd decided to experiment in an abandoned meetinghouse north of here, apparently haunted.

"I can only imagine them jumping at shadows, frightening themselves. Gerald no doubt hoping Grace would jump straight into his arms. And something went wrong, he claimed. He wouldn't say what—but it left Grace either witless and dying, or dead already. He panicked and fled. He panicked some more, only then returning to fetch Grace. Not to help her, mind you, to cover his own misdeeds. He rode through the storm to the only place he could think of to store a body: the shack by the fen. In his haste, he didn't tie up his horse and it wandered off. So he ran into town to fetch me as though I were waiting for nothing more than to help him out of such a ghastly mess."

Henrietta said, "You said Miss Stoughton didn't remain dead."

"No. She didn't."

"Tell us about that," I said. "In as much detail as you recall."

"Would that I recall less than I do. It started when we were arguing. Gerald insisted we bury her right then. In the fens, at the height of the storm, and thereafter claim ignorance. He met my objections with a sudden concern for our father's reputation and health. That didn't go over well with me, I can assure you. He then took half a step back from that immoral precipice and suggested we carry her to the shore to leave her down by the rocks. It would be a mystery. A tragedy. Unexplained. That's when I noticed the sounds."

"What sounds?" I asked, more than a little familiar with the ways of demons. From incoherent and primitive vocalizations, to insidious suggestions delivered in perfect diction, I'd heard the gamut.

"Yes. Sounds. Coming from Miss Stoughton. A thick groaning. You might imagine my relief—for she clearly wasn't dead, whatever we'd surmised. That was a lovely handful of seconds. I almost relaxed. Until she sat upright and twisted her head around nearly backward to look at us. She spoke—and not kindly. In fact, I've never heard such vile language." She met my eye. "I'm no delicate thing, Minister Finch. In my work, I deal with all sorts. Fishing hands. Sailors. The condemned. Thieves and constables. Soldiers. Prostitutes. Council members. I've spent enough time around those and more that I don't get the vapors at the first syllable of rough language. But what she said, well, Gerald put his hands to his ears and nearly ran from the shack."

"Personally offensive," I said. "Carnally suggestive. Delivered with an unmistakable malice."

"Yes."

"Likely a demon."

"But she was dead."

"The demon staked a claim."

"In her body?"

"In her corpse, yes. It can happen." I'd certainly seen enough of it. "What else did you notice? Did the temperature change—plunge, perhaps?"

"I was already shivering from the rain. But maybe."

"Fetid odor?"

"I assumed it was the fens. The mud. Or something dead in the shack. Dead before Miss Stoughton, I mean."

"Did any items move of their own accord or in a strange fashion?"

"Do you mean aside from Miss Stoughton? Or, as you say, her corpse?"

"Aside from her, yes."

"Not that I noticed—but my attention was rather fixed on the horror in front of us. By this point, my brother had chivalrously backed halfway out the door. I only gaped as Miss Stoughton clawed her way clumsily to her feet, watching me the entire time. Gerald begged me to get back and run."

"You didn't," I said.

"Of course I didn't. She hardly charged me like a Saxon warrior. More like a tosspot staggering out of the Pickett House down by the wharf. So I trussed her up like a runaway calf, using a dusty coil of rope hung from a peg in the corner. I found some sack cloth for a gag. Then we rode her to my house and, well, stuck her in the root cellar. It's the only place I could think of."

Had Mrs. Spenser grown a shade paler?

"If that were the whole of your story, Mrs. Spenser," I said, "I should be concerned, but not overly so. Demons are not to be trifled with, but they can be dealt with. Tell me more about this other Grace Stoughton. That part of your story troubles me."

"There's very little to tell beyond what I already have," Spenser said. "I saw her walking through the center of town this morning. The very last person I expected to see."

"Did you speak with her?"

"No. Lord, no."

"Perfect chance to clear things up," Henrietta said. She stood near the door, hands folded, head tilted. "Whether it made Miss Stoughton happy or not."

"Or," Spenser said, "a perfect chance for her to raise her arm in accusation, shouting to all within hearing that I'd kidnapped her, trussed her up, and locked her in my root cellar."

"Tell me how she looked," I said.

"As she ever does. She's young. She's pretty. On the short side. Fair hair, long."

"Her manner."

"As though without a care in the world."

"And what was she wearing?"

"A plain dress. Homespun. A dark cloak—the morning was chilly." She narrowed her eyes. "I think it was the same cloak."

"How did it look? I assume the events of the evening hadn't left it spotless."

"No, her cloak—at least when I stuffed her into the root cellar—was as muddy and soaked as my own. Worse, even." She paused. "All I know is that my heart practically stopped in my chest. I ducked behind the corner of the soap boiler's shop. Like something Gerald would do. Appalling."

"Where was she headed, could you tell?" I said.

"I don't know, and I didn't wait to find out. I lifted my hems and hurried back to my house, certain I'd find the root cellar door pried open somehow. And probably surrounded by the local constable and his men. But, no. It's still locked up tight. She was still growling behind it. Knocking into it. Kicking it. Unmistakably her."

"And Gerald?" I said.

"He spent the night—what little remained of it by the time we locked the root cellar—at my house. In a spare room. He's still there."

"I'll need to speak with him. I can be at your house"—I glanced at the clock by Mary's shoulder—"within the hour."

Mrs. Spenser rose. "I can count on your discretion, Minister Finch?"

I raised my chin and rested my fingertips on the table between us. "Protecting the province from any form of infernal threat is my charge, Mrs. Spenser. You did the correct thing in bringing this matter to my attention." I saw no premeditated culpability by Gerald—aside from a catastrophic lapse in judgment to meddle with the unseen. For the moment, I accepted Spenser's interpretation of the events as an accident, barring any evidence to the contrary. Should that not turn out to be the case, however, I would see justice done. Discretion only went so far.

Her gaze fixed on mine. "And my family name?"

"I'll do what I can."

She scrutinized me for a moment before turning to go. Henrietta saw her out.

MARY RESTED her hands on the back of one of the spindle-back chairs. She clicked her nails against the wood in quick triplets.

"You've a comment?" I said.

"The governor is no fan of Madeleine Spenser. Or her family. He might be pleased to have something against them."

"True. Yet he'll also insist I do nothing to help her or her family. Where will that leave them?"

"Exactly where they deserve to be?" Mary said. "Besides, the governor most likely already knows she's come to see you. He'll want to know why."

"How would he already know?"

"There are two people in Boston obsessive enough to know what's going on everywhere, all the time. You're one. And our ever-cautious governor is the other."

I turned to the window. "Mrs. Spenser needs a demon taken care of."

Click, click, click. Click, click, click.

"You may say what you wish to say instead of tapping it out in code upon the chair," I suggested.

Mary stilled her fingers. "Mrs. Spenser announced to the world two weeks back you're a witch. '*The Governor's Witch.*' An epithet now whispered across the city and farther. She's caused you trouble we're not even aware of yet. I'd have had Henrietta toss her out."

A trio of gulls rode the breeze over the harbor; if I were a gull, I suspected I wouldn't feel quite so suffocated. "Mrs. Spenser needs a demon taken care of."

When I added nothing further, Mary said, "Fine. I'll tell them to have the horses readied."

She turned and left. The fire huffed in the grate.

4

A STATUE OF ASHES

The door to Mrs. Spenser's house opened, revealing a man of about my age, his pale eyebrows raised. His face might charitably have been called cherubic. He'd clearly not shaved in days and faint golden stubble ran from cheek to throat. His eyes were a sharp blue, a clear contrast to an otherwise soft impression. Stained breeches. A too-tight shirt. Woolen vest.

"Gerald?" I said. "Your sister sent word we were coming, I gather."

He threw open the door and attempted to compose his collar while sweeping his arm inward. "Minister Finch. An honor and a pleasure."

I stepped inside, removing my hat. "This is my assistant, Secretary Whitelocke."

He swept back a lock of hair that had tumbled into his eyes. "Well known. Whitelockes of Boston. Also an honor, madame. I once played cards with your brother, Grayson. A memorable evening. I hope he's well. A genius at cards. And repartee. Please give him my regards."

"I'm sure he'll be delighted," Mary said.

"Mrs. Spenser is here, I take it?" I said.

The kitchen lay in the clutches of a riot of books, papers, notes. At the table, a half-finished work of point lace in an embroidery hoop, a spray of violet and lavender flowers extending from a basket. I found the last surprising; Spenser didn't seem the type.

"Sadly, no. An issue with our father called her away—as it is a day ending in the letters *d-a-y*." Gerald glanced outside at Mount Auburn Street before closing the door. "No soldiers come to arrest me—that's rather a relief."

"We don't need soldiers to arrest you," Mary offered. "We don't even need a warrant."

He swung his head to her, eyes wide.

"We're not here to arrest you," I said.

"I wouldn't put it past my sister," Gerald said.

"She helped you when you needed it."

"Self-serving, and don't believe a word otherwise. If it weren't for her concerns over our father—well, I shudder to think how tightly the manacles would fit around my wrists." He rubbed them as though the very mention conjured cruel iron. "Oh, she'll convince you how level-headed she is. It's her trick. Everyone finds her so impressive; such a sharp, intimidating, yet undeniably charismatic woman. Yet she's more trouble than you'd ever guess, which I may attest to as one who's known her all my life."

"Spoken like a loving sibling," Mary said.

"Yes, and I'd feel terrible if I weren't utterly certain she treated you to an even less generous depiction of me. Am I incorrect? Of course not. Gerald, the slavering fool, the reprobate, the disappointment of the Phipps lineage. As unfocused as I am unattractive. Stop me when I stray too far from what she told you."

A mug sat on the table. Ale fumes paced Gerald's words—which helped explain his going on like that while he had an undead woman in the cellar. From below the floor, a thump.

"Miss Stoughton remains in the root cellar?" I said.

He held out his hands, closing his eyes. "On second thought, whisk me to the safety of the Boston jail. It's all more than I can bear."

"Gerald."

"She remains in the root cellar. Her remains remain in the root cellar, as it were. Yes. She's there. This is the worst day of my life. And I've had more than my share."

"Tell us what happened."

"Can't we leave it at a generous '*And all hope died*'?"

"More detail might be useful."

"Fine." He opened his eyes and lowered his hands. "And it's not what Madeleine thinks, whatever she told you."

"She thinks you lured Miss Stoughton to a remote locale in order to scare her into your arms," Mary said.

"I—what?" His eyes widened. "Scare her? No. Ridiculous. She would think that though, wouldn't she? Inconceivable that I might possess even a few grains of native charm. Or talent. How could I possibly? I don't spend all my time hunched over a stack of deathly boring books, my eyes drying out, my teeth wearing down to nubs as I munch the sand that is the study of law. Yet another strike against me: I'm not compelled to work around the clock to better outrun the ghosts of the past, piously regarding even a moment of relaxation as a sinful indulgence."

I ignored Mary's glance in my direction.

Gerald continued, "And even worse, I no longer tremble at the thought I might not ever live up to our father's talent at whispering directly in the Lord's ear in between leaping from one great accomplishment to the next, as have done generations of Phipps men before him. Therefore, I'm not worthy. A failure. And what might a failure need in order to find a hint of genuine affection? A devious trap—a faulty one, in my case. Elementary."

"So you didn't?" I said.

He raised his arms to the ceiling. "Of course I didn't! I would never. She's infuriating, my sister. Tell me, Minister—do you have a potion or spell to do away with noxious judgmentalism coursing through a person's veins with every beat of their heart? She's about five foot five inches, let's call her one hundred and twenty pounds. In case you want the proper dose. But don't skimp, she's an extreme case."

A muffled howl rose through the floorboards. "Why don't you take us to the root cellar?" I said. "We can start there."

"An unpleasant place to start—though a worse one to finish, granted." He turned and crossed to a hallway extending from the kitchen, grabbing the mug of ale as he went. He took a pull. "A love trap. Ridiculous. Grace and I are friends. No more. Very good friends. Confidants with a penchant for the uncanny."

"What were you hoping to find?" I asked, following.

"Not a future for her groaning in my sister's root cellar. It's tragic."

"And the other Grace your sister saw?"

He paused before a narrow door. "Where to start? The ghost we'd been searching for? The ghost of hope? Perhaps the ghost of my sanity? Or maybe I'm the ghost." He gave me a harried smile as he opened the door. A dark stairway led to the cellar. "That's but a small sampling of my thoughts on the matter, Minister Finch. The production of which appears to be endless, pushing aside all else."

The groaning we'd heard in the kitchen grew louder. Gerald turned and descended into the darkness.

"You haven't spoken to her—the other Grace?" I said.

"Risky. Also terrifying. Neither appeals."

The stairs were of rough construction. Fieldstone walls and a dirt floor, though neat, exhaled a dank mustiness. The beams were low and swept clean of cobwebs. Mary followed me, her boots loud on the steps. A lantern burned on a small table in the middle of the room. In the far corner stood a small gray door set into the wall. The thick latch holding it closed had been nailed in place beneath a scrap of pine board. A far cry from delicate embroidery.

I sensed the demon immediately.

"She hasn't sought you out?" I asked.

"I've been hiding here. Too paranoid to even creep to the outhouse."

A strangled cry of frustration burst from behind the root cellar door. The door shuddered, struck again and again from the other side.

"Not that I particularly cherish my time here," Gerald added. He drained his ale and put the mug heavily down on the table.

"Let me out! Let me out!" came a hoarse cry, a voice strained to tatters. "He's kidnapped me! Ravished me! Please—help me, call for the constable, tell my parents!"

Gerald regarded the door without expression. "I didn't, of course."

"You did," the voice snapped. "And when your sister left, you dragged me out and lifted up my skirts, put your face there. Held me down. Rode me like a rocking horse!"

Gerald shook his head. "A lie."

"I understand." I approached the door. A current of frigid air grasped the back of my neck, my cheeks, my hands. "Tell me your name."

"Grace Stoughton. Please, I beg you. I beg you." The raspy voice collapsed into sobs. "I only want to leave. To see my parents. I won't tell anyone what he did. I won't make accusations. Anything to be freed."

"Tell me your name," I repeated.

"Grace. Grace Stoughton."

"Your middle name?"

"I don't have one. The eldest daughter in my family never gets one. Because of my great-grandmother."

"It's Susanna."

"That's what I said!" The timbers of the door frame shook as the slamming resumed.

I turned to Mary. "Hume's Third, if you would."

"I'd be delighted." With that, she peeled off her black riding gloves, folding them and putting them next to Gerald's empty mug.

"I smelled you the moment you set foot in the yard, witch," came the low whisper from the root cellar, the change in demeanor pronounced. "I know you. Oh, I've wanted you for so long. Send these others away. We can dance, you and I."

I ignored the demon.

"Just the two of us," the demon hissed. "You'd like to be touched, wouldn't you? The way you won't let anyone else touch you."

Mary stopped in front of the door, pushing back her sleeves. She paused for a moment, eyes closed. She lifted the crown of her head. Raising her hands, she spoke in a clear voice, "*Worhte wæpna smið, wundrum teode! Befongen freawrasnum, swa hine fyrndagum. Swa hine fyrndagum!*"

Nothing happened.

"*Mundum,*" I prompted.

Mary repeated the ward, a hint of color on her cheeks. "*Worhte wæpna smið, wundrum teode! Befongen freawrasnum, swa hine fyrndagum. Swa hine fyrndagum mundum!*"

A terrible shriek exploded behind the root cellar door along with a violent thrashing. For several seconds, the shriek continued—only to fade as though dragged to a great distance, diminishing to a faint hiss before disappearing. Silence remained. Mary stared at the door. She lowered her hands and flexed her fingers.

I closed my eye, concentrating, extending my senses. The difference between magic and witchcraft: magic could be learned with diligence, as Mary had done at my instruction; witchcraft was a gift, an inherited fluke of nature (some might say a *curse* of nature), one beholden more to wordless intuition and reflex than anything. "It's gone," I said after a moment. "Well done."

Mary fixed her sleeves. Wards weren't trivial.

Gerald stared at the root cellar door, then at Mary, then at me. "I'm sorry—is she—Grace, I mean—still there?"

"I expect her body is, yes," I said.

"But what just happened?"

"A demon. Likely one who occupied her body at the moment of death—there's a small window where it's relatively easy for them." I approached the door, paying it more attention than I paid Gerald. Extending a flow of my witchcraft, I detected no infernal presence. To be sure, I retrieved a planar compass from my waistcoat pocket. The readings of the device aligned with a recently vanished presence. Closing the lid, I slid it back into my pocket and turned to Gerald. "Are you comfortable with me examining her corpse? Or would you prefer to go upstairs?"

The poor man withered. He glanced at Mary, who regarded him calmly, having just banished a demon.

"No." He licked his lip. "I'm fine. I can fetch a pry bar."

"No need." I stepped to the root cellar door. Passing my hand over the slab of pine holding the latch, I spoke a spell of iron dissolution. The nails flared red for a moment, then dissolved in a tumble of sparks that fell harmlessly to the floor. I caught the board before it dropped and leaned it against the wall to my left. The latch lifted easily enough. Wood screeched in the frame as I pulled it open. A wave of chill air rolled out. Grace Stoughton lay on her side in the cramped space. Dress filthy. Eyes closed. Hair loose and strewn across her face, tangled with mud and pine needles. Her arms were tied behind her, the rope extending down to also bind her ankles. Skin cold. No pulse. Taking her by the shoulders, I dragged her partially out. Mary stepped up and helped me. We laid her out on the floor before the lantern. A small throttled sound escaped Gerald.

Fine-boned and pretty, Grace appeared younger in death than

her seventeen years. A stab of pity wounded me. She was only slightly older than I'd been when I'd first arrived in Boston from London. How close I'd come to ending up in a similar repose—on more than one occasion. The poor girl.

I knelt by her head. I pulled a small mirror from another pocket and incanted a spell by the magician Robert Venn. With the final couplet, I passed my hand over the glass, activating the *Lifeless Reflection*. The mirror shimmered. When it stilled, the view from the glass shaded indigo. I no longer saw my own reflection. Tilting the mirror, I confirmed that I no longer saw Gerald or Mary, either. I brought it close to Grace, seeing her as clearly as the beams overhead, the stones of the walls, the floor. Releasing the spell with a whisper, I said, "She's dead."

"They'll hang me," Gerald muttered. He put a surprisingly delicate hand to his eyes.

A hissing sound filled the cellar. Mary's gaze went to the floor behind me. I spun, raising my hands, Hume's Fourth Ward on my lips. Grace's clothing, her skin, her hair, all turned the gray of ash. Gerald looked out from behind his fingers and gasped.

"Stand back," I told him. I heightened my senses—but felt no demon, nothing. "What did you see, Mary?"

"It started on her arm, then her back. Then everywhere. As though it rose to the surface from inside her. I thought I was seeing things."

I knelt. I reached out to Grace's arm. When I touched it with the tip of my finger, it collapsed in a powdery cloud of gray that landed on the dirt floor with a soft huff, taking her hand with it. The exposed inside of the arm held no striation, nothing but a uniformity of ash; no sign of bones, veins, flesh or ligament remained. Her dress, her shoes, her hair—all assumed the appearance of day-old cinder. Nothing around her revealed a hint of heat or fire. No scorch marks, no crawling aura of soot.

She looked like a statue of ashes, carved with unerring accuracy.

5

ETERNITY VANQUISHED

A half-collapsed building came into sight where the lane petered out next to an overgrown lot. Brambles wrapped the remains of an old fence. A row of fieldstones formed a low wall behind the building, separating the lot from a wooded hillside. Gerald pulled up his horse. "That's it."

"It certainly looks ghost-worthy," Mary said.

"1624 or thereabouts. Built before the settlers crossed over to Boston to find better water." Gerald sat taller in his saddle. "Rowland Gardner was the minister. Not an easy man, if you read the surviving records. Though, to be fair, not an easy position. People by the harbor felt that they shouldn't have to pay salary and firewood for a minister so far out of town, while those closer by had little to offer. Gardner regularly threatened to resign, when he wasn't complaining about nearly freezing to death for lack of firewood. After he leveled some unconventional admonitions, a sickness spread through the farms out this way. So they hanged him as a warlock. Begging your pardon, Minister."

"An inviting location for a ghost hunt," I said. "What exactly did you attempt?"

"Rather less inviting now." Gerald stared at the rotted building, spots of color on his doughy cheeks. "Spirit writing, Minister. Seeking testimony to what lies beyond. Communicating with the dead. I'm sure you're familiar with it."

"The dangers of it."

"As am I. Now. But you must admit it all sounds rather harmless, in a way. Giving the dead their say. Writing. That's all. Correspondence with the afterlife."

The technique was far more complicated than that. For a human to deliberately open up an exchange with the unseen—well, who could know who or what might answer?

I led my horse through the opening in the old fence. "And how did you set about doing this?"

"A spirit-tablet," Gerald said.

"Which you acquired where?"

"I oughtn't say."

"Deliverance Bishop, in other words." The Amesbury merchant did a brisk business in illicit relics, questionable potions, and sundry paraphernalia of the unseen arts. Once or twice per year, I threatened to shut down her shop, yet the evidence of trade in such goods always cropped up again like toadstools after a rainstorm. And always led back to Bishop.

The flush on Gerald's face answered in the affirmative.

"Describe it," I said.

"It had a tarnished brass back, with a mechanism for holding a sheet of paper and a metal quill engraved with strange letters. It appeared to be genuine, even as I more often than not suspect Mrs. Bishop cobbles together her so-called special collection herself. Or perhaps she has her children do it. This one certainly cost me enough. And it had an uncanny air about it, so I had no reason to doubt it was a genuine article—even before I procured the additional ingredients."

"Of what sort?"

"This and that. Candles, sandalwood, earth from a burial yard, and silver coins."

"In other words," Mary says, climbing from her horse, "every tawdry cliché of magic."

"You may laugh if you want, Secretary Whitelocke," Gerald said, "but this wasn't a lark. Not some foolish escapade—though I hardly expect you to believe it. Ghosts, the unseen, manifestations of a greater reality, evidenced and documented. What could be of more interest? The law? Hardly. Printing snide opinions weekly? No, thank you. Shall I sleepwalk through life, only to find at the end that I've heedlessly slumbered it all away? No, I tell you. I find this far more interesting. Or at least I did. Before this disaster."

Moss decorated the remains of the meetinghouse. Splintered joists, gray with age, showed through the fallen sections of roof. The two miserly windows displayed cracked and missing panes. For all that, a power passed through it. Faint, yet powerful, like the steady vibration of an underground river, the air before a lightning strike.

Such sensations as manifest where the shores of one plane crashed up against another.

"AND YOU'RE sure romance didn't cross your mind?" Mary held her lips parted just so as she looked at him, knowing full well the effect it would have on poor Gerald.

"Well of course it did," he admitted. "As with every woman I encounter—isn't that what you're getting at? Yet I know better than anyone the actual height of those cliffs. And Grace made it quite clear that our shared interest in the unseen was the boundary. Which I respected."

I headed to the door. "Let's look."

Gerald made no move to get off his horse. "I'll wait here, if it's all the same."

"Best if you show us."

Mary got down from her horse and went to the door. "If he'd rather stay behind, I don't see why we shouldn't respect his comfort."

Which, of course, did the trick. Gerald sputtered, half apologizing, and climbed down from his horse, getting a button caught on the stirrup. He hurried to follow us inside. Pine needles huddled in the corners. Where the roof had fallen in, decades of seasons left their marks as water stains and warped boards. Animal droppings gathered beneath a bench fallen to rotted staves at the end of the gallery where the pulpit stood. I opened my senses to the scraps of energy spun throughout the meeting-house like fine strands of silk. I pulled out the planar compass and eyed the dial as I walked the length of the room.

"It would seem to live up to its reputation," I said. "Show me what you did, Gerald. And where you did it."

Gerald frowned, his fingers restless on the hem of his coat, a dab of sweat on his forehead. Should Mary have shed her clothing at that moment, I doubted he would have spared her a glance.

"Gerald?" I prompted.

"There." He pointed to a spot in the center of the space. "Where the roof is mostly intact."

Signs of the experiment remained strewn across the floor. "Tell me exactly what you did."

Gerald closed his eyes. "Spread the grave-earth evenly in a circle. Surrounded it with the silver, in this case coins I'd borrowed from my father's house. Lit the red candle in the center of the soil while reciting the Lord's Prayer."

"Go on."

"Once that was done, we took turns attempting to contact the dead by balancing the tablet on our knees and holding the quill lightly with our left hands."

"Did it work?"

"Not at first. Oh, I suppose we were both spurring it along.

Little scribbles accompanied by expressions of surprise. Jumping at the thunderclaps as the storm worsened. A tremendous downpour battered the building. We had to shout to hear one another. Grace had the tablet when the floor shook, surprising us both. I'd at first assumed it to be the thunder, but the candle bounced and I noticed something strange about the coins: they'd come to touch one another, edge to edge. And the circle of them was perfect, which was not at all the way I'd laid them out. I remember staring at them, puzzled. When I turned back to Grace, she scratched the quill across the paper hard enough to tear it, her eyes rolled back in her head, her mouth open."

"What did you feel?" I asked.

"Why, terror."

"No—I mean around you. A presence? Something malign?"

He'd described one of the hallmarks of possession. Not a subtle possession, and one I might not argue sporting.

Not every demon is refined, however.

"No. Just fright. And confusion," Gerald said. "Then everything went queer around us. I tried to get to my feet but felt twice as heavy as usual. The air was thick, as though we'd been dunked underwater. The coins jittered on the floor, still touching, and began to rotate as a group. Grace dropped the tablet, snapping out of it. She looked at me with wide eyes and called out, but her voice sounded muffled. I expected to see the room filled with spirits."

"Was it?"

"No. I staggered to my feet, the floor shifting, rolling like the deck of a ship in a gale. I reached for Grace, but without warning smashed my forehead into a wall—I suddenly wasn't where I'd been a moment earlier. You see the small room off the back there?" He pointed to an alcove near the far corner. "Not much more than a storage space, probably for firewood or coats or something. I'd hit that wall, with no memory of having crossed from the middle of the room. For a moment, it felt as though the entire world flipped upside down. I don't remember a moment more frightening in my entire life. The walls shook. Lightning flashed, one strike after another. Thunder filled the air."

He wiped the sweat from his forehead with the back of his cuff. I was relatively confident he wasn't under the thrall of a demon himself, having surreptitiously checked both when we'd left his sister's cellar, and a second time when we'd approached the meetinghouse. No, likely his nerves were simply getting the better of him.

"Bracing myself, I spotted Grace, crumpled in the corner of the storage area ten feet away from me. I called her, but she didn't answer. I crawled to her, my ears ringing, my hands numb. Her eyes were open and staring at the rotted ceiling. I called her name. Reached out and shook her arm. She didn't respond. I tapped her on the cheek with my hand. I—" His words caught. Once, twice, he tried to continue, his eyes filling with tears. He shook his head and whispered an apology.

"It must have been awful," I said.

"Beyond. She wasn't breathing. Wasn't...anything. I tried. I leaned her forward, pounded her between the shoulder blades. I tried to lift her to her feet, in a total panic. I had no idea what to do. The guilt nearly did me in. If I'd had a weapon, I might have turned it on myself in that moment. I leaned back, howling up at the storm to take me, to take me instead. I'm afraid I'm no good in a crisis."

"No?" Mary said.

"At least I know it," he shot back. "And can admit it. Along with all else I'm admitting, Secretary Whitelocke. I could have disappeared. Run off. Vanished. Headed west or south, taking this terrible secret with me. But I didn't. Yes, I panicked. But I also tried to do something—well, at least *en route* to the right thing, if not quite reaching it."

～

THE BRACING CURRENTS of energy puzzled me. Potent—yet so fine, thin. No overall pattern, just power, the wake left behind by a collision of planes. Mary forced Gerald to walk through his version of events again, probing at one point or another. In the back room where Gerald had found himself, I paused. A hint of color in the corner drew my eye: a scrap of cloth, pale in the shadows. Above it, the figure of a woman watching me from the corner.

I raised my hands, a ward at the ready.

Dress and shawl hung loose over her broomstick shoulders and ribs, stained with patches of white mold, gnawed at the hems and seams, threads dangling, buttons tarnished. Might it have once been plum? Hard to know. Faded petticoats, mildewed stockings puddling around the lower reaches of her tibia and fibula. Shoes in need of a shine, the buckles crusted over with green tarnish. And her hat, a delicate tricorn undertaking in vogue a century ago, once resplendent with gold trim, was draped with thick webbing long deserted by the spiders who tailored it. The dark eye orbits of her skull stared at me, framed by a cascade of gray hair.

"How you shine," she whispered.

I didn't sense a demon but remained more than a little wary.

"Have you heard the song of bones?" she said. "It's so lovely. May I tell you, dearie?"

"Mary," I called over my shoulder.

The woman leaned forward, hands on her knees as though telling a story to a child. Her tresses shifted. "The silence of the grave. That airless quiet where all hopes and dreams die—or do they? Such a sound to break the stillness, the ditty of bones. Heels dancing on the rough slabs. Femurs drumming. Tibia rattling. Ribs chattering. Teeth knocking. Such insistent celebration of the bones, in a melody and rhythm as wild as the downpour of a sweeping thunderstorm. If only you might have pressed your ear to the soft earth atop my grave. Do you know what you would have heard?"

"Mary," I repeated, louder.

"The sound of eternity vanquished. What gift under heaven, what clear sight within the wheels of the sun and stars could be more thrilling?" The figure tilted her head.

"Who are you?" I asked her.

The sound of Mary's boots came up behind me. The woman vanished, draining of color and cascading down like mist.

NO SIGN REAPPEARED as we searched the meetinghouse. During a second, more thorough pass, I read off the measurements from the face of the planar compass, watching the three thin hands move across the face in fine synchrony. Mary wrote down the findings. We scoured the accessible parts of the building, including the small alcove where the apparition of the woman had appeared. Beneath all else—the measurements, the age, the rot, the mildew, the abandonment—I sensed the faintest, most maddening hint of something I couldn't identify.

"Might I have them back?" Gerald squatted by the rough circle of silver coins around the perimeter of the soil. "They're worth a fair amount."

"Let me check them first," I said.

I passed the planar compass over the coins, concentrating. The hands turned in an odd fashion. I closed the lid of the compass and slid it into my pocket. A release of witchcraft from my hands stirred the silver. I reached for one of the coins.

And the room exploded.

6

HAUNT YOU

Drowning in a half-collapsed, rotting meetinghouse. Swept asunder, crushed beneath a riotous wave. Sent heels over head, pummeled by the churn of the planar energy. My witchcraft shielded me from the worst of it. The buffeting continued for what felt like minutes, but was more likely only seconds. Twenty, perhaps.

All around me extended the collision of two realities, each filled with flares of light, blinding. The most ferocious electrical storm I'd ever been through held nothing in comparison. Glimpses of the meetinghouse flickered back and forth with images of the same room, angled sideways, drawn in grays and blacks. My skin prickled with the touch of freezing, lifeless air. Beyond the strange visions, a vast wind howled. The pressure grew and grew and grew—and then it relented with a bone-jarring crack that cut off as though behind a door slammed shut.

Debris fell to the floor. I opened my eye to find a scattering of splinters, boards, crusted daub, slats, shingles, twigs, and branches all around me. Much of the remaining roof had given way. Mary lay sprawled ten feet from me, arms around her head, a section of a fallen joist across her back. Another section of roof lay across where Gerald had stood.

"Mary?" I called.

"I'm fine," she said. "At least I think I am. Good Lord."

As I got to my feet, the extent of the energy became clear to me: pockets of it pooled across the floor, in the air, snaking this way and that like smoke leftover from a cannon shot. I hurried to Mary and grasped her arm, helping her to her feet. She dusted herself off, one hand absently checking that her hair had stayed in place.

"Was it some kind of trap?" Her voice lacked its normal purr. "A setup?"

"How? Someone would have had to know we'd come here—all the while using Gerald as an unwitting lure."

"Or witting."

I dug out the planar compass and opened it. Looking at the readings, I froze.

Mary stepped next to me, wiping splinters from her sleeve. Her hand stopped when her gaze landed on the hands of the dial. "That can't be. Did it break?"

I passed a hand in front of it and the dials righted themselves to the neutral position. Releasing the reset, we both watched the hands spin smoothly around the face, quickly returning to the extreme reading I'd gotten. "It's working."

"But that's the *summa-praecento* band," Mary said. "Which I believe you once said is impossible."

"It is. Or, was. I don't know." I looked about. "I don't think we should remain."

Mary turned on her heel. "Gerald. Come. Wake up. It's time to go." She strode to the section of fallen roof. "Are you hurt?"

The dials on the planar compass shifted slightly.

Mary grunted, hefting the boards off Gerald. She paused.

I glanced over. "Is he all right?"

The boards boomed to the open floor next to her, sending up a plume of rolling dust.

Gerald was gone.

❧

I MADE a thorough pass through the inside, stepping carefully over and around the fallen roof and broken walls. Within the meetinghouse, outside, nearby—nothing, no sign of Gerald at all. Though the readings on my devices continued to register the trailing edge of a planar event, I could find no hint of what had become of him. Various other spells convinced me he'd truly disappeared, that he wasn't invisible, or otherwise shielded from detection. Leveraging an item from his horse—a glove from the saddlebag—I used Lerxt Hjelvik's *Intrinsic Dislodgement and Commutation of Essence*. The spell failed to generate a single glint.

Quite concerning, as even a corpse would register a directional flaring.

The figure of the woman I'd seen? Vanished, as well. Nothing within the corner she'd appeared registered differently on any of my devices.

The silver coins exuded no remaining magic I could detect, though they'd taken on a strange tarnished appearance they'd lacked earlier. With care, I nudged them into a kerchief and put them into a haversack I'd retrieved from my horse. I also gathered a sample of the burial yard soil and the candle. A spell of planar revelation only served to confound me further: the calibrated spectrum of colors keyed to the canonical order of the planes refused to settle, instead randomly shifting between hues. I made note of the order of the colors, so I might later study the pattern. A final extension of my witchcraft—a cautious one, needless to say—revealed more of that curious spindling of fine energies throughout the meetinghouse.

Before leaving the congregation hall, I put in place a series of light glamours—at the doors, near the fallen roof, around the spot where Gerald and Grace's ill-fated ghost hunt had culminated. Should anyone intrude upon or cross into the space, I would know of it instantly.

Outside, Mary approached, shaking her head. "Nothing. No tracks. Nothing in the trees, or the lane. I called for him, over and over. He's gone. I don't like this."

"Nor do I. You're not hurt?"

"Fine. Sore. Confused. Which annoys me."

"Same," I said. "None of this makes any sense."

"The woman in the back alcove?"

I shook my head. "It's as though I imagined her."

"A ghost in a haunted meetinghouse. Pity Gerald didn't get the chance to see it."

"It wasn't a ghost."

"Yes, you've told me the theory: ghosts aren't real. Just demons. Or imagination. Attributions of meaning to nothing more than coincidence. Et cetera." She smoothed out the front of her jacket. "Yet forgive me if it didn't sound to me as though you saw a ghost."

"I don't know what it was," I said, "other than an apparition—which might stem from any of a number of causes. Demonic presence, for instance. Planar intrusion. A subtle magic. Residual spellwork. Even some sort of temporal eddy. There might not even be a way to narrow it down."

"Then maybe don't cross *ghost* off the list just yet."

"You're not being helpful." I shaded my eyes, judging how much of the afternoon I had left. "I'm going to have to tell Mrs. Spenser."

"Careful she doesn't turn *you* into ghost," Mary said. "Then again, perhaps the next blazing essay to lift off her printing press will inspire Governor Reddington to do the honors. You're sure you want to tell her?"

I looked over the half-collapsed shape of the meetinghouse,

resting one hand on the pommel of my horse's saddle. "I lost her brother."

"You didn't lose him."

"Funny, because he's not here."

"You know what I mean."

"I'm not sure Mrs. Spenser will appreciate the distinction."

"Then hold off."

"No, I can't." I turned to her.

"Admirable. Let's hope not to a fault."

"There's no fault in the truth. Difficulties, yes. Fault, no."

"Ah, how silly of me not to see it." She tilted her head. "August Swaine and Ephraim Rush would no doubt have cheered on such ruthless honesty."

I swung up onto my horse. "Both of whom are no longer with us, you're implying?"

She put one boot into her stirrup. "Merely noting." She lifted herself into her saddle. "No question, they were both lovely gentlemen, equal parts influential and inspiring, who made you —and by extension me—who we are today."

"I sense a *yet*," I said.

"Well, there *is* a yet." She gathered her reins. "Because both of them barreled through their days with the certitude that being correct freed them from the need to manage or even acknowledge the expectations of others. Especially those whose influence or authority might also require the balancing of other considerations. As though being right allowed them to trample over any other objections, even those with genuine merit."

"I see."

"I'm not sure you do," Mary said. "Katie. Listen. I'm not asking you to ignore the truth. Or bend it. I'm just saying that we bring something to the table those gentlemen didn't. Empathy. Some grace. A touch of wiles. The extra attention we command. All of which can serve the truth—while making allowances for other people's vantages and needs."

"So I should lie to Mrs. Spenser?"

"Lie? No. I'm only suggesting that you don't have to ride over there at this very minute and drop the truth like a fieldstone on her notably large feet. And I know better than anyone how much you think of your mentors. How their memories overwhelm you. One might even say *haunt* you. But you've shown their memories as much respect as anyone might ask. You can both honor their memories and do things even better."

"Enough of your logic and good sense."

"I'm your right hand for a reason." Mary dusted off the knees of her breeches. "I'll ride back to Cambridge and continue searching for Gerald. I'll also see if I can't have a word with the walking-in-the-world-hale-as-ever Grace Stoughton. Whatever information I can find. You go back to Ten Gables. Look over your notes. Test the coins and the rest of it. Do what you do best. Then, you need to get ready for tonight's dinner with the governor."

"Must I?"

"Oh, you must. Don't even think about hiding in your books."

"It's so much more peaceful."

"It's musty. And lonely. Not at all worthy of a modern Minister of Magickal Sciences." She pulled the reins, turning her horse back to the lane.

"You'll be at the dinner?" I called after her.

"You trusted me with a demon. I think it high time I trust you at an official dinner on your own. But please have Anne Moorland pick an outfit for you. Something befitting." She gave the horse her heels and started off down the lane.

Befitting.

I watched her go, then left the meetinghouse to the quiet of the woods. What would Ephraim Rush have made of it all? Or August Swaine? I'd seen neither gentleman in four years, almost to the day.

Rush would have been pleased with what I'd made of the office, I believed. The work mattered. Dignity mattered. Perhaps

he'd have even been less concerned than I was at the thought of
me occupying his vaunted office.

As for Swaine? Mary wasn't entirely wrong. His drive for the
truth—the unreachable truth, the truth beneath it all—hadn't
won over many hearts and minds. Not that he cared a whit.

It had also killed him.

Mary's words echoed. *They haunt you.*

Yet I continued their legacy, the work they'd done. The work
mattered. Truth mattered.

Didn't it?

My horse's hooves sounded loud on the faint lane. Making
sure Mary was out of sight, I flicked a tear from the corner of my
eye and set off for Ten Gables.

7

———

CLAWING REACH

The headquarters of the Ministry of Magickal Sciences loomed over the middle of Queen Street. A magnificent construction three years in the making, Ten Gables announced its own importance without much subtlety, I'm afraid. Peaked roofs rose across those ten gables, covered in a riotous pattern of slate shingles, trimmed in baroque ornamentation that drew the eye. Black shutters stood watch by the many-paned arched windows. Painted the color of dusk, the building, in keeping with its mission, was said to appear and disappear more quickly than its neighbors at the touch of twilight. The tallest portion contained the council hall, while the wings of the structure spread out asymmetrically. Its unusual design pleased me, reflecting as it did the disciplines that had lifted me into my role in the first place: the logic and order of magic; the subtle connections of sorcery; and the wild flow of witchcraft.

The cost, however, had subjected me to a years-long, near-daily torrent of letters, notes, questions, second-guessing, and critiques from Finance Minister DeWitt. He wasn't the only one to take issue, either. At the time of its construction under the adzes and hammers of the city's finest carpenters, one wag at the *Boston Courant* likened its appearance to an unnatural act between a ship from the harbor and a cathedral from the Old World.

No accounting for taste.

Along with the audacious presence of Ten Gables, Queen Street had changed in other ways, as well. A new barracks across the way housed a company of soldiers who protected Ten Gables. The Fourth Company—colloquially known as the *Minister's Own* —resided there. Female, to the last, at my insistence.

Unheard of! Scandalous! The foundations of civilization assailed!

I'm still not sure how exactly I managed to extract that concession, but I was stubborn on the point, and at the moment of my maximum leverage, Governor Thomas Reddington acquiesced. Despite the public rending of shirts and wails of lamentation such a descent into madness provoked, neither retributive fire nor divine flood wiped Boston from the map.

In time, most citizens grew sanguine at the sight of the Minister's Own. Some—approximately half, shall we say—looked on with admiration, though sometimes under a requisite guise of disapproval. And those who regularly crowed about an alleged deficit of talent or skills—somewhat close to the other half—had yet to present a compelling shred of evidence.

Talent and focus mattered. As far as I was concerned, the conversation ended there.

I STEPPED through the double doors shortly before five o'clock. Secretary Anne Moorland rose from her station off the main foyer at my arrival. A slight thing at an even five feet tall, Anne nonetheless mastered my schedule with outrageous confidence. Her copper-colored hair tied smartly back, the crisp lines of her jacket hugging her slender frame, she matched my pace.

"We found her, Minister," she said.

"And she's where?"

"Waiting in the library, as you'd asked."

Instead of heading up to my workshop, I detoured to the library, at the far end of the eastern wing. Shelves of dark-stained mahogany rose along three walls; a matching step stool waited like an obedient hound at the foot, ready to assist in reaching the volumes along the top shelves. As I entered, Clara Dod turned from the corner where she'd been poking through a book. Long-limbed and more agile than I'd been at fourteen, she wore black breeches and a loose white shirt, her long hair hanging free. Anne shut the door behind us and stood off to the side.

"Where was she?" I asked Anne.

"By an alleyway off Clarks Square, Minister. There were two lads. And flames in the air."

"And they are now where? The lads, not the flames."

"They fled, Minister. I believe they were the only ones to witness it."

"Delightful." Only then did I deign to address Clara. "Well?"

Clara put the book back into its place. "It's not what you think."

"It's never what I think, is it?" I said to Anne. "As though I'm somehow in the wrong for merely considering the facts. A stubborn flaw in my thinking."

"Only they saw it," Clara suggested. "As Anne said."

"Yes, just them," I said. "And everyone else they'll tell. And then everyone else *they'll* tell. Well done, Clara. Your feet can never resist trampling a delicate situation, can they?"

"I didn't trample anything," Clara said, nothing delicate about her.

"Flames?"

With a glance at Anne, Clara said, "It wasn't as bad as she makes it sound. Just *Clawing Reach*. My best spell. Fully under control. And I didn't set anything on fire. Or anyone. The flames just circled them. Which got their attention. They're idiots."

"You're missing the point."

"You're the one who taught me the spell in the first place."

"And I trusted you to treat it with the respect it deserves. Respect. Everything I teach. Just as I do with Mary. When I teach her something like *Concave Illumination*, I don't expect her to immediately use it to find out what Eleanor Cabbot really thinks about her."

"She already knows: she's jealous of her," Clara said. "No mirror magic necessary. And by the way, what happened to *we should flaunt it*? I've only heard that a hundred times. Doesn't that make you a hypocrite?"

"Excuse me?" I said.

"Fine," Clara said. "I shouldn't have done it. Can I just go and finish my studies?"

"Not yet you can't. It's not that you used magic like that," I said. "It's that you did it before, and promised me you wouldn't do it again. You gave me your word. Do you remember?"

"It was just a little."

"I'm sorry, but did you carve away an exception for *just a little*?"

She curled her nose to the side three times, a peculiar tic she'd acquired in recent weeks. Since her stint in a haunted realm four years earlier, she'd cycled through any number of unpredictable physical or verbal twitches. None lasted much longer than a season before disappearing, only to reappear in some new guise soon enough. "No."

"Then why did you do it?"

"Now you want to hear?"

"You seem to think it will make a difference."

"Because." She waved a hand. "Because I don't know. I was just so annoyed. Thomas is so...rude. He's always cruel to Mena. Mocking her stammer. Telling her horrid lies. Claiming no one will ever marry her. And he doesn't stop. And worse, he looks for her. She avoids him. But I was helping her collect pins and cloth for her aunt and there they were. Thomas and his wretched friend. Following us. Taunting us. Mena started crying, even though she tried to hide it from them—she's not like Henrietta. So what was I supposed to do?"

Mena Brookshire was in fact not like her older sister: Henrietta was bricks, Mena sticks. One tough and fearless, the other intimidated by nearly everything the world threw at her. Remarkable that siblings could be so different.

"You turn around and tell them to leave," I said.

"Do you really think I didn't think of that? Because I did. More than once. But they kept at it. And I felt so terrible for Mena. And I was angry, I admit it. So I waited until we reached the alley. And then I did it. And I told them that if they ever said a cross word to either of us again, I'd burn the smirks off their faces. The spell just came out. As a way of making my point." She put her hands on her hips. "And I'd do it again. Even though you're going to yell at me."

"Am I yelling?" I said, whilst pointedly not yelling.

"Not yet."

Disobeying instructions. Acting rashly. Keeping secrets. I'd certainly done worse when I'd first learned magic. "I'm not going to. I don't need to. I've told you what I expect and why I expect it. You made a mistake. Again. Fine, it happens. You just need to understand why it shouldn't."

"I understand."

"I hope you do. This isn't a lark. What I'm teaching you is important—and not for public consumption. We walk a fine line in how we show ourselves. Never forget we're all being judged. All the time."

"Fine." She crossed her arms, still not looking away. "I do. But you weren't there."

Oh, how she could get on my every last nerve. "I'm going to

the governor's within the hour. And then I'm going to return and attend to some correspondence. I shall expect you to have spent at least two hours studying. Have you gotten far with your transelemental alignment?"

She kept her arms crossed. "Six pebbles, three on top, three on the bottom, a consistent circumference of air around each one. The water held the whole time."

"Now do eight."

"I don't even get a *well done*?"

I fixed her with my gaze. "You need to be more than competent, you have to be exceptional."

"Fine. I'll do eight."

"Twelve is mastery."

"Then I'll do twelve."

"Do eight first. And I'll want to see it this week."

She—luckily—bit back whatever other words gathered at the tip of her tongue and turned on her heel. Her steps to the door were louder than they needed to be. Anne made as if to speak, but I shook my head. Clara slammed the door behind her.

8

ARSENAL FOR THE UNSEEN ARTS

Mary was right that I'd much rather spend an evening alone on the top floor of Ten Gables than attending a trade dinner at the governor's manse. I felt most at home in my workshop. The smell of books—not at all *musty*, by the way—and the acrid tang of the morning's experiments still hanging in the air. The western windows of my workshop aglow with afternoon light. All perfect.

Yet peace: always fleeting.

With a sigh, I reached for my tea and found the cup empty. I stood, stretching. Crossing to the hearth in the center of the room, I built up the fire. It wasn't as though I hid in my workshop. No. I *worked* in my workshop. Those hours, carved ruthlessly away from my busy schedule, were invariably my most productive. Even those frequent hours when sleep eluded me—while my rivals on the council slept untroubled, no doubt—and I fled from the battleground of my blankets. Midnight lanterns glowing, research at hand, I could finally relax.

In my arsenal for the unseen arts.

Everything neat and organized, the arrangement meticulous beneath the slanting ceilings. Beyond the free-standing hearth stood a wall-to-wall collection of drawers of varying depths and widths, stocked with ingredients. Tinctures. Powders. Filings. Ashes. Bones. Minerals. Herbs. Rarities from the natural world, procured at considerable expense in many cases. Inks. Wax. Precious and more common metals in assorted states. Collections of unusual wood. Magicked coins, needles, knives. More.

Above the drawers, row upon row of bottles, all labeled in my clear hand. On the other side, shelves stacked with instruments and devices I used in keeping the infernal at bay across the province. Specialized compasses. Planar clocks, designed to trap demons. A number of lanterns, tuned to glow in varying intensity and color in response to the proximity of other planes and realms. A larger contraption similar to a spinning wheel, capable of gathering data from an arrangement of sensitive glamours and gauges I'd placed in various towns and villages bordering Salem. Next to it, a portable pendulum imbued with spells to aid in recording the results of such planar cartography onto wide folio sheets I had made expressly for the purpose.

On the near side of the hearth, my workbenches. Try as I might to keep them organized, they inevitably lost ground to the fullness of my schedule, accruing foreigners and trespassers willy-nilly. A pair of books on my device bench. The gearing of a planar clock trespassed on my spellwork bench. A magnifying lens here, a stray satchel there, a pair of silk gloves abandoned beyond. All signs of the relentless taskmaster that ruled me like a company of Anne Moorlands: time, and the general lack thereof.

As the spout of the kettle breathed a curl of steam like a dragon rousing from slumber, I turned back to my examination of Gerald's coins. They lay piled within the confines of a glamour; I'd handled them with caution, not touching them directly. On the opposite side of the bench, a second glamour contained a lone silver spoon, spinning slowly in the air.

A gentle knock at the door dragged me from my thoughts.

"Yes?" I said.

The door opened and Anne leaned into the workshop. "Thirty minutes until you're to be at the governor's manse, Minister."

"I can't politely demure?" I said.

"The delegation from New York arrived by packet this morning. The dinner has been on your schedule for weeks. I'm sorry."

"You're not really sorry." I took the boiling water from the hearth. "You're glad I won't keep you waiting patiently downstairs while I lose myself in my work for another six hours."

"Just six?" She eyed the floating spoon as she gathered the pair of books on my device bench and considerately returned them to the shelves along the wall.

"It's cursed, probably. Certainly distinctive." Adding tea leaves, I said, "Through a principle known as *reflective entrainment*, it may give me an indication if the coins on the other side of the bench also share the quality of being cursed. Not that it would tell me much more than that, but we must start somewhere."

"Naturally. And they're all silver?"

"Silver is a restless metal," I said. "Eager to take on a new role. Malleable. Capable of great luster. Beauty, utility, flexibility—we might find much to admire in silver."

"I never thought of it that way, Minister."

I put the tin of tea away. "It gets better. In the unseen arts, the possibilities expand. Silver is keen to store magic. Absorb it. Transfer it. It can serve as a bridge between the planes, its presence extending subtly beyond sight. And—to our more immediate concern—silver can be enchanted to any number of caustic effects. Opening a channel into another world. Physical explosions, splintering into piercing needles. Minor and major curses. Location triggers designed to spring secondary magic. Ensorcelled silver can release a virulent pox. Or a demon. Or several demons."

Anne's gaze narrowed as she regarded the spoon and coins. "I see."

"Not that there are any demons with this, I don't think." Unlike magic and witchcraft, the art of sorcery was entirely focused on the manipulation, harnessing, and defenses against demons. Given my office and province in which I served, I kept my skills at sorcery well honed. I motioned with my hand and the spoon fell to the workbench with a chiming clang. "Though I will say unraveling its riddle would certainly be more interesting than a fancy dinner."

Moorland barely flinched, stepping aside as I left the workshop. She walked beside me. We crossed the arched landing and headed down the wide staircase. At another landing, we turned to the hallway where the private residence of Ten Gables extended beneath the workshop.

"Any word from Mr. Twelves?" I asked.

"He assures me all will be ready by week's end."

"I believe I heard the same last week."

"True. But his wife is due with child."

"That's my fear," I said. "Brilliant clock making is no doubt even slower with a squalling babe tucked in one arm."

"I assume Mrs. Twelves will handle the squalling."

"Then you don't know Mrs. Twelves well enough. She runs her father's mill, an endeavor she views as the equal to Mr. Twelves's work, as far as the family's industry goes. Furthermore, she has not wavered in her opinion that men are perfectly capable of changing a nappie. What else?"

"Councilman Seward stopped by earlier and requested an audience," Anne said.

"Again?"

"He was rather charming about it. In that graceless way of his."

"Oh dear." We passed along the long eastern hallway to my quarters. "Find some time for him next week. And not a time near the end of the day. Nor near midday. I don't want to have to, yet again, refuse to take a meal with him."

"I'll find a suitable time," Anne said. "Also, Theodosia Wilfred dropped in."

"Poor thing. Demons?"

"How they trouble her."

"I don't have time."

"I know. I was gentle about it."

"Well done." We crossed into my dressing chamber, a small room with damask-patterned paper hangings on the walls. While the rest of Ten Gables—especially my workshop—reflected my needs entirely, Mary had taken a hand in decorating the rooms of less interest to me. "How formal?"

"Official attire. But—no dress or gown." She scanned my wardrobe. "They're a dour bunch. You shouldn't quite join them." She traversed the racks and pulled down an ivory shirt, a brocade sash, a heather vest with matching buttons, a dark green coat, black breeches, ivory stockings, and a cream cravat, matching them up against one another with efficiency. While she laid them out for me, I switched my black eye patch for a peacock-blue one that went better with the vest she'd chosen.

"One of the gray ones might work better, Minister," Anne said.

"The blue doesn't highlight the coat?"

"Not...particularly."

"Fine," I said, changing the eye patch. "Governor Jansen can't stand me. When I met him last year, he refused to shake my hand."

"Terribly rude." Moorland retrieved a pair of dark shoes for me. "To what end?"

"My guess was that he didn't want to get stained with any of the ink I'd used to sign away my soul." I shrugged off my coat, vest, and shirt, slipping into the new outfit as Anne handed me each next piece.

She tutted. "He's just jealous. And Dutch. And paranoid. But I repeat myself. He's upset his colony doesn't get the attention we do."

I tugged on the breeches. "We don't always get it for the right reasons. As our own governor regularly reminds me."

Once I'd stepped into the shoes, Moorland helped bring my hair under control as I adjusted the cravat.

"Hat?" I said.

"Of course."

She selected a tricorn with a low profile; black, edged in satin. I angled it on. And in a private tribute to my predecessor—his having been on my mind as a result of Mary's earlier comments—I pulled down a walnut box from a high shelf and took out Ephraim Rush's old watch. I slid it into the pocket of the heather vest. Buttoning my coat, I asked, "Not dour?"

"Dark green is your color, Minister."

"Now you're just flattering me. You've said that about dark blue."

"I'm not." And I could see she wasn't. She flushed prettily when flustered and flustered easily, which was why I flustered her with some regularity. "Those colors work for you. On the other hand, you should never wear yellow. It makes you look like a sweaty candle. Pink isn't your friend, either, unless you wish your eyebrows to stand out in an unkind fashion. Any shade of light blue should exist only below your waist, lest it wash you out and make you look like a scullery maid."

"That's more like it."

She folded her hands behind her back. "As I said."

"A scullery maid?" I looked myself over in the tall oval mirror. Attire befitting the Minister of Magickal Sciences. Yet beneath it, I still saw the old aprons and sturdy cotton dresses, hemmed and patched as needed. Clothing designed for work, not for show. Worn through usage. Unassuming—like the hat of the miller I'd seen that morning.

"You might be too tall to be a good maid," Anne said.

"And too graceful."

"Well—you move with confidence, we'll say."

"Delicately put."

"Should I have them bring the carriage around?"

"It's only two streets over." I adjusted the hat. "The walk will clear my head."

Like silver, I was restless.

9

———

DOGGEREL

At the governor's manse, I was escorted privately to the Map Room, where Governor Thomas Reddington awaited me. The room had maps, of course. Books: unread as far as I could tell. A fine table of polished cherry. All of it together contributed to the air of authority. Reddington turned from the window. He stood several inches shorter than me, the gray hairs dusting his temples the only break in his otherwise youthful aura. Trim, athletic, Boston's best horseman by all accounts, Reddington was a man of intense discipline. Like me, he kept his staff functioning like the quick spinning gears of a watch, so much so that Mary had once described him as *"a Finchier Finch."*

Reddington dismissed the aide who brought me. When the door closed, he said, "If it isn't the Governor's Witch."

"Sir?"

"Here with the most corrupt governor in the besotted history of Massachusetts governance, should you believe everything you read from our critics." He put his hands on the table before him. "Tell me, Minister—is it you?"

"Is what me?"

"The source of the doggerel peeled from the presses of the *Provincial Gazette*."

"Of course not, sir. I'm as livid as you over it."

He fixed me with his stare. "Then I can only assume you met with that woman today to glamour her barrels of ink to never reveal the words *Reddington* or *Finch* ever again. There could surely be no other reasonable explanation."

Not that glamours worked that way, an error I prudently let slide. I said, "She came by Ten Gables on unrelated business. A family situation."

"I trust you then arranged for the gaping maw of Hell itself to immediately widen to consume the entire Phipps lineage." The vein on his right temple was visible. Not a good sign. "What a brief and pleasant conclusion to the story."

"I agreed to help her."

"Help her? That woman is disgusting. The bile she writes, thick with lies and insults, is a constant series of thorns in my backside. She told the world you're a witch. And I've a room full of delegates from New York who question—again and again— why they should do any business at all with a colony with a Minister of Magickal Sciences in the first place. That was bad enough. Now thanks to that vindictive harpy, the word *witch* is on half the lips of Boston again."

"Sir—"

"Don't help her. Don't lift a finger, don't speak with her again. I don't care what she needs. Until she retracts every last word of insidious libel she's plastered the town with, she's dead to us."

Governors and their moods: always tricky. Not certain how heavy the cannonade might grow, I ventured a few steps out from under my shelter. "But if she realizes the utility we bring to the citizenry—whomever they might be—maybe the commentary she publishes will change in our favor."

"What a charming thought," Reddington said.

"The work I do—"

"The work I let you do. Go on."

No wonder so many wilted under the stony gray of his eyes. "Is of interest to us all."

"Even those who strive to cut us down at every opportunity? To sabotage every effort we undertake? Ridiculous."

"My duty is to protect the province from the infernal, sir. Demons don't care who says or does or publishes anything at all. They're a danger to us all."

The clock on the mantelpiece chimed the hour. Reddington adjusted the lapels of his jacket. "I don't care if Mrs. James Spenser is being stalked by the Prince of Hell himself. Far too late for her to turn to us for help. Let her rot. Am I clear?"

The words welled up behind my lips: *He could find a new minister.*

The unending slings and arrows of the politics of Boston required the constant application of hypocrisy. Even Clara had seen as much.

I could leave it all behind, for good. Retire to the house Swaine had left me in Andover. Fill my days with books. Research. Playing the harpsichord and singing. Gardening. Peace and quiet enough to really focus, integrity intact.

Instead, I said, "Of course, sir. I understand."

"Excellent, Finch. You're my favorite minister for a reason. And now we need to impress. I'm chafing at London's leash—and this is how we might eventually slip free altogether. Let's make these humorless, vain New Yorkers feel at home. Convince them all that doing business with us in no way commits anyone's soul to the flames. Overwhelm them with our considerable charm." He motioned to the door. "After you, Minister."

10

WITH A STEADY PULSE

The Indigo Room shone with candle and oil lamp, light glinting off the chandeliers. At the sight of the governor, the trio of string players in the corner shifted their tune to "*Hail Glory's Reach.*" Unabashedly earnest, verging on cloying. I often found myself singing it in jest—much to the chagrin of my staff.

The guests rose. A polite wave of applause swept the room, cresting as we reached the head table by the hearth. I took a spot beside Alfred Cross, our envoy from the court of London. Before us, the three dozen guests beamed. Council members with their wives or husbands, dressed in evening finery. Enough satin and silk to upholster several households' worth of furnishings. Jewels. Thin glasses of wine, cut-glass decanters, servants with trays of brandy.

At the far side of the table, the New York delegation, led by Governor Pieter Jansen, stood in greeting. For his part, Jansen flashed a polite smile. A portly man, he wore his hair trimmed close beneath his bald dome. No wig. Gray hair, gray eyes, gray coat over dark breeches.

The dinner guests raised their glasses, taking a cue from Reddington.

"I think Governor Jansen will find no less admiration anywhere he might go in Boston tonight," he said to the gathering. "As for the rest of us, well, we might only hope to possess a small fraction of the approbation throughout the colonies he has so rightfully earned. To our honored guest."

Words of assent rose. Glasses clinked. Jansen bowed his head quickly, with a murmured "Thank you."

With a signal from Reddington, the musicians resumed their bowing on an innocuous tune as people took their seats.

COURSES WERE CARRIED out with precision; no one would leave hungry. Reddington and Governor Jansen discussed news from New York. At the far end of the table, the wife of Newton Endecott—my least favorite member of the council, and he no great fan of mine—chatted politely with one of the New York merchants, a wide-faced gentleman with a pair of spectacles perched on the end of his nose. Cross surveyed the guests as the meal progressed.

"They pretend to not see you at all," Cross said. "Yet they mark your attention every time you're not looking. Does it bother you?"

"I'm quite used to it," I said.

"And every time you're not there. Well. They aren't subtle gentlemen."

Endecott—as well as the Finance Minister DeWitt—were no one's idea of subtle, attempting, at every opportunity, to sabotage me.

"They lack the wiles of a woman," I said. "For which I should be grateful."

A voice cut across the table. "As if all they needed to double their business was a witch," Endecott's wife, Helena, said.

Her final word landed like a dead cod in the midst of the table. Conversation paused.

Endecott's gaze flicked to me, then back to his wife.

She continued: "It's one thing after another with them, isn't it? As though their problems were more beguiling than anyone else's. Is that the right word? *Beguiling*? In any event, it's crass. I'm sure she has better things to do."

"You were saying?" Cross said.

I cleared my throat. Helena's glance lifted to my face. A deep blush rose from her décolletage and consumed her throat and face. In the silence at the main table, the sound of forks on porcelain plates, the chatter of the other guests, and the scuffling shoes of the servers only deepened the moment's discomfort.

Her husband noted Reddington's displeasure, after ignoring mine altogether. "Helena," he whispered.

Reddington looked at me and raised an eyebrow. At my nod, he would have had her escorted out. Or, I could have requested that Helena finish her thoughts about merchants and witches. I could have done any of these. Instead, I looked at Helena and said, "It's fine, dear. It was rather crass of them to ask for my public patronage of their shop, given the rumors."

"I'm—" Helena began, her gaze fixed on the table before her. "Thank you, ma'am."

I turned to Governor Reddington and Governor Jansen and changed the subject.

PERHAPS MY ACT of social charity toward Helena Endecott changed Jansen's estimation of me, for he afterward acknowledged my presence, gracing me with an agreeable word or two as the dinner progressed. The New York governor, it turned out, had a sharp sense of humor, even though he kept it sheathed more often than not. By the time the main course arrived, he'd even shared with me a tale of his wife banning him from consuming pickled foods in an attempt to stem his snoring.

Reddington, no doubt pleased to see the thawing, sat back and let his favorite minister charm his counterpart. Jansen and I both landed on a shared admiration for Addison and Steele's *The Spectator*, each having acquired the seven volumes of the original run of the paper. His gaze focused on me with even more intensity from then on.

As Jansen, tracing a point in the air with the tip of his knife, explained to Reddington his reaction to the story of "Inkle and Yarico," the pocket watch in my vest vibrated. Once, twice, and then with a steady pulse. I paused.

The watch had activated at my own presence after Rush had bequeathed it, and much else, to me in his last will and testament. I'd counteracted the spell with one of my own so that I might be near the watch without it vibrating senselessly off the shelf I normally kept it on.

I might have suspected Dr. Rush's watch of malfunctioning, had I not also been on edge since entering the room. I'd assumed Reddington's demand, coupled with the pressures of setting the New York contingent at ease, had been the cause. Yet some other, more subtle sensation had nagged at me, just below the surface.

The watch continued to knock in my pocket. I scanned the Indigo Room.

There was another witch present.

11

A PUBLIC DISPLAY OF MAGIC

My face, my demeanor, gave away nothing. Yet in short order, I narrowed the list down to three candidates—though they were barely more than guesses, so cleverly did this witch cloak. If I hadn't worn Rush's pocket watch, I might never have suspected anything whatsoever. Though the device activated at a proximity of one hundred yards or thereabouts, it gave no finer exactness. Little good in identifying who was the witch.

To the list.

A new serving girl. I hadn't seen her on the governor's staff before, and she seemed ill at ease. She strained not to look too blatantly at the wealthy and important guests, myself included, but her gaze darted about unceasingly. A few stumbles in protocol here and there, discreetly corrected by a butler.

Next, a slender gentleman fiddling with spectacles. A witch could be a male, of course. Rarer, to be sure, but possible. This young man sat at a table of council officials and merchants I'd crossed paths with on occasion. Dark hair, a lock draping his forehead. Waxy skin, a nervous sheen to his face. Fingers, long and restless. He stared at the New Yorkers from time to time, a touch of furtiveness clear even from across the room. His posture had a tension to it, as though he was prepared to be discovered a fraud at any moment. I'd never seen him before.

Third came a woman with the visiting New Yorkers. Unlike the other two, no hesitant wallflower was she. She charmed those around her—holding forth, chatting agreeably, a touch of aloofness to her. The wife of one of the delegation, I guessed. A paunchy fellow next to her, louder than his compatriots, occasionally leaned and whispered to her. Something about this woman's manner nagged at me.

All three drew my scrutiny, each a little off.

So as custard and coffee were served, I surveilled my suspects whilst sharing a word, a compliment, a jest with the other guests. Governor Reddington's father spilled wine across the white silk of his breeches when he stood to bow at my approach, the breathy fumes of several drinks too many notable from three feet away. At the next table, the slender gentleman fiddled with his dessert spoon. He stared so intently at his spoon I wondered if he weren't trying to turn it to gold. Not once did he glance at me.

As I was about to force an introduction upon him, a voice spoke directly behind me. "I see you haven't yet wilted under the scornful glare of the governor of New York. Good for you." Grayson Whitelocke, dressed in an expensively tailored suit of moss green satin, his hair of fashionable length held back with a wide ivory ribbon, appeared at my elbow.

"He actually finds me delightful." I reached over and flicked a crumb from his collar. "And I him. Once I got past his defenses."

Changing my plan for the slender gentleman, I led Grayson away from the table.

"You'll have to tell me your trick," he said, following. "What with the way he eyes everyone and everything around him as though studying a ledger. Still, if he can get past the impression of you being Satan's bride, I have more of a chance than I thought."

"Perhaps I can give you some lessons in charm one of these days," I said. "But not now. I need your help."

"Then you shall have it. And while we're on the subject of assistance, do any of these New Yorkers know Giles Walcott, the silversmith?"

"Grayson, this is important."

"I saw some of his work on my visit to New York last fall. I must admit I was staggered. His artistry is spectacular. Idiosyncratic."

The difficulty of stopping a Whitelocke in Boston, and all that.

"I've no idea," I said.

"But you wouldn't mind introducing me to them, so I might further my inquiry?"

Grayson had over the past few years shed his fixation on women and brandy and instead applied himself to building a reputation as one of Boston's most tasteful importers. To his sister Mary's annoyance, he'd also become much sought after amongst the highest social circles of the city, a gentleman with an eye for the latest fashions and a nose for profits. Unmarried, yet. I certainly had no complaint as to his sobriety. Moreover, I appreciated his connections within the book trade, made and maintained, as far as I could see, for no one's benefit but my own. I often found him early in the day breakfasting at the tavern near Ten Gables, waiting for me with a tale or two he'd heard of an infernal nature. He was also just as liable to corner me for my impressions of this or that merchant, council member, or an inquiry into the governor's latest thinking. His own romantic triumphs and setbacks were yet another cornucopia of commentary, delivered with coffee-fueled gusto. On occasion, he even asked how I was doing.

"I'm a little preoccupied, thank you," I said. "I need—"

"Don't tell me all your running around chasing demons and

whatnot has obscured your commitment to always being on the lookout for your dear friend Grayson's needs."

"Fine, I'll ask around," I said.

"That's more like it."

"But first I need something from you. Do you know everyone who's here tonight?"

"Beg pardon?"

"All the guests. Everyone."

"Many. Most, I should think. Why?"

"The man at the table behind us," I said. "The one with the spectacles. Who is he?"

Grayson casually glanced back in that direction. "Don't tell me that after all these years, the woman who would rather wear her one good eye down to a nub in an obsessive pursuit of, apparently, reading every word printed in every book, ensconced in her garret every evening in the company of no one but her loving tea kettle—this successful and attractive woman who might have her pick of nearly any male suitor in Boston has at last revealed what her type is?" He frowned. "And it's...that?"

"Not for romance."

"There we are. World in proper alignment again."

I leaned close to his ear. "There's a witch here," I whispered.

"Rose Donlon."

"No. An *actual* witch."

"How is that possible?"

"I've no idea," I said. "But I mean to find out."

Grayson gave the man a second look. "No. Don't recognize him. Though he's next to Henry Greene, who runs the mercantile at the end of Brattles Street. There might have been mention of a nephew or cousin coming here to attend Harvard. You think he's a...you know?"

"Something about him seems off." When I pointed out my other two suspects, Grayson's gaze lingered on the woman from New York.

He adjusted his collar. "I suppose I can drop by. Do some digging."

"Just don't make it obvious."

"I'm not my sister. Fear not."

ONCE GRAYSON SET OFF, I strolled the perimeter of the room while the strains of an up-tempo waltz filled the air. Blazing fireplaces enlivened the shadows. Hutches and serving trays lined one wall, great windows with blue satin curtains another. In my vest pocket, the watch continued its steady *tock tock tock*. As I neared the back of the room, the candles and lamps in the Indigo Room appeared to shudder, their flames wavering as on a gust of wind. For the briefest of moments, sounds and sights blurred, the air around me rippling like clear, flowing water. Some delicate energy brushed my skin.

As if I wouldn't notice.

With a gentle deflection, I parried the probing energy, the expression on my face as pleasant as could be. Witchcraft has a unique texture to it. While I'd grown familiar with it in dealing with Salem, I'd never encountered it in the context of a living witch. That said, I wasn't a novice. I followed the deflected energy with a strand of my own, an insistent thrust. I caught sight of Grayson making his way toward the head table. Next to him, the maid dropped a glass, the high tinkle of its shattering rising over the sound of the violins. Nervous man slid his spectacles up his nose and lifted his head at the sound, turning in that direction. Wife or mistress rested her fingers beneath her chin, smiling.

Barely a moment later, a glint of magic near one of the chandeliers just to my left caught my eye. Twining, twisting.

"No you don't," I whispered. I had only a second to make the choice: let the fixture crash down upon the unsuspecting guests, or make a public display of magic.

Just as the chandelier tore free of its mounting, sending down a cascade of plaster and slats, I extended my witchcraft to catch it. I stopped the weighty fixture and debris a yard above the cups, plates, bowls, and startled guests. A wind rose, spinning with enough force to lift my hair, the tails of my dress jacket, the brocade sash over the waist of my breeches. Conversation halted, replaced with gasps.

I hunched, taking on the weight of the chandelier, directing it instead to whirl and set down on a stretch of empty floor off to the side. Wax spilled, flames snuffed, crystals clinked. After a beat of startled silence, Grayson put his hands together in applause. A moment later, Governor Reddington stood and joined in. Soon, the rest of the guests—especially those who had been seated beneath the chandelier—added to the applause.

REDDINGTON TOOK control of the situation with immediate concern for the guests, leavened with good humor. Servants—including the new maid—quickly appeared, clearing up the mess, carrying out the fallen chandelier. People moved away from the nearest tables, gathering in small groups, some leaving, others rearranging their seating. Henrietta stayed near me, discreetly off to my side.

The scurry of servants created an intermission of sorts in the evening. In the commotion, I lost sight of the slender gentleman. The New York woman remained with her compatriots, her attention most brazenly on me. I was tempted to wiggle my fingers at her in return.

Grayson approached. "That's your idea of not being obvious? Duly noted."

"What did you find?"

"The young fellow isn't Greene's nephew. He's one of his nephew's friends. James Breckenridge. Came up from New York just ahead of this lot, apparently. Middle son of a middling merchant. Sweaty hands." He wiped his palm on his thigh. "The woman with the New Yorkers, however—she's a cask of black powder with an enticing fuse. Penelope Bayard. Of the Bayards of New York. As near as I can glean, she's been toying with the paunchy fellow next to her for some time. He's wealthy enough—though not Bayard wealthy. She's been the bane of half the entourage here tonight at one time or another."

"How did you—"

"I have my ways. Now to the maid, who managed to spill wine across my new shoes, then spread it to my stockings with a clumsy attempt to dab it dry. Underfed crow of a thing. Joined the staff a fortnight back. Distant relation of Mr. Hastings. Somewhat to his dismay, I'm coming to understand."

"He's useful, every now and then," Henrietta observed.

"And I don't even have a sidearm," Grayson said. "What next?"

Summon the guards. Bar anyone from leaving. Question every guest. Have the suspects brought to Ten Gables for further questioning.

The reasonable course of action, in other words.

Governor Reddington approached, tension around his eyes. I whispered to Grayson and Henrietta, "Find out what else you can about them."

"Let's see who's the more useful, shall we?" Grayson said to Henrietta. She simply stared at him, a trick that invariably unnerved him. He shook his head. They fanned out into the crowded Indigo Room. As Grayson passed by Reddington, he pointed at the fallen chandelier. "Mary used to swing from that one in the wilder days of her youth. I'm sure you can tender the bill to her."

"And face her scorn for the next decade?" Reddington said. "The books will record it as wear and tear."

"A Whitelocke specialty," Grayson said, continuing on.

Reddington approached me and said quietly, "Well done, Finch. Anything concerning?"

Just another witch, sir. Perfect timing, really.

"I think not, sir. But I'll confirm. Did Governor Jansen say anything?"

"The man sees everything yet says very little," Reddington said. "Save to you, apparently. That little display of yours may have worked. Quite a show of utility, hardly a hint of Hell's fires. His people certainly took note. Some of whom have expressed an interest in chatting with our Minister of Magickal Sciences. I'm happy to let them see firsthand that you're charming, witty, and—"

"Actually human."

"I was going to say well versed in the state of the province, but human is fine, too. Happy to see the rumors disintegrate at the touch of reality. You don't mind?"

"Of course not, sir. I'd like to get to know them better."

One of them in particular.

12

WITCH BONES

Dipping a quill, I returned to the covering letter.

I hope this chapter will meet with your approval, I wrote. *My thoughts ran rather roughshod across the concept. Still undecided on whether these interstitial planes are the result of two existing planes merging in some fashion, or if they grow from "cold" energy pouring in from neighboring planes reaching a point of destabilization, potentially leading to undetectable planes. Well, from such doubts spring new frameworks of thought. Or so we hope! In any event, I took it upon myself to fashion a stretch of new terminology related to the intersections of the luminous and dark structures: substratic deflection, destabilizing illuminescence channels, and (my favorite) the inversionary mirroring of degree. Bold! Haughty! I might as well simply admit it: I was in high color last week, and I refuse to bend to a calmer perspective, even now. I trust you'll appreciate the spirit.*

I scanned the letter before closing with: *I hope this finds you well, Georgina, & Look forward to your withering deconstruction of my errors in logic. Yr obnt srvt, K. Finch.*

With that, I sanded the letter and folded it, sealing it with a dab of melting wax. I placed it atop the pages I'd had copied from my original. They were bound for Georgina Rush of Philadelphia, the youngest and only surviving sibling of Ephraim Rush. Still spry in her seventy-fourth year, Georgina had maintained a prolific correspondence with her older brother for more than half a century. Spurred on by his voluminous commentary and research into the planar circumstances regarding Salem, Georgina had reached out to me seeking a better understanding of her brother's final efforts and heroic death. A delightful correspondence ensued, eventually leading to two trips to her home in Philadelphia. From that had sprung not only a valued friendship, but the idea of a collaboration. Three years of said collaboration had brought us perilously close to finishing a volume together. The chapter I'd completed being one of the last, with luck.

A knock on the door to my private study brought me back from my thoughts. "Come," I called.

Mary opened the door. "Look at you sitting nearly in the dark. It's not healthy for your eye." She came inside, tutting. "And it's never a good sign to see you attending to correspondence this late in the evening."

The fire in the hearth guttered. A single candle on my writing desk. "It calms me. Clarifies my thoughts."

She put down her satchel and draped herself on the settee across from my writing desk, loosening the top buttons of her riding jacket. "Are they clear?"

"There's not enough correspondence."

"Clara?"

"Oh, you know. Tossing fireballs around in public. And who knows what else. Yet I'm the hypocrite in the scenario, apparently."

"Despite all you've done for her."

"Someone put the idea in her mind that she should flaunt a brazen attitude. One with no apologies. Every bit as confident as any man in the colony."

Mary shrugged. "It's not as though I'm the one who showed her how to toss about fireballs."

"Bringing us back to it being my fault." I put my quill away. "It probably is."

"Now, now. She owes you everything. And she's grateful—even though she'll never show it."

"Little has been easy for her. I'm trying to make room for that. Smooth out her rough edges when I can."

"Back to joinery, I see."

"Except straight and true might not be possible in this situation," I said.

"How was the dinner at the governor's?"

I put my face in my hands. "Keep the correspondence coming."

ONCE I'D TOLD HER, Mary looked at the ceiling. "Unexpected. Thoughts?"

I gave her such thoughts as had occurred to me, the entire motley grab bag.

"It must have been that Bayard woman," Mary said.

"I'm not sure of anything."

"If only we had some way of detecting the presence of witches. Say, spread throughout Boston."

"Lovely," I said. "Thank you, indeed."

Amongst the other changes I'd overseen in the heart of Boston, the witch-poles that once stood in unending vigilance had been taken down at my order six months after my appointment. All sixty-six of them. Relics from another era, or so I'd thought.

"The threat to the city wasn't—nor has it ever been—witches," I added.

"Until tonight, apparently."

"We'll see," I said. "What about you? What did you find?"

She sighed. "To start with, no sign of Gerald. Not at the room he lets on Dunster Street. Not at his sister's house."

"You went back?"

"No one saw me, you can be sure. I also visited the home of Judge Phipps. One infirm elderly man, two servants, no Gerald."

"Mrs. Spenser will hear of it."

"Mrs. Spenser will most certainly *not* hear of it. Trust me, darling—I have my ways. I also visited three taverns frequented by our Gerald on the advice of one of said servants. The Three Loaves, Rose and Crown, and the Drum. No one's seen him in a few days. An unusual absence. Credit to Gerald for consistency. And I believe I rather burnished his reputation, asking after him so. Side note: he apparently owes handfuls of money to various gentlemen. I'm not the only one looking for him. Just the most attractive." She stretched her legs, crossing her boots at the ankle.

"I'm going to have to tell Mrs. Spenser we lost her brother." I dreaded the thought.

"By her own accounting of him, she ought to shake your hand. Though I'm sure she'll instead return the favor by savaging us in print."

I closed my eye and rubbed my temple. Reading in the dark did bring on my headaches.

"Grace Stoughton hasn't seen him, either," Mary said.

I opened my eye. "You spoke with her?"

"I did, in fact." She leaned forward, elbows on knees, pursing her lips in thought. "Frightened little thing; I believe I could have burst her hummingbird heart if I'd yelled *boo* at her after I introduced myself. But I calmed her down."

"How did she seem?"

"Confused."

"Physically."

"Nothing outwardly odd," Mary said, resting her chin on her fist. "Sleepless, worried. I cast that version of *Unseen Ripples* you taught me as she walked ahead of me. The faintest hint of golden lines clung to her, so fleeting I wondered if I'd imagined them. But clearly nothing more."

Given the planar activity we'd noted at the meetinghouse, the surprise would have been if Grace Susanna Stoughton *hadn't* borne any hints of that powerful energy. "Go on."

"The first half of her story aligned precisely with what Gerald told us," Mary said. "Save for the lovely impression she painted of Gerald as an impressive intellect. Confident and inspiring. I think Gerald was wrong about the likelihood of romance; Grace finds him admirable in nearly every way."

"Gerald?"

"Who would think, yes."

"And the second half of her story?" I asked.

"The peculiarities started when she was using the spirit-tablet —she took it with her, by the way."

"She did?"

Mary reached over to her satchel. "Here." She pulled out a brass mechanism of about the same size and shape as a child's spelling slate. Every conceivable banality of magic was etched into either side: stars, eyes, nonsense runes, broom-sticks. On the front were a spring and clip designed to hold paper.

"Any magic?" I asked.

"Nothing I found."

Passing a hand across its surface and opening up my witch-craft, I didn't sense any overt magic. Still, something about it felt odd. "We'll have to test this in the workshop. What were the peculiarities she told you about?"

"The sound of the storm grew muffled," Mary continued. "And she saw the coins behaving strangely. Moving, as Gerald said. But Grace also claims they doubled. Two layers of them, one atop the other, partially intersecting the first. This second layer then spun up. Like a spinning hoop coming to rest, she said—

except in reverse. Curious, she reached out to touch it, and that's when Gerald vanished."

"Gerald?"

"Yes. Gerald. She saw no sign of him. By the sound of it, she panicked. She called his name and searched the meetinghouse, terrified at being by herself at the height of the storm. She didn't find him, so she fled." Mary raised an eyebrow. "But those coins, I found that strange, so I pressed her. She'd harbored doubts about them before they'd even set foot in the meetinghouse. Care to know why?"

"They weren't his?"

"Oh, they were his. Or, his father's, rather. But where he got them isn't nearly as interesting as what he *did* with them before they went to the meetinghouse. Poor Grace turned pale as I wrung the story from her, convinced I was going to arrest her, then and there."

"Arrest her for what?"

"For trespassing into Salem."

"Excuse me?"

"Yes. Apparently our friend Deliverance Bishop suggested that for the spirit-tablet to function optimally, a handful of accompanying silver need to spend a night buried in a graveyard in Salem. A rather glaring omission from Gerald's tale, wouldn't you say?"

"First of all, they couldn't have gotten past my glamours without my knowing. And secondly, there aren't any graveyards in Salem."

"Gerald isn't as foolish as he looks," Mary said. "For it seems he uncovered a hidden record of the place, possibly in the form of some official records in the archives. Maps. Correspondence. A Governor Hawthorn—this would be some fifty years back—had a number of headstones removed from Salem and sunk into the ocean just beyond the mouth of the Merrimack River. The site of the graves was then planted with trees and covered with boulders and fieldstones."

I knew of a few spots in Salem matching such a description, not that I ever gave them much thought. "Why?"

"Apparently a small, illicit trade had emerged of people attempting to dig up witch bones in order to sell them. Souvenirs, trophies—who knows what—often sought by wealthy individuals in other colonies."

"Ah, depravity," I said. "Considering all else the witches were subject to, I'm hardly surprised."

"So the two of them traipsed into Salem."

"I would have known of it." The loft at the far end of my workshop held a series of illuminated lanterns and bells linked to the magic I'd put in place around Salem, precisely for that reason. Last I'd checked, they all worked fine.

"That I can't explain—but they went there. Gerald first, to bury the coins. Then he brought Grace the next day to retrieve them. Gerald had a map and plotted out a route that kept them well away from the stationed soldiers. The woods beyond Tapley Brook brought them across the hills. Gerald rolled his ankles in the briars, but they made it, coming into Salem at a hill crowned with tall maples. The burial yard was on the far side of the hill." She shook her head. "The girl was terrified, and no wonder."

"It couldn't have been more dangerous," I said. "And how exactly did they avoid being attacked by demons?"

"I'm not sure. Give Gerald credit, he got them safely in and out. He got his coins. He won the heart of Grace, it would seem. Until he disappeared."

"What else did he leave out of his story, I wonder?" I said.

"I don't think much. As I said, most of what Grace told me matched what he'd told us." Mary sat back. "In many ways, the mirror of Gerald's tale—save that Grace found no sign of her companion. Giving in to panic, she grabbed the spirit-tablet and fled back to her home in the lashing rains, sneaking into her room undetected to spend a fitful night of regrets and worry, pacing her room, tossing and turning in the safety of her bed."

"And she thought to tell no one?" I said.

"That she snuck into Salem? That Gerald had vanished whilst the two of them performed magic? Of course not. She's barely seventeen. In the morning, she went looking for Gerald again. I imagine that's when Mrs. Spenser saw her—though hardly without a care in the world, as she'd inferred. As for Grace, she's clearly terrified of Spenser. I'd wager she'd march back into Salem again before she'd face her."

I looked at the spirit-tablet. "What about the coins?"

"What about them?"

"Why didn't she take those, also? Or the candle?"

"I'm not sure. She wasn't exactly calm." She looked at me. "What are you thinking?"

"I'm thinking I like Miss Stoughton's tale even less than I liked Gerald's."

"What next?" Mary said.

Placing the spirit-tablet on my desk, I said, "Reddington told me to drop it. If it involves Mrs. Spenser, I'm not to lift a finger."

"He doesn't need to know."

"He'll find out. He knew she came here before I told him. And I told him I wouldn't. You didn't see him."

"Is he strangely in love with her, do you think?"

I looked up. "In love with her?"

"You haven't considered it?"

"Considered it? Why would I? She's plastered half the province with essays calling him a liar, a fraud, a shirker. Also inept, arrogant, narcissistic, lazy, selfish, and dim-witted. A month ago, she announced him below average in height, fragile-boned, and a mediocre horseman."

She waved away the evidence. "Ignore all that. Why he wouldn't be in love with her? Widow. Successful. The most influential woman in the province—after you, of course. Rather attractive in spite of herself. Driven like he is himself."

"The vein in his temple nearly burst at the mention of her name."

"He might be one of those boys who mistakes love for annoyance."

"Boys?"

"They're all boys."

13

STRAIGHT AND TRUE

As I left my study half an hour later, the silence of midnight filled Ten Gables. I made my way up the narrow stairs to the hallway to my bedchamber. Moonlight sprayed across the gleaming floor from the side windows.

Straight and true.

I wondered if I were being too demanding of Clara. While I attempted to provide her with the same sort of guidance August Swaine had given me, I also tried to leaven it with more compassion, more understanding of the difficulties she'd been through. Then again, maybe I wasn't being demanding enough.

The question didn't lend itself to easy answers.

I shouldn't have been so curt with her earlier in the day. The fickleness of any one moment eventually dissipates. And what was left, in the end? I thought of the four years that had passed since Swaine and Rush met their ends, and how much I'd missed them.

Before going to my room, I paused outside of Clara's chambers. A line of light shone beneath the door. I listened. A quill scratched across paper. A crinkle of a page being turned. Maybe she had responded well to the pressure after all; encouragement was what she needed. That I could give her. I rapped my knuckles softly on the oak door. "Clara? May I come in?"

The soft strokes of the quill continued. I put my hand on the brass knob and turned it. Her sitting room, turned into her study, glowed in the light of the lantern on her work desk. Embers smoldered in the grate.

She wasn't there.

I stepped farther into the room. The door to her bedchamber stood open, a dark square beyond. "Clara?"

A page turned in the book on her writing desk.

Looking more closely, I frowned. No hand touched the book. Next to it, a quill danced in the air, the nib—free of ink—sliding across a sheet of paper in random circles, then lifting, shifting, and setting down again to repeat the pattern.

At least she was clever.

Her studies of elemental magic had clearly not been wasted. Something akin to Bernard Lachlin's *Bending Breath on Branch* to turn the pages of the book. The quill? The obvious approach would be a reciprocating echo of mirroring materials: her own gesture, imbued into the quill, set to repeat until she stopped it. I'd given her some lessons in that area a year ago. As I looked more closely, I noticed a certain grace to the way the quill formed its nonsense loops, an agility to the motion. Was it possible she'd tapped into the nature of the quill itself, using elemental magic to revive the airlike qualities of flight within it? Now that would impress me.

I went to the door to her bedchamber and glanced inside. Bed, draped in rumpled blankets, as ever. Clothing tossed about in profusion. A dressing table loaded up with whatever she had in hand when passing by: coins, cups, ribbons, an ivory-handled brush, a stale heel of bread, a cork, a locket, one shoe, two belts, one of my books, what looked to be a musket ball, a silk kerchief, a brooch, a dried rose, spilling its petals.

Yet for all of its essence of Clara, no Clara.

The window, however, stood wide open. Curtains rippled with the night breeze. The streets and rooftops of Boston stretched away beneath the heavens. The dark of the harbor glinted with the moon's reflection. To the right, a slight incline of roof, leading to a lower overhang. Twelve paces along that would bring a person to the next gable down, which would take them to the flatter roof of the stable. A short drop, and one would find themselves happily standing on Queen Street.

I rested my fingertips on the windowsill, the strain of the day culminating in a moment of purest aggravation.

14

THE ACHE IN MY HEART

The mind is a liar, is it not?

An unreliable witness. A fabulist, churning out ream after ream of fairy tales. Excuses clumsily bolted on after the fact. Flimsy arguments, rehearsed and set to memory. In so many ways, we're all putting on a performance to the smallest, least-critical audience of all: ourselves. And each play is the same: we are the hero, reacting smartly to events, doing the noble thing. Of course. We bask in our own applause.

So it was with my arrival in Salem the next day.

The matter would drop, of course. Mrs. James Spenser was on her own, as I'd agreed.

In riding to Salem, I was only being prudent. Thorough. Verifying Grace Stoughton's story made sense, if merely to tie up the loose ends. Why, even Governor Reddington would agree to that much.

Not that I would bother him with such detail; he had a province to run, after all.

A sound story. One I'd begun constructing the moment the mention of Salem had crossed Mary's lips.

By late morning, I found the spot where Grace and Gerald had dug up the silver coins.

Not far off, trampled grass led back through to the edge of the forest. All night, I'd puzzled over how they'd gotten past the glamours I'd maintained around the abandoned town. What I found confounded me even more, for the glamours had been neutralized, three of them. They exuded no hints of residual countermagic. Nothing. My unease deepened.

The burial yard yielded no further clues, unfortunately. No magic, or witchcraft.

I stared down at the planar compass for several moments after jotting down the readings. A lovely mechanism. Gearing and movement, inerrant. The brass casing bore a patina of fine scratches, burnished here and there from untold collisions with the other long gone passengers in August Swaine's pockets: coin, key, medallion, fine tools, magnifying lens, or any of the dozen other instruments he'd absently jam in alongside the watch when his attention reared and galloped off with the full force of his unstopping genius. I closed the lid, running my fingers across the surface. At first, it had felt wrong to carry the watch, like a child taking something unearned, putting on airs; perhaps one reason why Mrs. Spenser's criticism stung so deeply.

Satisfied the graveyard held no residual unseen energies, I put the compass away and returned to my horse. I ran a hand along her neck. "You remember this place, don't you? Still lonely, I'm afraid. At least there's grass to munch."

I got my foot to the stirrup and lifted myself into the saddle, the familiar creak of the leather loud in the silence.

I'd stayed away from Salem for too long.

Not intentionally, so I told myself. Something always cropped up. Got in the way. A soliloquy of excuses, at the ready.

I set my horse toward the lane. My gaze lifted to the rise of land to my left. The manse where I'd lived with Swaine stood mute atop the hill. Windows staring toward the ocean, empty. Sagging roofline. Paint along the second-story windows more peeled than ever, revealing the gray wood beneath. The little fence along the side where I'd tended a garden, half-collapsed now, likely from the heavy snowfalls of the prior two winters. The garden itself fallen to a hopeless collection of weeds. Might rooting around in it still yield a stray carrot or turnip? Possibly.

It might also reveal how deep the ache in my heart ran.

The barn next to the manse—our former workshop— looked to have held up better. Big doors still locked fast, as far as I could tell; I'd certainly glamoured it well enough. The roof appeared intact. As I passed by on the lane at the foot of the hill, I still found it odd to not see the slight figure of the revenant atop the roof: the corpse of a young lad, fused with a demon under Swaine's control, turning every quarter hour, keeping watch for stray demons. I'd buried the corpse in a stretch of soft earth behind the barn, along with the others. No revenants remained in Salem. As with most all else from that time in my life, they'd become a memory, buried for good.

Had I really been that person?

THE WATER of the harbor dallied amongst the rocks, lifted into spray by a strong wind. A flat stretch of land stood beyond the bridge that crossed the North River. Even four years removed, my stomach clenched at the site where the sorcerium had stood—a building extruded from the nether realm of hidden magic known as the demonmere.

The spot where my mentor perished just before all the planar magic collapsed back into a world not our own.

Nothing but large boulders—placed there by soldiers at my direction—marked the spot. Off to the side, a small doorway set into the earth stood as the last known entrance into the demonmere. While it had been a good ten months since I'd last visited Salem, it had been longer still since I'd opened that door.

During those first years after Swaine's death, I'd made a habit of writing him letters and leaving them on the first step beneath the door. With each one, I unburdened a little more of my grief and guilt, loosened the unwieldy knot of anger, frustration, and despair that was the other inheritance I'd been bequeathed.

Painful, but helpful. And doing so left me more room, in time, for the thankfulness, gratitude—and, yes, love.

Not just for how he'd taken me in when I'd been bereft of a single living soul for me to call family or friend. Or for how he'd helped me discover my true nature as a witch.

But for *all* he'd taught me.

About magic, witchcraft, and sorcery—yes. But also about life. Dedication. Discipline. Enthusiasm. An infectious embrace of mystery. Unbridled passion for nurturing the intellect. The way in which a day might offer a nearly endless banquet of opportunities. He'd lived with boundless energy, all parts of life, highs and lows, alike.

I wouldn't be who I was without his influence.

And at some point along the way, I'd stopped writing those letters. Not just when I'd discovered the prior letters gone, though that had been a shock. Yet as much as my mind wanted to turn it into a spark of hope that he'd somehow returned and collected them, well—a few moments of clear, Swaine-like thought on the matter discounted the possibility.

If he'd returned to get the letters, he'd have returned. Simple as that.

The demonmere itself caused the letters to vanish, in all likelihood. Its shifting nature. Its strange sentience. Other causes were even more unsettling: some other wanderer in that treacherous world stumbling across the letters and stealing them. Reading them. Somehow using them to reach through to me. An unkind spirit or demon. The possibilities grew darker from there.

So I'd stopped writing those letters.

As the cold wind from the north flapped my coat and my hair, I decided I might find time—somehow, given how buried I was beneath obligations, both personal and professional—to write Swaine another letter.

One to tuck away amongst my books, many of which had been his. At some point near to his death, no doubt even then in the throes of early demonic possession, he'd written out a comprehensive will leaving his entire estate to me, even going through the formalities of having copies made and witnessed by a lawyer in Andover. A considerable sum of money. Tools. House. Books. All of which had served me well.

With a glance back toward the manse, I almost turned my horse to leave—but then, on a whim, started her off in the direction of the bridge. Just to ease my mind.

Twenty-six planar gauges fed their readings back to Ten Gables. Significant shifts triggered alarms I'd rigged up, though there hadn't been one of those in over a year. One of the gauges stood just opposite the bridge, the tripod legs sunk solidly into the soil, a plum bob suspended on a twenty-inch chain beneath the wooden casing containing the mechanism itself. Like the others, it looked fine.

Approaching the grounds of the former sorcerium, I found the glamours as strong as ever—even a more recent one at the near corner, which I'd had Mary instantiate.

Her skills had flourished over the past two years, once she'd finally conquered her inherent laziness, a campaign I'd waged ruthlessly, laying into her with shoulder, sharp tongue, and measured taunting. Swaine would have been proud of how I'd taught her, using the very same principles he'd used to teach me —though he'd likely have passed out at the thought of teaching Mary Whitelocke to do any magic whatsoever.

Satisfied that all was in order, I hesitated once more before leaving. By the largest of the boulders stood the small doorway, set flat into the ground. My skin prickled as I passed through the glamours. Even with such precautions in place, the footprint of the former building hummed with a curious planar instability— a looseness, the feeling that it all might give way without warning. The calculations I'd done convinced me it would stay that way for at least the next three thousand four hundred odd years, accounting for the expected shifts in the various grand planes.

Not that it put my mind at ease.

The square door nestled between granite slabs, level and flush with one another. No handle nor fingerhold of any sort graced the upper face of the door itself, a construction of tight planks of stained oak, three foot by three foot. Hinges attached on the underside. No pry bar could open it. No fire nor explosion might damage it. It was immune to the elements.

Only I had the key.

I squatted before it and stretched my hand out. A whispered spell unlocked the first of the bindings, sending an intricate pattern of sparks tracing the surface of the wood, mirrored in four directions. My witchcraft did the rest, extending out to activate the four channels of metal inset between the oak of the top and the crosswise rock maple planks of the bottom side. Spirals of iron, silver, steel, and copper came to life at the touch of witchcraft, each requiring a slightly different degree of pressure.

From the other side—coming up from the demonmere—only the lightest touch was required, once the proper words were spoken. And those words? Well, I'd had my clockmaker friend

Robert Twelves carve two letters into the underside of the door. Twelves being Twelves, he also fashioned a brass plaque with the letters embossed boldly, which he secured to the wall right next to the door, at the top step.

The letters: *KF*.

I manipulated the metals and the bindings released. With a hiss, the edges of the door sundered their connection with the granite. The far end lifted, the hinges smooth and silent. I readied myself for the exhalation of frigid air.

It didn't come.

A patch of earth bore the impression of the underside of the door—complete with my initials.

The stone stairs descending into a stubborn darkness between walls of curiously lifeless plaster the color of bone?

Gone.

No sign of the opening remained, even when I dug my fingers into the earth, heaving it out and off to the side. Even when I used a spell to hurl out three feet, four feet of soil, I uncovered nothing but more soil and small rocks. To the side, the same. Nothing.

After a half hour of searching, I stood, wiping my dirty hands on my legs. The hole I'd dug stared back at me, empty.

The demonmere?

Vanished.

15

____

MYSTERY THE FIRST

By the time I returned to Ten Gables, dusk settled. I fended off all requests, messages, and attempts to detour me, trailing word that I wasn't to be disturbed, save for a meal to be left outside my workshop door. My first order of business: confirm the planar gauges around Salem retained their proper calibration.

Glamours entrained the mechanisms in Salem to a long row of devices at the far end of my workshop. Each device displayed a reading within a black-faced dial ringed with brass numerals. The precise regulation of the measurements was fascinating, one of my most sophisticated advances, though to judge from the blank expressions on the faces of Mary and Clara when I explained it to them, not quite as thrilling to a wider audience.

A pat on one's own back must sometimes suffice.

Innovative theory and masterful technique aside, the devices tracked planar fluctuations in real time to produce a daily average, displayed within a small window in the faces. Those I recorded by hand. The readings also fed into a larger contraption in the corner, centered around a perfectly weighted plum bob that spiraled slowly in and out above a three foot by three foot map of the northeastern portion of the colony. Readings above a specified level caused a glamoured quill to extend downward, leaving a mark on the map. I changed the map once per week (keeping my favorite map maker happily in coin for the privilege) and maintained a series of large folios with the recordings, divided into three month increments.

The devices all appeared in order, functioning as well as they had when I'd first set them up and glamoured them. Each spell remained intact. Current readings displayed properly.

Satisfied, I cleared off my main workbench to make room for the prior six months' worth of record keeping. Smaller ledgers, folios. With such data before me, I attempted to piece together a narrative of what had happened in Salem over the previous months. I went over all the numbers, scanning the neat columns arranged by date. Against these baselines were the measurements I'd made at the site of the sorcerium hours earlier.

The picture made little sense.

Mystery the first: a *slight* planar shift could be divined from the daily readings—yet even that was ambiguous, given that the numbers fell within the expected range of imprecision. Had the demonmere then disappeared without leaving as much as a ripple, when its appearance four years earlier had initiated a massive shift in planar activity?

Mystery the second: the localized readings captured above the door to the demonmere presented a puzzling coincidence. A notable spike within two unusual bands of planar frequencies was evident, neither of which fell within the standard measurements detected in Salem. In itself, I wouldn't have been overly concerned by those spikes—such deviant energies weren't altogether uncommon, especially in a location as inherently unstable as the site of the former sorcerium, the locus of a massive planar convergence four years earlier.

What stood out, however, was that both of those bands lay within what's known as the Helmstrom series. The series—

whose repeating waves formed predictable steps consisting of fractions of the fundamental frequency known as *harmonics*—presented one of the oddities of planar theory. In a discipline wherein dysregulation was the norm, where the relationship of the planes was notably obscure, the Helmstrom series suggested a level of order, of connection, between the planes themselves unseen elsewhere.

Would you care to guess what other reading was precisely within the Helmstrom series?

The strange fluctuations I'd recorded at the spot where Gerald disappeared: the *summa-praecento* band.

Having detected two such results might have been no more than a startling coincidence. Three such readings ventured well into the realm of improbability.

And when all three spikes registered within two steps of one another along the Helmstrom series?

Unheard of.

I CHECKED, double-checked, and triple-checked every reading, as well as the calibration of each device. Finding no error nor flaw in either group, I sat back with a stretch of my arms overhead and an unladylike cracking of my knuckles. The flame of the lone taper on my bench wavered. Workshop, otherwise dark; I'd done it again. Hearing Mary scolding me for straining my eye, I used a minor spell to ignite the wicks of six other candles nearby. Two lanterns also leapt to brightness.

My stomach reminded me noisily that I'd not eaten since the morning. Outside the door, my dinner, left as instructed, waited for me on a tray. Small round of cheese, two cured sausages, heel of dark bread, small jar of glazed apricots for dessert, fresh tankard of water. A meal that might sit perfectly well untouched for hours, in other words. My staff knew me well. I'd often done the same for Swaine.

Carrying the tray back to my bench, I spotted a note wedged between the jar and the tankard. I put the tray down and took a monstrous bite of sausage before lifting the note. It looked to be on ministry stationery. I unfolded it. The handwriting within, strong and neat, read:

Minister Finch,

Your staff continue in their terrible habit of keeping important guests standing around, so I must trust this note will in fact reach you. Secretary Whitelocke dodges my inquiries with that infuriating smile of hers. When you finally lose patience with her, I should be glad to put her in my employ so I might have the pleasure of such a loyal watchdog fending off unwanted intruders upon my time: ministers, perhaps.

My brother?

Yours, etc.

Mad. Spenser

I read the note again—and then again. My supper remained untouched for some time.

16

AN AIR OF JUDGMENT

Along the back of the main room of the *Provincial Gazette* loomed three printing presses, tall contraptions of wood and iron. Tools hung behind them. Barrels of ink and buckets of grease by each press. Opposite, a row of windows faced Mount Auburn Street. A pair of men at benches set type with practiced movements, a rhythm of delicate sticks and deft slotting, each new metal character accompanied by a satisfying click. The smell of ink permeated the air. A workshop of words, magic of another sort.

I passed behind the type-setters unnoticed, my entrance forgotten as soon as it had registered. All those I'd passed since I'd left Ten Gables had slipped into reverie potent enough to erase my passage from their mind. A variant of the spell *Spiegelumhang*, or "*mirror-cloak*," triggered a burst of heightened reflection on whatever train of thought the observer carried with them. Most only need the gentlest nudge.

Mrs. Spenser worked in the office beyond the print room. She stared at a sheet of paper, frowning, quill at the ready. A strand of hair sprung loose from the ribbon that held the rest back framed the left side of her face. She wore an ink-stained canvas apron over a gray dress of plain cut. The room around her was either the product of a disordered mind, or one that operated on a system only grasped by an extraordinary one. Pressings and texts hung tacked to the walls, or lay in complex arrangements on the table and desk, the floor in some instances. Quills, stamps, blades, hand-rollers, gluepots stood at the ready. Stacks of correspondence here. Maps there. Scraps of paper, scrawled with notes in the same strong handwriting I'd read the night before.

I closed the door behind me. "I see your work engulfs you with some ferocity. Truly, I feel your pain."

Spenser looked up, her mouth open in surprise. I released *Spiegelumhang.*

"You'll forgive my intrusion," I said. "Best if no one knows I'm here—the governor has forbidden me from helping you in the slightest. You haven't been kind to him."

I confess enjoying the moment of confusion on her face, though the look of vulnerability didn't last long.

"My job isn't to be kind to those who govern us."

"Job well done," I said. "'*A Governor Without Sensibility Ensures Government Without Sense.*' '*Governor Reddington's Abdication of Truest Principles.*' '*A Footnote in History Rides His Horse Well and Little Else.*' Oh, they caught his eye."

"I'm not wrong."

"Wrong? Your opinions are your own. Now, informed versus misinformed: that might be a conversation."

"Then how are my essays misinformed, if that's your delineation?" she said.

"Governor Reddington is a man of ambition, true. Vigilant in his concern with social standing. Prickly toward perceived criticisms." I looked over a collection of what appeared to be proofs. "He thinks he knows better on most matters than those he surrounds himself with. He holds everyone to a standard which —not coincidentally—aligns rather precisely to those areas in which he excels. Obtuse to his own shortcomings, unforgiving of those in others. You've known ambitious men, have you not?"

"I was raised by one," she said.

"Then you might appreciate that our governor also possesses a set of beliefs held with integrity. Thinks carefully about his responsibilities to the province. Knows his place in history and shoulders the burden with determination. As for those who work for him, such as myself, he's unfailingly encouraging. Demanding, of course. We get on well. Maybe because of that, in fact."

"Governor Reddington should forbid you from helping me more often," she said. "It might improve his standing in my estimation."

"Did you know Gerald trespassed into Salem?" I said.

"I can't say I find it surprising, given his endless supply of poor judgment." She tucked the stray lock of hair behind her ear. "He's in jail, then? My contacts there claimed otherwise."

"He's not in jail."

"Then where?"

"I'm not precisely sure. The same potent disruption that temporarily resulted in two Grace Stoughtons appears to have also resulted in zero Gerald Phipps Jrs."

"Wait—you lost him?"

"Not on purpose."

"Should that be comforting?"

"My job isn't to be comforting," I said. "I'm not without hope of getting him back."

She pointed to the office door. "You noticed those three presses out there? Just think of what I shall peel off them if you don't."

"That won't help get him back," I said.

"What will?"

"I need your cooperation. Gerald left more out of what he told you than we suspected."

"I don't see how—"

"I'll preserve your family's reputation, as I'd agreed earlier. But I need your help."

THE PHIPPS HOUSE loomed astride a low hillside, clapboard sides painted a somber gray, a black fence of cast iron along the street. A dozen windows overlooked the surrounding homes with an air of judgment. Mrs. Spenser said nothing as she led me beneath the towering boughs of a chestnut tree, then along a path of slate steppingstones winding to the back door. The sky to the west dimmed with a surly line of storm clouds, trailing faint veils.

Spenser stopped at the door. "My father is not well. I don't wish him disturbed."

"Of course."

Her gaze lingered on mine for a moment before she opened the door. The older construction of the house spoke of generations. Low ceilings, stained floorboards, thresholds worn. Soot marked the stones of the hearths. Walls showing hints of earlier coats of whitewash beneath, faint webbing of cracks atop earlier fractures whispering of sagging joists. And throughout, the relics of the Phipps lineage. Somber portraits stared down from prominent walls. Old flintlocks. Fur rugs. A ship's wheel. Medals framed in dusty glass. Wooden carvings of native design. With the past taking up so much of the present, little wonder Gerald Jr. longed to escape such weighty expectations.

"My brother's room is this way," Spenser said. She'd seen me eyeing the decor.

We passed through a dim hallway. Across from the stairs to the second floor, a library opened, the shelves of books arranged beneath yet another portrait.

"Deborah—is that you?" came a voice from the library as we passed it.

Spenser paused, leaned her hand on the doorway. "It's Madeleine."

"Again?"

"Madeleine, Father."

"Madeleine? Of course. I was thinking of your mother."

"You shouldn't be down here, sir. Not without Bess."

"Always telling me what to do, that one," he said. "Not the first. Do you remember Charles Everett? I could never stand him. Insipid man. Thought he could school me on tenure of lands. Bills of review. Dandridge has a few things to say on that, in point of fact. I quoted liberally. You should have seen his face. You should have seen it, Deborah."

"Father."

"But I can't find it. Have you seen it? Dandridge. Let us pray Gerald hasn't taken it—though he could do worse. Though Dandridge could do better, couldn't he?"

The gentleman tottered to the doorway of the library. Barrel-chested, well into what appeared to be his late eighties, Gerald Phipps Sr. wagged an unkempt beard across his collarbones, his skin and chest hair visible beneath the unbuttoned shirt he wore. A faded pair of breeches, likewise unbuttoned, clung to his notably thin hips. He shared little of his features with Gerald Jr., save for perhaps in the arch of the brows. His eyes, however, resembled Spenser's in color and form. As well as in their sharp and immediate judgment.

"Who's this?" he said, staring at me.

"This is Katherine, sir. A friend of mine." Embarrassment radiated from Spenser's throat and cheeks.

"Judge Phipps," I said.

"What happened to her eye?" he said, staring.

"Let me get you back to your room, sir," Spenser said.

"A fellow at the Rowley court back in the Oughts wore a patch. Peake was his name. Randall Peake. I always thought that amusing. Peake. Peek. Do you see?"

"At least his name wasn't Van Winkle," I suggested.

He pointed a gnarled finger toward me. "See? Kathleen finds it amusing, as well. I told you."

Spenser bustled her father past me, hand on his elbow, steadying him.

"Make sure Gerald returns my Dandridge," he muttered. "And tell him to stop knocking about in his room. All bloody night. Slamming his drawers, doing God knows what. Not studying, I'll wager. Tell him to keep his breeches on. Used to be a cherub, that one. Now he looks like my mother's sister Constance. Did I ever tell you how I put her in her place when she accused me of getting the better of her thin-wristed Henry when I sold him that land? You always said I enjoyed myself a little too much when it came to humiliating him. Well he deserved it. Just like your sister did."

Spenser avoided my eye as she led her father to the stairs. I waited by the gloomy library as her father's voice drifted up the stairs, unceasing.

FAT RAINDROPS STRUCK the glass at the end of the hallway, followed moments later by the roll of a downpour on shingle and clapboard. A crack of thunder rattled the morning outside. When Spenser returned, she apologized for her father's behavior.

I said, "I hope my presence didn't distress him."

"He's already forgotten."

"What was he talking about?"

"Anything and everything from about 1650 until about five years ago. I'd rather not discuss my father, thank you."

"No. About Gerald. Knocking around in his room last night."

"Minister Finch," she said, brusque. "My father's condition is unpleasant and demeaning and ultimately heartbreaking. He was once a great man. No longer. His awareness of who he's with is as unreliable as his sense of what month, year, or decade it is. One day he recognizes me, yet thinks I'm fifteen years old. The next, he thinks I'm my mother. The next, I'm a servant bent on tormenting him. Or he simply stares at me, baffled. Whatever he may have said about my brother may fairly be dismissed."

The rain drummed on the windows. "I'd still like to look at Gerald's room, if I might."

"Fine," she said. "This way."

GERALD'S ROOMS—A sitting room adjacent to a bedroom—surprised me not at all. Whereas Spenser's office reflected a mind agile enough to make acute organization resemble chaos, her brother's accommodations demonstrated nothing more than anarchy. In no fashion did I mistake such disarray for genius of any kind.

Clothing, in profusion, and nary an item within a whisper of a chest or vanity. Books here and there, most in need of rescue or excavation from beneath saucer, lone shoe, pitcher, or in one case the bone of a Sunday ham. Writing implements. Lenses. Pipes. Ceramic mugs filled with coins, corn kernels, soil. Pieces of a clock. Two walking sticks bound together with twine. A burlap sack filled with river stones. A gray wig that no doubt looked ridiculous on Gerald's wide head. A milk box of hammered tin, stuffed with sheets of paper covered in what I took to be Gerald's unkempt scrawl. Not a square foot of either room appeared free of the castoffs of his ever-changing whims. He made Clara look like an ascetic.

"Maybe he's in here after all," Spenser sighed. "How would we even know?"

"I'm no longer surprised by the diametrically opposed temperaments of siblings, I may confirm." I poked around the sitting room, unsure what I was looking for. A woolen nightshirt draped the stock of a musket shorn of its barrel.

"Do you have any?" Spenser asked.

"Siblings? I did. Brothers, six of them. They're all deceased."

"I'm sorry."

"They were a terror and a torment. They were also my closest friends. I miss them more as the years get on."

"Growing up with so many brothers must explain your comfort amongst ambitious men."

"In part, I suppose." An angled writing stand held a stack of pages filled with notes pertaining to the law. I wiped a finger along the top sheet and came up with a skim of dust. Perhaps not as bold a testament to Gerald's diligence as he intended it to be, though I gave him credit for the effort.

Spenser remained in the doorway, not deigning to enter the physical manifestation of her brother's personality. "Your work with August Swaine, then."

"Did you ever meet him?" I asked.

"James met him years back. Twice. I'm not sure how they ran into each other. It may have been at one of the booksellers'. He helped him acquire some maps. James's brother Arthur is a cartographer in Gloucester. Mr. Swaine left a strong impression."

"He would." I picked my way into Gerald's bedroom. "May I open the curtains?"

"Go ahead."

The dim light of the storm didn't make it much easier to search the chaos. Scraps of paper held random notes. Beneath a mustard-brown waistcoat poked the edge of a map. I pulled it out to see it illustrated the western edges of Salem. It held no additional markings from Gerald. A discreet wave of my hand revealed no presence of magic. Searching more closely where I'd found the map, I came up with nothing more of relevance. A collection of lone keys. A penknife. The reed to some instrument or other. Pressed flowers slipped into a folded sheet of paper.

When I returned to the sitting room, Spenser said, "Do you not like to talk about him?"

"Pardon?"

"August Swaine."

"He saved me from great peril. He mentored me. And then he died with little fanfare. What else is there to say?"

"I would assume more than that." She watched me leave her comment unanswered, then added, "You've made no secret of your relationship with him."

"I was his assistant. Maybe even something of a friend. I trust you're not implying anything more than that."

"I only meant to say your public acknowledgment of your studying with him is a form of tribute. Fanfare, of a sort," Spenser said.

"Most certainly not enough of one, if that's the case," I said. At the foot of a stool lay an empty velvet bag with a drawstring. I picked it up, folding it between my fingers. "Where does your father keep his coins?"

"Coins?" Spenser said.

"Silver coins. Like the ones Gerald took. Spanish. And no need to look at me like that; I'm not hunting up a commission. I only wish to see them."

～

THE DRAWING ROOM opened behind a pair of pocket doors off the stately dining room. Like the rest of the large house, it dedicated itself more to the past than to the present. Another dark portrait of a Phipps man above a sideboard. A silver serving set arranged before a row of scrimshaw carvings. The wall opposite held an imposing harpoon in brass mounts.

"My brothers would have found no end to troublesome uses for that," I noted.

"This room wasn't for us children," Spenser said. "Though I used to sneak in and look at the carvings."

"And so began your peering behind the curtains of power?"

"I just liked the way they looked." She stopped before an armoire of carved mahogany stained the color of soil. A small iron key sat within the lock on the righthand door. She unlocked it and swung the door wide, feeling for the latch at the top of the other door before opening that, as well. "The coins are in here. Alleged to have come from a ship of brigands in the last century. Our great-grandfather Alfred Phipps commanded a frigate."

She withdrew a decorative wooden box of an Oriental design, large enough to house a pistol, and carried it to the sideboard. "They were kept in here."

"May I?"

"Of course."

I slid aside the small hasp that kept the top closed. The box smelled of aged varnish. I stared at the contents as a rumble of thunder rolled across Cambridge.

"Has anyone touched this since Gerald?" I asked.

"I can't imagine why anyone would."

Within the box, twelve silver coins lay arranged in a perfect circle, edge touching edge. I immediately sensed the seething planar energies, just like those at the meetinghouse.

Spenser stepped next to me, peering over my shoulder into the box. "What is that?"

"If I'm not mistaken," I said, "it's a message."

17

PERFECT CIRCLES

Back in my workshop, I examined the silver coins. A complex web of glamours spun over them. The state of the silver confounded me. The coins reacted strangely when subjected to a series of spells, starting with the most benign magic-detection cantrips and working up to more serious probing of planar influence. Some of my tests glanced off them leaving them entirely untouched, when they ought to have shown a mark, a shine, a movement. Other tests displayed similar results. I didn't think them cursed, however. Three separate attempts to reveal such magic came up empty. Although glad to knock that worry off my list, my concern only deepened as the afternoon lengthened.

Most striking, I couldn't determine who'd handled the coins last. Any number of spells can illuminate association, key in on identity, or in some other fashion demonstrate a link between an individual and an object. Some of these I'd known offhand, others I'd needed to research and practice to apply to the coins.

None gave me even the slightest answer.

Other spells along those lines, ones that might trace the path of an object through its past hours, days, and weeks referencing a map, likewise gave me no results.

Changing tack, I exposed the coins to a suite of basic elemental magic. Heat, cold, electricity. Spells designed for silver. Spells designed for a broader grouping of metals. I tried glamouring them.

In all cases the results defied my expectations.

The application of a freezing spell led them to sizzle. A faint steam rose from them when I applied the essence of lightning. I could move them across the workbench untouched, but I could no longer get them to link to one another as they been when I'd found them. When I left them spread out, they remained still, but when I stacked them carefully, the stacks would not stand for long, soon enough tumbling down.

Delving into sorcery, I cast a series of wards, investigating the possibility that the strange behavior arose from the presence of one or more demons: objects could become fixations for demons, they could be used as lures by demons. The history of sorcery was rich with bizarre examples of infernal entities being bound within physical objects.

The difference between a cursed object and an object infused with a bound demon? Subtle indeed.

Yet none of the wards I cast seemed to influence the behavior of the coins. No infernal malignancy came to light, no hint of demonic presence.

The trail of my intuitions went cold.

Unexpected. Unexplained. Unstable.

Worse, the planar readings I took around the coins demonstrated small but noteworthy spikes within the bands and frequencies I'd detected earlier. Even within the well-protected confines of my workshop at Ten Gables, I was loath to trigger the kind of planar event the meetinghouse had experienced.

Thus, my guesswork and theories tided themselves into intractable knots.

MY VOICE DANCED around the small parlor at Ten Gables as my fingers danced on the keys of the harpsichord. When a stubborn problem cluttered up my mind too much, singing and playing had a way of creating space, of making way for ideas to come through.

A knock at the door behind me stopped the next verse halfway through.

"Yes?" I said.

Henrietta entered.

"How's my singing?" I asked.

"It's getting—" She paused. "Better."

"Better?" I said. "Don't be one of those. My singing is not so bad that *better* is the kindest thing one might say."

"Of course not, Minister," she said. "How does *almost there* suit you?"

"Closer to the mark. And I shall cease stretching your manners to the breaking point," I said. "How are we doing?"

"We have most of them in place," she said. "Everyone is out of sight, as you'd ordered. We've positioned them in attics, cellars, warehouses. A few are outside, under cover. We kept it so nobody could really see what we were doing, so I don't think we have to worry about that."

"Excellent. How many more do you have left to do?"

"We're down to the last dozen. We should have those done by the end of the day tomorrow."

I'd ordered Henrietta to have her soldiers reinstate the witch-lanterns throughout Boston, not mounting them back on top of the poles where the public might see them, but rather in discreet locations. I needed to find the other witch, get a sense of where she—or he—had gone. I'd set Clara to installing a series of numbered candles in the far corner of my workshop, their wicks glimmered to ignite at the activation of the corresponding witch-pole. While there was some chance the witch might possess some method to evade such detection—I'd done so myself throughout much of my first year in Boston—I thought it unlikely. I'd benefitted from a magicked pendant fashioned for me by August Swaine. I doubted the witch had access to such mastery.

"Does Anne have the list?" I asked.

"She does," Henrietta said. "And she'll have the rest tomorrow."

"And our suspects?" I'd also made use of the Minister's Own for surveillance. Though I hadn't seen nor sensed a hint of further witchcraft, I wasn't taking any chances.

"Mr. Breckenridge seems to want to see everything there is to see in the city," Henrietta said. "I have two soldiers in plain clothes following him. He seems a restless sort. He's been at some of the booksellers' and jewelers', the library at Harvard, and talked with various merchants. He sleeps late, takes his dinner midafternoon, and seems determined to compare the ale of every tavern in Boston before he leaves."

"Who has he been dealing with?" I asked. "Anyone of note?"

"Not that I can tell. Mostly young men his age."

"And the others?"

"Ms. Bayard is an interesting one. She draws people to her. A bit of a queen bee it would seem. Mostly men, sniffing around. She clearly enjoys the attention."

"Just the New Yorkers?"

"She's cast her net wider than that. Several of the council members have been to see her."

"Has she been traveling? Moving about anywhere?"

"Not particularly," Henrietta said. "She's staying at the Harrimans' guesthouse. She's gone out a few times to take a meal in the company of others, but that's it."

"Nothing at night?"

"A steady stream of guests. Meals. Drinks. A tailor from

Newbury Street visited her. But nowhere at night that we've seen."

When I talked to Bayard, she'd intimidated me more than I'd seemed to intimidate her. Pleasant enough, well mannered, spoke admiringly of me. It wasn't hard to see how she charmed virtually every man who crossed her path. And it was no wonder she had most of the New York delegation falling over themselves to be in her company. We'd chitchatted for short time at the governor's behest, and while I'd seen a hint of curiosity glimmering in her eye the whole while, if she possessed any witchcraft, she cloaked it extremely well.

"And the other one? The maid?"

"Easiest of all. Kizzie McCormick. She's been at the governor's manse since arriving last month. A quiet one. Since we started watching her, she went out only once with two of the other maids to fetch several boxes of pastries for a meeting the governor had scheduled with the New Yorkers yesterday morning. Other than that, she hasn't gone anywhere. She keeps to her duties, takes her meals with the house staff, and shares a room on the top floor with one of the other maids."

"Have you been able to find out any more about her?"

"Very little," Henrietta said. "As I said, she appeared about a month back, coming up from New Jersey. A township not far from Trenton. She's the daughter of Mr. Hastings's cousin. Word is that he offered a position to her after her mother died late last year. Her father remarried a woman with a rather large number of children, and everyone thought it would be best to make more room in the household. So off she came to Boston. By all accounts she does a mediocre job."

"She should be easy enough to keep track of," I said.

"They're all easy enough to keep track of."

"One other thing I need," I said. "I want you to increase the watch along the borders of Salem. I detected an incident there and it's best if it doesn't happen again."

"Incident?"

"Nothing you need to worry about and no fault of yours or the troops. A small failure of my own devices, but I just want to make sure it doesn't happen again."

"Of course, Minister. I can shift one of the companies to spend more time up there. I'll have them head out as soon as I get back."

I ran my finger across the ivory keys of the harpsichord. "Do you play?"

"Not the harpsichord. I can scratch out a few notes on the violin."

"And do you sing?"

"I'm not much of a singer, Minister."

"Don't let that stop you, Lieutenant Colonel. After all, I'm almost there."

RETURNING to my workshop after my conversation with Henrietta, I eyed the silver coins arrayed across two workbenches with even more suspicion. Talk of Salem put yet another idea in mind—one I'd been avoiding.

Witchcraft.

Conscious of what had happened to Gerald, I approached the first workbench with trepidation. Sixteen silver Spanish coins, arranged in four rows of four. The faces on their fronts, the uneven stamping on their surfaces, reflected the flames of the lanterns.

I raised my right hand and held it out above the coins, palm down. Concentrating, I let slip a fine misting of energy. Not the quick, tumbling stream I'd released when I'd half-attentively investigated them at the meetinghouse. This time, I focused all my attention with control and precision.

Witchcraft ran down my arm in delicate rivulets. Using the

visualization I'd trained myself in, I held an image of a foggy clearing in the forest at dawn. Air scented with fresh rain, the perfume of the soil beneath. The finest, faintest touch: more than a shadow, less than a raindrop.

And so flowed my witchcraft.

As it rolled across the faces of the coins, all sixteen coins—as well as the twelve coins on the adjacent workbench—snapped together, forming perfect circles. The simultaneous clinking of their edges filled my workshop with a metallic snapping.

The dials of my devices on the corners of the workbenches spun up. The needles quivered. A glance confirmed which frequency bands they hovered in: the Helmstrom series. I stopped the gentle rainfall of witchcraft. The coins remained in their circles.

Everything remained, just as it ought to have been. No surging of energies, no discomforting shifting of reality.

Instead, I had the curious impression of behavior by design.

But to what end?

This time I held both hands out over the coins, palms down. The mist became a trickle, as I directed my witchcraft into a more intricate webbing to wrap the coins. More pressure. A more insistent nudging.

The coins slipped in and out of focus.

Not vanishing nor disappearing, but sharpening then blurring. Hints of movement flitted across them. A strange pressure charged the atmosphere in my workshop. Bottles on the shelves rattled to my right. The delicate dials of the planar devices registered a spike. I eased off, considering.

This time, instead of pouring down witchcraft across the coins, I opened up my senses.

Strange glimmers of light flickered to life above the coins. Wisps. Tatters. For a brief moment, I caught glimpses of features. A face in profile. The quick sweep of a hand. Motion. Once again, I eased off.

I took a series of measurements, using a ruler and a marked chain. The arrangement of the coins—two circles, one larger than the other by dint of being comprised of four additional coins—was true. Perfect circles.

That spoke of intention.

Their surfaces shone brightly. One could imagine a servant in the Phipps household whiling away hours polishing the family coins once or twice a year. And while they all appeared to be of Spanish origin, it was a motley collection from across many decades, the imprints and faces of varying size and design.

I held the tip of my index finger above the nearest coin.

I tapped my fingertip to the coin.

Nothing exploded, this time. The workshop remained the same. The coins retained their arrangement. I laid my fingertips down on the coins, the silver cool beneath my skin.

And no, Gerald did not miraculously reappear, befuddled and sputtering at my shoulder. I let go of that faint hope with a pang of regret.

A KNOCKING at the door to my workshop pulled me from my thoughts. "Yes?" I said.

The door opened a hand-span. "I have the next two lanterns," Clara said.

"Fine. Yes, bring them in."

Her footsteps—never quiet—ascended the stairs leading up into the workshop. I could have told her I was busy and to come back later, but she'd been on a noteworthy streak of diligence, which I wanted to encourage. No doubt she was doing it all to distract me from the fact she was climbing out of her window late at night whenever she felt like it, but at least I was seeing some progress. She wore her hair back in a braid, and wore a dark outfit—ready for mischief, clearly. I said nothing. I had work to do.

"You checked the calibration?" I asked.

"Just like all the others."

She crossed behind me, glancing at the coins arranged across the workbenches. The lanterns in her hand were small, six inches apiece. She brought them to the far wall and worked them into their fixed bases.

"You're probably doing those in your dreams by now," I said.

"I'm getting faster at them. They're still hard, though."

"But look at how many you've already done," I said.

Clara stood back, hands on her hips, regarding the four rows of lanterns arranged against a portion of the wall. Each one glamoured and calibrated. Her nose twitched, one, two, three times.

"Not an easy feat," I suggested. "You couldn't have done them a year ago. A double threaded, reflective glamour? With a substrate of entrainment? You picked up the practical side faster than Mary did. Between you and I."

"She's too impatient for entrainment work," Clara said.

"We all have our strengths and weaknesses."

In some ways, Clara had more potential than Mary in the unseen arts. More of a natural talent. A greater ability to focus—when she chose to, that was. Mary had to be coaxed: purely feline. Clara, on the other hand, required stronger guidance: a bull. Both were useful, both were challenging, and both sometimes made me wonder why I'd ever decided to try to teach them magic in the first place. Still, one worked with the tools at hand.

Clara looked at the coins arrayed on the workbenches. "I heard you singing earlier. Is this what's annoying you?"

"I can't just sing?"

"Not usually." She lifted her right shoulder quickly: one, two, three. I hadn't noticed that twitch before. "Why are they all smudged like that?"

I looked to the workbench. Each coin bore a discoloration—

one that hadn't been there moments earlier. Nothing had changed about the surfaces of the coins save for the way the light struck them. Each coin now bore a darkened area across the lower two thirds of the face. At first, I took it to be some sort of print, a marking left by some unseen pressure or force or touch.

"Who is that?" Clara said, seeing it before I did.

What I'd taken to be a dark print of some sort was in fact a reflection. I moved my hand over the coins and released the glamours. "Stand back for a moment. Within that glamour over there." I pointed to the circle scribed into the floor in front of the second workbench. Clara immediately stepped inside.

I lifted one of the coins, removing it from the circle. It came away effortlessly, with no force of magic connecting it with the other coins. It took me a moment to decipher the details of the unchanging reflection. Only so much was revealed: the indistinct figure of a person, hand outstretched, features faint and blurred.

Every last coin held the same image.

18

QUITE A RIDDLE

The Crown and Comb on Queen Street made up for hours of lost sleep with the aroma alone: strong coffee, light notes of tea, and the soft, sweet scent of cakes and rolls. I inhaled deeply. A two-minute walk from Ten Gables, the Crown and Comb was my usual destination when I took my meals away from the ministry. The clientele was a delightful mix of craftsmen and soldiers from the Minister's Own, some off duty and others in their uniforms. I headed toward my usual table at the back, glad for the change of pace after all the time I'd spent in my workshop.

Lawrence DeWitt stepped in front of me like an unwanted apparition. "If it's not the Governor's Witch," he said.

"Councilman," I said.

"Tell me, Minister—are you paying Mrs. Spenser to bolster your reputation, or threatening her to cease her relentless lobs at you? I can't decide which—poor choice of words, sorry—answers the riddle that's obsessed me since yesterday."

"I'm sorry—what are you talking about?"

"My nephew sets type for her, you see," he said. "And he

swears up and down he saw you at her shop yesterday. As I said: quite a riddle."

"Some find it odd you spend so much time thinking about me," I answered. Not the best I could do, but it was early.

"You'll come to regret I do, I'll hazard."

He raised a hand to someone he knew and brushed past me as though I'd been swallowed by the floor. I could have had the floor open up beneath him; I knew just the spell. Instead, I ground my molars and headed to my table.

"Ah, there you are. A vision in studiousness." Grayson White-locke sat at the table, his back to the wall, a cup of coffee and a berry tart in front of him.

I slid onto the bench across from him. "You look chipper."

"And you look exhausted." He lifted a hand and motioned with his fingers to the owner. "None of your tea. It's a coffee morning for you, my dear. My treat."

"Am I to take it I look as terrible as I feel?"

"Terrible? No. You would have to work a lot harder—and have a much less impressive staff—to ever look terrible. But you need to learn to sleep now and then. And don't plaster me with excuses. I can tell when someone's been up all night rambling about her workshop, determined to do just one last thing before going to bed. And then never going to bed."

"You look well rested."

"Clever. I'll have you know I'm rather busy." He pushed the hair away from his forehead. "Busier than ever. Can you see it on my face?"

"I see a crumb on your face. Right there."

Grayson wiped the side of his lip with the white linen napkin he held on his lap. "Blame it on my carefree heart," he said.

The owner of the coffee house came to the table and offered a good morning, setting down a tall cup of coffee and a tin plate with two rolls and a slab of fresh butter. I thanked him.

"Delilah Cabot?" I asked.

"Heavens no. I'm not nearly of good enough breeding for her family."

"That other one? Rebecca Brewster?"

"It turns out she's unexpectedly boring. And if there's one thing I can't stand."

I took a sip of my coffee; the various rooms of my mind began to throw open the curtains and get ready for business. "Not exactly vivacious, is she?"

"She'll make someone a perfectly adequate wife someday. Someone unimaginative and boring himself." Grayson sat back, extending one arm along the back of the bench, gazing about the crowded room. "No, I'm graced with a touch of infatuation. A little enraptured. The pitter-pattering of my heart providing me with a lovely melody. That's all."

"Oh Lord." I tore one of the warm rolls in half and spread half of the butter into the warm crannies.

"Yes, it's that bad, I'm afraid."

"And you're not going to tell me who she is?"

"You know I'll tell you almost anything."

"Just not this," I observed. "And all for some complex, unfathomable, politically sensitive, deal-related reason, I'm guessing."

"Something like that."

"Your New York endeavors?"

"I have more than one iron in that fire, true. But I'm much too discreet to make it that kind of iron." He leaned forward. "Unlike that James Breckenridge fellow you had me sniff out. Something of a hanger-on, I've learned. No longer welcome. A situation of unrequited love. Questionable behavior. Lurking. Still, I'm much too happy to be bothered."

"Well I'm glad for you. Whomever she may be." I took a bite of my roll. "And do know I'm here for you when things go wrong."

"Now, now. Things don't always have to go wrong. You're just seeing the world through the thicket of your own insecurities."

"You may tell yourself anything you want. I'll still be here for you." I gave him half a roll.

"Did young Miss Clara mention I ran into her the other afternoon?"

"Was she standing in the middle of the Haymarket, turning it into an inferno?"

"Oh, dear."

"I may come to regret having ever taught her any magic at all. She finds a way to turn even the most innocent cantrip into mayhem. Mischief trails her like her own shadow."

"She certainly looked guilty, now that you mention it."

"What did she do?"

Grayson raised his hands. "No one's hurt. No one's dead. Nothing burned down."

"An encouraging start."

"I was on Brattle Street after finishing a meeting with some gentlemen from Philadelphia. As I'd seen them off at the wharves a quarter of an hour earlier, I'd been thinking about a meal at the Admiral Vernon. The best fish stew in town. Yet as I'm passing by that little market by the chandler, I caught a glimpse of a familiar, light-haired young woman. And when I hailed her, you might have thought I'd interrupted her plans for a kidnapping."

"Naturally," I said.

"Far be it from me to look askance at the ribald spirit of youth —but I thought the situation called for a measure of mature guidance."

"And to whom did you bring her?"

"Touché. I was diplomatic. I treated her to a delightful fish stew, liberally garnished with the wisdom of her elder. She may have even listened to a word or two."

"How did she seem?"

"Discomfited. Embarrassed. A touch annoyed."

"Lucky you," I said. "I seem to get the reverse ratio, these days."

"You'd think she'd find it in herself to show a generous amount of gratitude after all this time."

"It's complicated."

"Fair enough."

"And it's a difficult age, in any event," I said.

"Even the second time through?"

"As I said."

"Then I shall leave the situation in your more-than-capable hands. Try not to kill her."

"I'll endeavor to contain myself," I said.

Grayson reached down to the bench and unclasped the top of the satchel next to him. "And speaking of containing yourself, these are yours." He pulled out two books and slid them across the table to me. "You left the first in that carriage we shared several weeks back. The other I found sitting on my dining table. It must've been there for a good six weeks, I'm afraid. Although maybe it says something about our friendship that so much time would pass since you made a social call."

"I think it says more about how busy I am, my dear," I said, taking the books and adding the volume I'd brought with me on top of them, stacking the pile next to me. While I had a precise memory for the content *within* books, I often lost track of the books themselves amongst the many demands on my time.

"Would you like to borrow my satchel?"

"I'll be fine, thanks."

Grayson stole another half of one of my rolls. "If you're that busy, I won't mention the tavern out on Haymarket."

"Mentioning it is a funny way of not mentioning it."

"Well, you know how these things are. People talk."

I rested my hand on the stack of books. "It's Boston, yes."

"The Three Loaves," Grayson said. "Not a bad tavern. Ale is usually fresh. The owner can be a touch ingratiating. Nor would I put it past him to launch exactly this sort of rumor, drumming up business with a tale of titillation."

"Titillation?"

"Let's just say if you were going to hint your tavern was haunted, you couldn't pick a more appropriate haunting: apparently there's talk of a spot within the tavern, somewhere near the back of the public room, where a mug of beer will refill itself, over and over."

"Endless beer? I must drop everything and investigate." I shook my head. "Yet why do I have the feeling that if the Minister of Magickal Sciences suddenly appears to investigate this eternal spring of beer, that might be exactly what he wants. Sorry. I'm a little too busy."

Grayson raised his hand, a bite of roll pinched between his finger and thumb, speaking around a mouthful. "Not suggesting, merely relaying. You may file it away as you see fit. Or not." A pair of well-dressed gentlemen took their seats at a table across from ours, hailing Grayson as they did. He offered them a snappy greeting, then turned back to me. "Speaking of mysteries, have you had any more luck with, well, your little problem from the governor's dinner?"

"Oh, I have a plan," I said. "I doubt very much the governor's most interesting guest is going to remain mysterious for much longer."

Grayson leaned forward. "Does your plan involve Mrs. James Spenser?"

"Pardon?"

"Word has gotten around. I just thought it curious. What with all she's written about you, after all."

"A different matter entirely," I said. "Though what have you heard?"

"Only that you've befriended Mrs. Spenser—as a prelude to having her arrested."

"Ridiculous."

"Ah, one of those rumors." Grayson finished his coffee and dabbed at the corner of his mouth with his napkin, afterward folding it and placing it on the table. He wiped his hands together and adjusted his collar, then said, "It's been delightful as ever, but if you'll excuse me, I think those gentlemen over there are in possession of a decent sum of money, some of which I think might be mine in the future."

"Don't let me hold you back." I patted the stack of books beside me. "And thank you for these. You should start charging me a finder's fee."

Grayson stood and patted my shoulder affectionately as he headed over to the other table. "I'll no doubt retire quite wealthy in that case, Finch."

19

NOT MY FINEST MOMENT

The lanterns vexed me.

Not all had come out of storage working properly; some only flared intermittently, others not at all. Out of the sixty-six lanterns Henrietta's troops had dispersed, only sixty-two worked reliably. I painstakingly narrowed down the four that didn't work—a process that took most of the day—then set about rerouting the connections amongst the working ones.

When I was done, I looked over the corresponding map. Lines, numbers, letters, a box at the bottom where I kept the key to it all. Various scratchings crossed out. First attempts, second attempts abandoned. While it made sense to me at that very moment, I worried it was all going to collapse back into the confusion it had taken me seven unbroken hours to get out of.

Before I did anything else, then, I would copy all of the working information cleanly onto another sheet. I reached my arms overhead, balling my hands into fists and stretching to the left, to the right, lifting up onto my toes, then setting my heels down with a sigh. I hadn't eaten since breakfast.

As soon as I had everything properly documented, I'd eat.

That hope in mind, I double- and triple-checked the

numbers. When I went to make more notes, I found my work-bench inkwell nearly empty, which annoyed me, as I had just filled it the day before. My mood didn't improve when I couldn't find the new blank book I'd set aside. Yet another habit I'd learned from Swaine—though my own handwriting was considerably neater than his barely legible scrawl. My collection of notebooks from the previous four years stretched a respectable yard along a shelf at the back of the workshop.

But after the day I'd had, I was in no mood for hunting.

I stepped to the door. "Clara!"

"What?" she called back from down the stairs.

"My new book for notes—did you take it?"

"Sorry?"

I strode to the top of the stairs. "My blank book. Have you seen it?"

"Book? No. I didn't borrow any book."

Which was of course what she might say as she was frantically trying to hide it. Or disassemble the mechanical spell simulating her hard at work—which, it occurred to me, would be a perfectly irritating use of the only remaining blank book I had at Ten Gables.

I headed down the stairs, not slowing at the door to her room. In my more restrained moods, I always respected her privacy, to be clear. This time, I simply pushed it open. "Well I can't bloody find it and I need it. So unless you think I feel like transforming into a magpie to flit about the Ten Gables, gathering a scrap of paper here, another scrap there, all so I might get on with my actual work, please think again because I can assure you I don't."

Clara knelt by the edge of her bed, a look of purest guilt on her face. Her braided hair fell across one shoulder. A high-collared shirt beneath an open silk vest was untucked above a pair of green breeches.

"Oh, is that where you're hiding it?" I said.

"Really. I didn't take your book."

"Of course not. Why would you need a book for notes?"

"What hornet crawled into your bonnet?" she said.

"Excuse me?" I shot back. "Are you referring to the work of the province filling my days and nights? That hornet? Or is it the time and effort I carve away from all of that to poke, prod, and nudge you half an inch farther along in your studies and experiments, all for your meager or nonexistent thanks—unless it perhaps consists in your semi-impressive contrivances designed to trick me into believing you're working harder than you actually are. Is that the hornet in my bonnet you suggest I'm reacting to?"

She sat back on her heels, clearly not having read my mood correctly. "I don't—contrivances? What?"

I crossed the room. "Look, do you have it or not?"

"I told you. I don't."

"Then what *do* you have?"

She stayed where she was, which told me all I needed to know. I half expected to find a young lad beneath her bed by that point.

Which might have upset me less than what I did find.

She scooted back when she saw I wasn't kidding. I put one hand on her bed and leaned down. As with the rest of Clara's room, the territory beneath the bed had surrendered to the invading army that was her daily presence: a stray shoe, papers, an old walking stick, three mismatched empty cups from the kitchen. And next to those: an ivory-handled looking glass, glimmering with magic.

I gave her a frown and pulled it out. "Really?"

"You want me to learn mirror magic, don't you?" she said, without much hope in her voice.

"You're not ready for mirror magic." I didn't even bother looking at the glass, simply waving my hand across the surface and dissipating the activation. "Does Mary know you have this?" She started to bleat some excuse or another, but I shook my head, silencing her with a similar wave of my hand. "I'll answer that for you. No. Of course she doesn't know. Unlike you, she's been diligent about her studies. Unlike you, she's making impressive progress. And unlike you, she's earned my trust with potent magic."

"Trust?" she said. "You'll never trust me. I can try to prove a thousand ways I'm not the same person I was, and it doesn't matter. You look at me, and you see the past."

"That has nothing to do with it," I said. Really, I ought to have warned her not to push me any further.

"It has *everything* to do with it. And because of it, I'll never be good enough for you. The slightest mistake on my part is just more proof of how broken and unworthy I am—while Mary can get away with literal murder before you give her the slightest reprimand."

"That's not true," I said. Though it might have been true.

"I wasn't even doing anything terrible with it," Clara continued. "Other than getting inspired. Which is a lot easier to do with something like that than by staring at four pebbles floating above four blobs of water."

I straightened to full height. "Of course. You're entirely correct. That's what's missing here: inspiration. I do hope you'll forgive my massive oversight in the custom curriculum I've put together to teach you the unseen arts. Now if I only had my blank book I could make a note of that: *more inspiration.* Transelemental alignment, the harnessing of innate unseen energies to manipulate the natural world: *not inspiring.* A rethink is clearly in order. Perhaps I ought to rig up a cannon for you, designed to hurl great bolts of colored fire from the rooftop—would that be inspirational enough? Or maybe you'd just light up at thought of flying across the skyscape of the city on a magicked broom, trailing golden sparks? Would that be *motivationally dense* enough for you?" My voice had risen to something approaching a shout.

She stared at me, eyes wide and mouth smartly closed.

"Well?" I insisted.

Her gaze went to the floor.

I turned and headed for the door. "Do let me know when and if you're prepared to get serious about any single thing I'm willing to teach you. Otherwise, it's probably best if we give each other some distance."

With that, I left her room, slamming the door behind me.

Not my finest moment, I'm afraid.

20

WHERE ARE YOU, WITCH?

By the time I'd documented all of the connections and rerouting I'd done for the network of witch lanterns—crisp handwriting across blank pages in my fresh book, found where I'd left it atop my dressing table—my left hand ached. I flexed my fingers and got up from my writing desk. An easel in the corner next to it held the map of the city, freshly transcribed with the numbers corresponding to each lantern. The ink I'd used for the numbering was magicked: enchanted to illuminate to the same degree as its paired lamp along the wall, giving me an accurate display of what the lanterns throughout the city registered.

Next to the wall of lamps, a small box of clockwork gearing stood beneath a glass dome. The brass base nestled within a glamoured grid of thin steel wires; wherever they crossed, a pair of spells linked to an individual lamp. Modeled after Rush's original contraption for maintaining the witch-poles, my version relied on a form of entrainment capable of occupying a much smaller space.

I instantiated the preliminary stage of magic, casting the activation spell with my hand above the glass dome. Within, the gearing came to life, the main flywheel in the middle spinning, driving the rest of the gearing, generating the field of transferent energy to regulate the spells contained within the steel wires. Each intersection came to life, pairing with its partner lamp on the wall.

As the system of spells came to proper strength, the lamps along the wall lit up, one after another. With each illumination, the numerals upon the map flared one after another, a brilliant blue. These flashes danced across the expanse of Boston, in no particular order. I found the effect quite lovely.

As the sequence finished, the final lamp against the wall dimmed. I held my breath. Faint pulses of illumination flowed across the wall and the map. The gearing beneath the dome continued to whirl, steady and smooth. Throughout that corner of the workshop, magic wavered, the faint and colorful lines of it, subtle gradations in my vision.

For a few moments, I was convinced I was a genius.

Where are you, witch?

The numerals on the map lit dimly, shifting slightly in brightness, like embers in a fireplace. After a few moments, the number 23 brightened, corresponding to one of the lanterns along the wall.

The far end of Princess Street.

There you are.

But before I could congratulate myself much further, another numeral illuminated, this time across the city, down near Windmill Point. Number 41. Both numerals remained bright. A third joined them soon enough. Number 16, over by Treamount Street. Each numeral flared and then remained steady, along with the numeral indicating the lantern next to me.

Three lanterns, three locations.

Three witches?

As I studied the map, I watched the 23 fade, the number 51 light up instead.

A moment later, halfway across the city, right at the edge of Haymarket.

The numeral down by Windmill Point also faded, soon replaced by the number 11 at Orange Street, near the Neck. I watched the numbers brighten and fade, replaced by others. The lamps along the wall followed in synchrony.

"Clever," I said. "But maybe not as clever as you think."

I stepped over to the contraption with the gearing. On the base above where it met the steel strings was a dial with a triangular indicator standing out from it. I reached out and turned it to the right. As I did, the gearing under the glass spun to a halt. I spoke seven lines of a spell, and then turned the dial one more notch to the right.

The entire network of lanterns, lamps, my map, and the magic that undergirded all of it shifted. The lanterns could of course be tuned to more than one frequency. Rush had been the world's expert in planar cartography; I'd studied his writings exhaustively.

As a result, I knew more than some random witch.

By turning the dial, I switched the lanterns over to the frequencies known to be quite sensitive to the presence of witches, a subtle channel of energies.

As the gearing spun up, the lanterns ran through their initial sequence a second time. The numerals on the map, this time, glowed a ruby red. Sparkling, glowing like embers. Across the city they flared. As I looked at the map, the numbers resumed their faint glowing, this time cycling at a quicker pace.

It didn't take long.

Soon the number 27 lit up until it glowed brightly. Number 27 corresponded to the attic above a chandler shop, just at the end of Queen Street.

Less than a quarter of a mile from where I watched the map.

21

A MAGIC MIRROR

Queen Street stood quiet beneath the stars. A few lights burned at Ten Gables, a few at the barracks of the Minister's Own across the way. I took a back way, so as not to be seen. I also disguised my movements with a spell of obscuration. In my hand, Rush's pocket watch. More to the point, I kept my senses wide open, looking for my clever witch. Guessing—or better—that I might reinstall after some fashion Boston's legendary witch-poles, they'd concocted a method for manipulating the readings.

Not exactly trivial—though still not good enough.

I also had to assume they were, and likely had been for some time, watching Ten Gables closely. Fair enough. That also confirmed my suspicion that their presence in Boston, their appearance at the governor's dinner, wasn't just happenstance. They knew who I was, they'd heard what I was, and they were here to take a closer look.

Thank you once again, Madeleine Spenser.

I stayed off Queen Street. A narrow lane ran behind several of the businesses, along the same side of the street as Ten Gables. As far as the witch knew, I had no idea—or more specifically the wrong idea entirely—where they were. I passed behind the old jail, crossing through a small yard fresh with new grass, and paused out at the edge of Church Square. The old church stood on its own, the steeple reaching up to stab at the full moon riding high, at the meeting of Queen Street, Cornhill, and King Street. A fancy carriage rolled by, giving me a brief glance of an attractive woman in the lantern light within—had it been Penelope Bayard? I pressed myself against the bricks of the wall to the churchyard, staying hidden.

Once the carriage passed, I stepped out and watched it fade into the midnight shadows. What had she been doing? Before I might puzzle it out further, footsteps broke the silence. A figure hurried along the dark street, a cloak pulled tight against the chill. I recognized her instantly.

Clara.

I watched her pass me by, then scanned the rest of the square.

"Dammit," I whispered.

I followed, keeping a distance. She took several streets turning east and north until she approached the mill astride Mill Creek, where a stream sluiced into the great pond separated from the River Charles by a stone dam, a line of shadow.

Clara stopped and looked around. "Mena?"

Shadows slipped from a corner of the mill. "I thought you'd left me shivering here. Forgotten." The young lass with thin face and worried eyes was Clara's friend and trouble accelerant.

Not that Mena would ever cause any trouble on her own. Henrietta would tolerate nothing of the kind, firstly. Further, the poor girl flinched at the squawk of a seagull, a sound only heard ten thousand times each day in Boston. Yet there was something in her character that inspired Clara to embrace trouble.

As she was no doubt doing at that very moment.

"You-know-who was in a mood," Clara said. "It was trickier than I thought." With that, she pulled a handheld looking glass from inside her cloak.

My anger knew no bounds.

"But luckily for us, I don't give up," she added.

The looking glass wasn't the one I'd taken from her. Not that she wouldn't have dared sneak into my workroom to take it back, I suspected. But this one was clearly of a different shape. Had she made a second enchanted mirror? And had the plan been to use two, but now they were just making do with one?

"Is it really going to work?" Mena asked.

"Would I have made it if it wouldn't work?"

"The first two didn't work, you said."

"Well this one does. And it might work even better than I'd planned." Clara added: "It might even kill him."

"Kill him?"

"This is probably the end of him."

Mena looked like she was about to dart off. "But...you...said." The poor girl struggled to get the words out, the affliction at the root of what was going on, I imagined.

"Don't tell me you wouldn't want to see him dead," Clara offered.

"No. I don't. Not...dead."

"Mena: I'm joking. I'm not going to kill him. And thank you for thinking I might so casually become a murderer. I didn't know you thought so little of me."

Clara was difficult, even to her friends. Poor Mena.

"This is why my sister doesn't want me spending any time with you," Mena said.

The dismissive sound Clara made was clear enough. "Your sister would run him through with the bayonet—but I'm the problem. Fine. As you say. But I'm not going to hold back from taunting him. Nor from enjoying what we're about to do. He's cruel. He's idiotic. I'm not going to quake in my stockings at the sight of his foolish face. Are you?"

"No." Whining tone, still there.

"Good." Clara looked around and led Mena off to the corner of the mill. "Then let's have some fun."

The two girls paused by a stack of empty baskets against the back wall of the mill. The stream rolled around the large water-wheel to splash down a small step of stones and into the mill pond. Starlight glinted off the shifting currents.

"We'll do it here." Clara knelt and threw back the hood of her cloak.

Mena knelt across from her. "How do you know it will work?"

"Because I'm a magician, obviously. It's a simple matter of translocational manipulation initiated through the principle of monoplanar entrainment. Did you really have to ask?" Clara said.

"How do you know all that?" Mena said.

"My studies of the unseen arts."

"When do I get to study them?"

Clara looked up from the mirror. "Mena—I adore you. I *knew* you wanted to."

"I'm probably too terrified to, actually."

"Nonsense. You're nearly as smart as me."

"Nearly?"

"Fine. You're much smarter. Just too timid." She reached over and gave Mena's hand a squeeze. "If I can do it, you can do it. Trust me. Really. If Mary Whitelocke can do it—pretty much anyone can do it."

Oh, really?

"She's everything I want to be," Mena said.

"Stop that right now, I might throw up."

"She's elegant. Graceful. Forceful. Powerful."

"Well dressed, yes," Clara added. "With her shining hair, her wonderful perfumes, and the way men lose their wits around her. But don't get carried away—I see much more of her than you might imagine. She's fine, mostly. But also peckish, judgmental, lazy, and unendingly gossipy."

"Aren't you being gossipy right now?"

"You started it. Besides, you're much more like Katie. Over-thinking everything and caring about everyone's opinion. And actually rather shy."

"The minister is not shy," Mena said.

"Oh, but she is. Nearly as shy as you. She just hides it better."

"If only I could hide it that well."

"You should."

"Do you really think I'm like her?"

"I really do." Clara lowered the looking glass to her lap with a sigh. "You're both conscientious and concerned about me. And the two of you somehow manage to put up with my—whatever you might call it."

"You could listen to her," Mena said. "More than you do, I mean."

Good for Mena. I'd always rather liked her.

"I should," Clara said. "But I don't. We're always—I don't know. Crashing into each other when we should have learned to pass by each other. And it is *not* always my fault."

"Like stealing off with a magic mirror?" Mena said.

"Fine. Sometimes it is my fault. Can we get on with this? I'm going to be in enough trouble already."

With that, she lifted the mirror. Paused. Appeared to slow her breathing, as I taught her. Mena's gaze leapt from the mirror to Clara's face to the mirror and so on. The passage of the creek amongst the stones was the only sound. After a minute, Clara raised one hand and held it above the surface of the glass while whispering the words of the enchantment. She spoke quickly, confidently, until streaks of light poured from her fingertips, spreading out like bright silver ink in water above the mirror.

The glass flickered with tiny concentric rings of illumination, the marks of an unseen fall of glowing rain. Soon the entire surface shimmered. Mena put a hand to her mouth, her eyes wide. A spiral of faint light lifted from the surface to dissipate in the air between the two girls—and the mirror showed a curiously warped view into a darkened room.

"You did it," Mena whispered.

"Of course I did it," Clara whispered back, putting a finger to her pursed lips. She tilted the mirror to and fro, peering into it. "I see him. Look. He's in his bed."

She leaned back to give Mena a better view. Mena barely brought herself to look, mostly covering her eyes with her thin fingers. A bare hint of a room and a sleeping person shone in the glass. Though by then I suspected nothing more than a prank, I was ready to step in if anything got out of hand.

The pocket watch in my hand ticked, taking on a steady pulse. My attention shot across to the other side of the creek, drawn to some hint of motion. I focused. A figure stood at the edge of the tumbled remains of an old foundation.

"What are you going to tell him?" Mena whispered.

Clara brought the mirror closer to her face, speaking into it. "Thomas. Thomas Cabot. Wake up. The time for reckoning has arrived. Awaken."

Mena stifled a yelp of surprise.

The hackles rose on my neck. Was that the brush of witchcraft?

Clara flashed Mena a look, then returned to speaking into the mirror. "That's right—I'm here, watching. I've been watching you. I always watch you. You just don't know I'm here, for you're too dimwitted to sense me."

I focused on the figure on the other side of the creek, my hand resting lightly on the bark of the chestnut tree where I crouched.

A muttered voice spilled from the mirror. Clara enjoyed herself. "No, you listen to me, you unwashed, foul-breathed coward—the mouth to Hell awaits, yawning wide to consume you. I hope you fall into its sulfurous maw, but I have been forced to warn you. One slip, one failure to heed my otherworldly warning, and your soul is ours. We will take you to the fires. Your taunting ends. This very midnight. Your cruelty."

In spite of myself, I had to give her credit: it was a fine way to handle a tormentor.

The lad on the other side of the mirror reacted badly to her threats, no doubt confused and terrified at hearing a discorporeal voice speaking at him from the midst of his dark bedroom in the middle of the night. Mena watched in rapt admiration as Clara went into delicious detail about the fate waiting for Thomas Cabot if he didn't mend his ways.

As I looked more closely at the figure by the foundation, I made out the form of an adult male—eyes shone with faint light, peering from his drooping face. Hints of clothing, scorched and tattered, hung from thin shoulders. Old-style pants down to ripped stockings and burned shoes. My mind went back to the apparition I'd seen in the meetinghouse.

Have you heard the song of bones?

Behind the figure stood six or seven more spirits, all staring at me. Their eyes shone like stars. Outfits, as well as I could make them out in the dim light, were also of an older generation. All of them shared the unusual scorch marks, some worse than others. Were they victims of a fire, a tavern fire? Was that the foundation they stood around?

I crept over to the creek. The figures stood on the opposite bank, waiting for me.

The very definition of a trap.

Oh, the witch was a clever one.

I sidled over to the right, following the edge of the creek. The presence of witchcraft tickled my core as I moved to the back of the overgrown foundation. I leapt the creek at a narrow spot, then passed through skirts of tall weeds and briars. The touch of witchcraft brushed me again: the same power I'd felt at the governor's manse.

But this time, I wasn't standing amidst the most influential of

Boston's citizens. This time I wasn't standing in a ballroom filled with weighty chandeliers and blazing hearths.

I had more options.

With a gentle flexing of my witchcraft, I slipped into the *occulta prolou*, the planar eaves: hidden, interstitial passages where planes collided. For not being seen in a particular location, they were just as effective as the most potent cloaking spells—with the added benefit of making me undetectable.

The timing would be tricky, but anything else would tip my hand. I stepped out behind the ghosts, slipping out of a side channel of the planar eaves. As much credit as I gave the witch, there was no way she—or he—would've anticipated this move. Coming out from the half realm shadowing this world, I searched for the witch with an intense burst of probing from my witchcraft. I felt the tickle of the trees, soil in the earth, the stones of the foundation. All the while, the sensation grew stronger.

Hints of essence, almost a warmth as I closed in.

There—the nervous fellow with the spidery fingers, Breckenridge. He crouched at the corner of a fieldstone wall that bordered the pond. Better still, he hadn't seen me.

Now, I could have rendered him unconscious. Part of me wanted to—though perhaps that was the frustration of the evening. To have him chuckling at how I fell for his little trap one moment, and the next moment he'd be unconscious.

Satisfying.

But not the most satisfying. As Mary might say, if you can't bring a touch of flair to your time in the world, why be here at all?

So instead of rendering him senseless, I appeared directly behind him.

"Did you need some help finding me?" I said.

He whipped around, eyes wide. Yes, it was him. Dark hair, a stray lock hanging across his forehead. Slender. Sallow cheeks. Same dark breeches and coat. James Breckenridge wasn't wearing the spectacles he'd had on in the Indigo Room, but he was none-theless unmistakable. His hands flicked up in surprise.

"You did well," I offered. "I think we both had our fun."

He lifted from a crouch, extending his hands toward me. Before he could release any witchcraft, I hit him with a spell of binding, the equivalent of yards and yards of rope coiling him from shoulders to ankles.

"But I had more," I said as he fell to the ground. Taking a step, I stood over him. "And now we're going to have a little conversation."

Fine, yes. It was a bit much. Melodramatic, showy, unnecessary.

But I'd been so annoyed with this witch. And, yes, he bruised my ego.

Not being in control tries me.

Moonlight shimmered on the surface of the creek. Wind sighed through the overgrown weeds by the old foundation. I knelt next to Breckenridge. "Let's start with your name."

He didn't answer, just stared up at me. I reached down and put a hand to his chest. "This doesn't have to be difficult."

For a moment, the light around him queered, shimmered. I struggled to focus on him, steadying myself with my hand. His eyes didn't track me. They remained dumbly fixed on the stars overhead.

"Hey." I tapped his cheek lightly, the touch of dread in my chest preceding my understanding by a few moments. He didn't move. I held the backs of my fingers in front of his nose and mouth and felt no breath. I reached down and pressed my finger-tips to the side of his throat: no pulse.

Dead.

My mind spiraled through the possibilities. Had the surprise done him in? Was it some exposure to the planar eaves? Had the spell of binding interacted with his witch nature in some unexpected—and fatal—manner?

I rifled through the pockets of his coat. Nothing, at first. No billfold. No pocketknife. No coin. No spectacles, which was marginally curious. Finding a narrow breast pocket, I slid a finger through it and came up with a folded piece of paper. Opening it, I saw two words clear in the starlight, dead center on the page:

Oh, dear.

Oh, dear? Oh—dear? My eyes flicked over the pair of words several times until the meeting kicked me in the gut.

I looked at the body and opened my senses. As my witchcraft ran across him, I detected no signs of his; he had no witchcraft. I extended my natural magic around the body, the ground, the stone wall. A hint—there. A faint trail of witchcraft. Leading back past the stone wall.

Enough to suggest exactly how outsmarted I'd been.

Oh, dear.

As I lifted my gaze to the gathering of spirits standing beside the foundation of the old tavern, they each raised one hand, placing the other at their midriff. And, like a troupe of actors finishing a performance, they bowed in unison. Before they could rise again to the applause only they could hear they dissolved into falling mist, vanishing.

The creek burbled under the light of the heavens.

And by the time I turned back to James Breckenridge, he'd turned to cinder.

22

SET TO MURDER SOMEONE

Rain drummed on the roof of Ten Gables, a steady spring downpour. I searched the top drawer of my dresser, looking for my favorite eye patch. "Have you seen the dark green one?"

"Perhaps Clara made off with that, as well," Mary said. She rested her hip against the settee in my dressing chamber, immaculately dressed as ever, boots polished.

I lifted a plain black patch and placed it over my deflated left eye socket, adjusting the thin band beneath my hair. "Good enough?"

"They're all fine, darling. Unless you go truly unreasonable. Which I've mostly trained out of you, you're welcome."

I shrugged on a moss-colored waistcoat. "This witch is three steps ahead of us."

"I'm not sure she's that good," Mary suggested.

"She guessed—correctly—I'd use the witch-poles to hunt for her. Took it as an opportunity to confound me."

"She didn't guess you were going to be searching on more than one frequency. Perhaps she's not the infallible genius you are giving her credit for."

"I still don't like it." I adjusted my waistcoat with a glance in the standing mirror.

Mary took it upon herself to tug down the back of the waistcoat, leveling out the hem. Satisfied, she patted my shoulders, urging me not to slouch. I forced my shoulders back. We passed into the hallway heading to the stairs. Rain lashed the windows on the right-hand side of the corridor.

At the rear foyer of Ten Gables, the woman at arms stood near the foot of the stairs, an officer's dress sword at her side, the shoulders of her uniform damp from rain. "Your brother is in the dining parlor, Secretary Whitelocke." The captain opened the doors. "Minister."

"I didn't invite him," Mary said as we crossed through the open double doors and into the dining parlor. A fire burned in the grate. Grayson sat at the table, a cup of coffee steaming before him, half a buttered scone on a fine plate next to it. He wore his hair down. A soaked hat hung from the back of the chair.

"Ah, two glorious rays of sunshine to relieve the gloom," he said. When neither of us remarked on his observation, instead going to pour ourselves some coffee as well, he reconsidered. "The both of you look set to murder someone. What have I missed? Shall I send a search party after young Miss Clara?"

"A little too close to the mark," Mary said.

"Now what?"

"I'd rather not get into it," I said.

"That bad?" Grayson said.

"You're looking well." As I took my seat, a server entered with a covered platter of fresh eggs and ham, along with a bowl of spiced apples in cream. He placed them at the table and uncovered the lids. A far cry from my days of hanging a bowl of mush to warm in the hearth before the dawn.

"What's not to celebrate?" Grayson said. "An invigorating night. Strong coffee. Deals to be had. My closest friends to share it all with."

"He wants something." Mary took a small portion of eggs and apples.

"You do want something," I said.

"Well, don't we *all* want something, most of the time? And fear not, it's nothing extravagant." He rubbed his palms together. "A few moments of your time. The aura of your fame, aimed in a particular direction."

"We're busy," Mary said.

"And I have nothing but respect for your work," Grayson continued. "But hear me out. After all, this started when I attended a certain governor's dinner wherein a candle-laden fixture nearly crashed atop a table of dignitaries—whose evening if not their lives were spared by the quick-thinking Minister of Magickal Sciences. Impressive. Noteworthy. An event which has spiked an insatiable curiosity in the mistress of an incredibly talented silversmith in New York by the name of Giles Walcott."

"And." I sipped the hot coffee.

"Not intriguing enough? Well, let's just say Giles is a true artist, in every sense of the word," Grayson said. "A man of tremendous sensibilities, finding muses in the most unlikely, one might even say, *inconvenient* places—yet helpless to turn away from inspiration. Ruled by his passions."

"I take it there's a point in there somewhere?" Mary said.

"Ignore my impatient sibling," he said to me. "Miss Penelope Bayard and I have rather bonded over the past few days."

Mary and I exchanged a glance. "Penelope Bayard?" I said.

"Yes, that Penelope Bayard."

I raised an eyebrow. "Is she the one for whom your heart was pitter-pattering? And please say no."

"I don't know why the two of you have to assume my every interaction with a beautiful woman is going to leave me tripping over my own feet, love-struck. I'm a merchant. Miss Bayard is a merchant of the heart, of some sort. Fascinating woman. Sharper than you might guess."

"You do remember she's on my list of suspects, don't you?" I said.

"Of course I do. Why do you think I dug into this in the first place? And don't thank me yet, because it gets even better. One might even say delicious. She's fascinated with you."

"Or actively stalking her," Mary said.

"She wants to meet you," Grayson said. "Secretly."

"Does she?" I said. "Do you think this time she'd care to do it without killing anyone, causing anyone to vanish, or swarming me with spirits?"

Grayson looked back and forth between Mary and me, his hopes of his next great deal dimming as he took in our expressions.

GOVERNOR REDDINGTON and I rode along the banks of the Charles. Just the two of us, in contrast to prior weeks when Newton Endecott and Lawrence DeWitt had joined us—only to behave in manner and word as though it were just the three of them, perhaps trailed by a shadow, or a faint garbage smell. I couldn't tell if their absence was a good sign, or a bad one.

The rain had changed to a fine mist that turned to beads and baubles on my outfits, my saddle, my horse. Fog blurred the far banks above the lead-colored waters, matching the hemmed-in mood of my morning. Reddington rode with the ease of an expert horseman, dressed in a black coat, dark brown breeches, and tall boots. The muscles of his stallion looked as though they'd been carved from marble.

"Yesterday's skewering from Madeleine Spenser," he said. "Have you read it?"

"No, sir."

"Rather an interesting headline. '*Such Trust as to Be Beyond Measure, Squandered in Reckless Governance,*'" he said. "Little about the piece is much kinder. Cutting depictions of ministerial dysfunction interspersed with pointed attacks on the practicalities of your office. Let's not forget the insinuations of a lack of attention on my part to the issues of the day, in favor of horse riding and hunting. A few linger in my mind, Finch. '*An invidious mendacity permeates every strata of our feckless administration.*' And there was also: '*Reddington's casual disregard of detail and nuance.*' And, '*More gifted in the saddle than in the seat of power.*'"

He held the reins easily. Our horses' hooves squelched in the damp grass and soil.

"And so on," he continued. "But don't worry, she saved a few shots for you, as well. Pointing out you didn't have anything resembling a doctoral background or accreditation. Nor do you provide me with a swatch of skirt to hide behind, even as I persist in propping up your useless office. And, of course, she couldn't resist making it personal, claiming that the continuing diminution of the stature of the governorship has been brought on by my fancy for the temple of bodily competition, a result of my overcompensation for my own lack of physical height."

My gaze flicked to his face. His lips had all but disappeared into a tight white line.

"Now remind me," he said. "Was there any ambiguity in my instructions to stay away from Madeleine Spenser?"

"This isn't an attack on you," I said. "It's an attack on me."

"Interesting then that it's my name she mentioned seventeen times."

"She references me clearly enough, sir."

And just as clear: she was letting me know that if I didn't find her brother, she would do her best to take down the governor and the Ministry of Magickal Sciences with him.

Reddington shifted the reins to his other hand. "There's more than my pride at stake here, unfairly battered and bruised though it be. This is about prying London's hands from around our throats. I haven't spent two years wooing that cold, judgmental

Dutchman for my own amusement. And now Jansen may pick up stakes and return as early as this afternoon. He's back to questioning the wisdom of even talking with us at all."

We passed by a man leading a dozen sheep. The man raised his hand, and Reddington greeted him in return.

"This business with that Breckenridge fellow," he said. "It's not helping. Neither is this talk of the Three Loaves and its haunted beer mug. Or the bookshop down the street, with their window showing night outside when it's daytime. Or daytime when it's nighttime. Whichever it bloody is. People's seeing shadows of ravens passing in front of the wall—but no ravens. I need it all to stop. Now. Today."

He jumped his horse over a wide puddle, galloping out ahead of me. I frowned and gave my horse my heels, splashing through the puddle to catch up.

When I did, he said, "Tell me—do you require anything for Ten Gables?"

"No, sir."

"And do you lack for any support with the council?"

"I don't."

He said nothing.

"I'll take care of it, sir," I said. "All of it."

Reddington picked up our pace. "Nothing like a ride to clear the mind."

I stayed at his side. Serving a man like Thomas Reddington meant delivering for him: every time, whatever it took. Doubt became liability. Liability was not tolerated. His message to me was quite clear: *I made you, I can unmake you.*

23

SPIRIT WRITING

The rain cleared out by midafternoon, leaving the patch of Cambridge where I waited glittering with a hundred thousand drops of rain. Phantoms of steam rose as the sun warmed the air. I sat on a bench near Waterhouse Street.

If only the rain could rinse out the stain of politics. Everyone wanted something, and everyone viewed those around them as tools with which to get what they wanted. A dirty business. Perhaps if I simply sat, not thinking, my misgivings might burn off like the morning rain and fog.

Difficult.

A number of sheep spread out across the large swath of grazing commons across from me. I watched an ewe who seemed to be quite enjoying herself. What had she to worry about? The skies had cleared, the grass was fresh, the sun was bright.

But what did I know?

Everyone looked so calm from the outside. Yet weren't most of us stumbling about in a kind of fever-delirium: tangled in the briars of the past, or gazing obsessively at the faint horizon of the future? Not sure I could answer that question, I watched the sheep.

Grace Stoughton came into view. On her way home from the schoolhouse where she volunteered, the young woman leaned forward as she walked, a bundle of books pressed to her chest, a distracted look on her face. It wasn't difficult to see why Gerald could be smitten with her. Her face had a sweet quality to it, framed in dark curls. I stayed on the bench. She didn't register me as she approached; I guessed her as lost in thought as the rest of us.

As she hurried past, I said, "Grace?"

If I'd released a wall of flames—possibly with some lightning thrown in, and a thunderclap as well—I don't think she could have been more startled. A yelp burst from her lips and one of the books she carried fell to the street. She looked at me with wide eyes.

"I didn't mean to startle you." I leaned forward and picked up the book she had dropped, wiping the mud from the cover. A Latin primer.

Her eyes remained wide as she stared at me. I stood, offering the book back to her.

"You are not in any trouble," I said. "But I do have a few questions."

She started to shake her head, then seemed to change her mind. "I didn't—I haven't—I'm sorry."

"Why don't we just take a walk? That's simple enough, don't you think?"

"Simple? Of course, yes."

A graveled path cut through the field, half of which had been turned into a common where a white gazebo stood framed by two tall elm trees.

"This is about Gerald, isn't it?" she asked.

As I glanced at her, I tried to square the vibrant, anxious set of her features against the filthy corpse I'd pulled from Madeleine Spenser's root cellar. Or the cinder version of said same corpse.

I liked the living version next to me so much better.

"You've been through a lot," I said.

She pressed the books even more tightly to her chest. "Every morning when I wake, if I've slept at all, there's a moment where I think it's all a terrible dream. And for just a second, I'm so relieved. Isn't that awful?"

"I know that feeling." The gravel crunched beneath our steps. The ewe I'd been watching earlier raised her head and noted our passage. "A cruel forgetfulness."

"Yes, it *is* cruel," she said. "And it's made me realize that when you're younger, you think everything is just as it should be. The world clean, fresh, interesting, and carefree."

Grace Stoughton still looked quite young to me, but I said nothing.

She continued, "But then you start to see all that's unpleasant. And you start to see what a horrendous lie it all is. It's as though we're walking on the thinnest sheets of paper, painted over beautifully, but bound to rip beneath our way eventually. And that's it for us, when it does."

Maybe she wasn't quite as innocent as she appeared. "Now that's rather bleak."

"It is. It's terrible. It's why Gerald and I tried so hard to see what else there is. Even though our families would find it all so silly. I find nothing more interesting—don't you?"

I recalled the sight of her demon-inhabited corpse and the vile suggestions spewing from its mouth. "It has its moments."

"I don't believe he's gone."

"It's hard," I said.

She looked up at me. "No, not like that. I don't mean *I don't believe he's gone* in the sense of...of grieving disbelief. I mean I don't believe he's gone. I think he's somewhere. Somewhere nearby. And he's trying to get back."

We neared the gazebo. The fresh whitewash glowed in the sunshine. "Why do you think that?"

Grace stopped. She crossed her arms, gazed to the sky, her lips set. Then she looked at me and said, "Because he told me so."

THE RIVER GLINTED in the distance. Songbirds filled the air with their melodies. Grace held the railing of the gazebo, her soft features tightened into sharp concentration. "I'm not helpless. My family thinks I am. They never fail to remind me so. But Gerald and I—well, we are more alike than either one of us would have guessed. He doesn't treat me like I'm some delicate porcelain doll. Or a seven-year-old. He treats me as though I'm every bit as smart as him."

"Are you?"

She shrugged. "Possibly. But certainly not in every area. And Gerald himself is smarter than, well, than he looks. And he's certainly smarter than he's given credit for. Mostly by his family. Just because he doesn't want to study the law doesn't make him lazy. It just makes him interesting, as far as I'm concerned." She leaned her waist against the railing, staring out across the commons. "Which is why I knew he would reach out for me."

"Reach out for you how?"

"Well, I wasn't sure exactly how, not at first. But I knew he would. When he disappeared, I was horrified, of course. But he'd warned me that something of the kind might happen."

"Did he?"

"Of course he did. Tampering with the planes isn't without risk," she said.

"Indeed," I said. "What else did Gerald tell you about the planes?"

"Everything he knows. He gave me one of his books to read. *On Planar Cartography*, by—"

"Ephraim Rush," I said. "And yet, this was all connected to spirit writing?"

"Gerald believes the afterlife might in fact be the transmission of consciousness from one plane to a different plane. And if the proper communications could be established, that would be proof. That would change everything, wouldn't it?" The color in her cheek was high.

"But he knew the risks."

"He did. So we made an agreement before we started at the meetinghouse," Grace said. "We agreed that, should something happen, the one of us it happened to would reach out to the one remaining and offer up a signal."

"Rather bold," I said. "What kind of signal?"

"We settled on three. A spectral manifestation, if that was at all possible. Spirit writing, of course. And—"

I waited for her to finish. She stared at me, gnawing at the corner of her lip. "And the third?" I prompted.

"Witch bells, ma'am."

"And what exactly are 'witch bells'?"

"Well, I assumed—that being—well, that you would know."

"I assume them to be some paraphernalia purchased from Deliverance Bishop?"

Grace flushed. "I—I think so. Yes. But they're supposed to be genuine. Small handbells, used by the witches to warn each other of Christians."

Bellcraft had a long place in the unseen arts. I'd explored it myself. Whether the witches of Salem ever used them to warn of Christians, or of greedy and fearful Bostonians, was another matter entirely. But I suppose the markets for fake or lightly magicked bells could rise even more in value if the word *witch* were attached. "Go on."

Grace clicked together the nails of her index finger and thumb on her left hand. "Well, the physical manifestation obviously didn't happen. Not that night when I fled the meetinghouse. Not when I went back the next day searching. Not when I went by Gerald's father's house. Not at night in my house. So I don't think that's going to happen. I tried spirit writing, even though I didn't have the tablet. But I tried with what I had. A goose quill, paper, special ink. Gerald and I had them made."

"Quite a little magic duo the two of you are," I observed.

She didn't meet my eye. "I suppose you think us ridiculous. Being the Minister of Magickal Sciences."

I reached out and rested my hand on her shoulder. "I actually think the two of you did quite well, all things considered. And if I'm being honest, it all sounds far less immature than I expected. Dangerous, though. But I think you know that now. Tell me what happened with the spirit writing."

"You have to understand I wasn't exactly eager to hold a quill in my hand and open myself up to the spirits again," she said.

I contained the shudder that wanted to ripple through me at the naïveté with which she and Gerald approached opening up just such channel into the unknown.

She continued, "But it's what we agreed on, I reminded myself. It was my duty. I waited until the rest of my family went to sleep, and I set everything up as Gerald had taught me. I lit a pair of candles inside a circle of soil on the floor. I used a normal writing tablet to hold the paper. At first, I didn't think anything was going to happen. Maybe that's because nothing ever happened before—except at the meetinghouse, I suppose. What more horrendous proof could I need? I relaxed my mind, my thoughts, and tried to picture Gerald. I resisted the urge to start moving my quill across the paper. It's easy to fool yourself. You just start circling with the nib, spinning it out into doodles, maybe those doodles start to feel more like words—but all the while, you know you're really the one doing it, and try to convince yourself."

"Did you? Convince yourself."

She looked at me, her hazel eyes fixed on mine, direct. "No. Because I wanted to hear from Gerald. I kept all those silly urges in check. I'm sure of it. Which is why I sat there for at least half an hour with nothing happening. If nothing happened, then that would be a signal of some kind, at least. Which is exactly what I thought was going to happen—nothing—when the quill jumped in my grasp. It was different than at the meetinghouse. Then, it was as if I had slipped into some daydream, my senses gone funny. But this time I was as aware and as fully in control of my thoughts as I am right now with you. It was the quill. It seemed to come alive in my grip. And it scratched out two words on the page before the quill itself fell to pieces in my hand, as though it had been peeled apart. And just as it happened, the witch bell I kept on my nightstand tumbled off and landed on the floor."

She looked earnest enough. And she sounded self-aware enough. But people could see and hear what they wanted to, if they were desperate enough.

"What were the words?" I asked.

"Snow Hill." Grace lifted her arm and pointed out at the river. "You can just make it out from here."

I looked in the direction she pointed, squaring it with my knowledge of the area. "Do you mean the windmill?"

"Yes. The one near Ferry Way, across from Charlestown. Near the burying place."

"Is that somewhere the two of you searched?" I asked.

"I've never been there. In fact, I don't remember Gerald ever even mentioning it to me."

"I'm sorry, I don't understand," I said. "Why would you think it was Gerald in that case?"

"Because it's on his list of locations he thinks haunted. Places he thinks worthy of investigating. Like the meetinghouse," she said.

"And you know this how?"

Grace leaned down and pulled a slim book from the middle of the stack of books she'd carried. She held it up for me to see. "Because he wrote of it in his journal. Here."

I took the slender volume and opened the covers. On the

front plate was written: *The Property of Gerald Phipps Jr. Private. Peruse at Your Own Peril.* Beyond that, the pages brimmed over with Gerald's handwriting. The ribbon mark lay between two pages, one of which contained the list Grace referenced. Number two on the list was: *Snow Hill, windmill.* A parenthetical after it read *Explosion and fire, 1694. Four perished. Rebuilt 1697. Reports of hauntings ever since.* I scanned farther down the list. *Old stone church (Charlestown). Alder Field Cemetery (Reading). Pompy's cabin & watchtower (Andover). Site of the Drum (Gloucester).* Sundry others of that nature.

I flipped through some of the other pages, and my gaze paused on one note in particular. In the marginalia, Gerald had written, and underlined, the name of a tavern, a little mug drawn next to it.

The Three Loaves.

24

WISPS AND CURLS AND TATTERS

By the time I reached the windmill atop Snow Hill, the afternoon had lengthened. I'd taken pains to keep my passage unnoticed as I'd made my way over from Cambridge. If the other witch had thought to follow me, or ambush me again, I'd made that impossible. The lowering sunlight glanced off the leaden braids of the river. A ferry made its way back from the Charlestown bank, the ferryman poling the vessel across the current.

A warm breeze snapped at the fabric of the windmill's four tall sails, locked in place, the grinding wheels silent. I made my way past the grain house and round to the back. A squared-off entrance wore what appeared to be a relatively fresh coat of paint. I paused at the door, cocking my ear for sounds from within. Hearing nothing, I tried the door. Locked. Not a problem. I held my hand by the iron latch and whispered a simple enchantment of release. The iron tumbled within. I pulled the door open and slipped inside. The air smelled of ground barley. I touched the end of my nose, stifling a sneeze.

Above me loomed the great axles of the mill, gearing extending down to the stone grinding wheels in the center. A fine skein of dust covered the floor and every other available surface. Tools hung along one wall. By the millstones leaned various implements for shifting and directing grain. Somewhere off in the corner, a mouse skittered. A breeze outside sent the sails to thump gently, the sound within deep and reverberating.

The energy felt strange.

My witchcraft vibrated like the string of a lute just plucked. Nothing appeared out of place, yet my wariness deepened. I withdrew the planar compass from my pocket. Though I hardly needed the confirmation, the dials registered a significant disturbance, peaks rising in the unusual frequency bands I'd noted at the meetinghouse.

"Gerald?" My voice sounded strange in the large space. "Can you hear me?"

The mouse or mice in the corner stilled. Splashes of deepening sunlight rose along the eastern side of the interior. My presence had agitated the fine motes of grain in the air, and they spiraled and danced where the sun caught them.

No faint voice reached me. No witch bell knocked from a nightstand. No tool tossed out of place, a signal.

Clearing a spot in the middle of the floor between two large bins that brimmed over with ground barley, I rested one knee on the floorboards. From my satchel, I pulled a small glass bottle. I unstopped it and poured a small stream of high-grade silver filings into my left palm. Setting the bottle down, I lifted a pinch and let the silver fall in a thin stream to the floor. Concentrating, focused, I created a circle of about a foot in diameter. When I connected the ends, I brushed off the remaining flecks of silver into the middle of the circle. Nothing changed.

Joists high above creaked, the building coming to rest as the temperature cooled. Gulls cried out from the river. The mouse resumed her endeavors.

I extended my hand over the circle of silver filings. Carefully, I extended my witchcraft, the most delicate of touches.

As it brushed the silver, the filings shifted, aligning themselves to one another, bringing the circle into precision. A glance at the planar compass I'd set down on the floor next to me confirmed yet another jump in the frequencies.

"Gerald?"

The strange energy pressed me, twining, coiling within the space. I released more witchcraft, letting it seek its way across the silver, embracing it. The particular essence of the metal ran from the filings on the floor up into my hands. I tasted it in the back of my throat. Likewise the wood beneath the silver, with its long-ago memory of sunlight and the quenching waters pulled in through its old roots. Even the tiny flecks of barley grain, the dust between the silver in the wood, bloomed inside me as impressions: wind and rain, the blazing growth of the earth, awakening in springtime, the drive to rise and expand.

And something else.

The shifting, coiling energies blotted out my awareness of the other materials. What I felt, I didn't care for. It was as though I'd been walking, lost in thought, only to catch myself when my foot stepped past the edge of a cliff I hadn't known was there.

An immense void, the sensation dizzying, overwhelming. Before I could tumble headlong into it, my other knee slipped to the floor as I put a hand out to catch myself. My palm skidded through the silver filings, disturbing the circle. The entire windmill shook. Beams and boards strained. The millstones knocked against one another in a quick triplet of sharp, stony clunks. Feathery rills of dust fell from a dozen spots on the walls and ceiling, from the gears and axles.

The needles on the planar compass pinned all the way to the right, quivering. Under the weight of my hand, the silver rippled like a powerful stream, tickling my skin. Flares of light spun across the walls, as though tracking half a century's worth of the passage of the sun through the days, from rising to setting, as though the universe spun on its axle all centered on the windmill.

Tools near the millstones fell and clattered on the floor. The grain in the bins vibrated, spilling over the edges to bounce and dance on the floor.

In the midst of the disturbance, figures appeared. Four of them, then six.

Their features blurred. Then came into focus then blurred again as though I were watching them through strong currents of clear water. Five men and one woman. All of them drained of color, from their skin and flesh to the rustic work shirts, breeches, and buckled shoes. Their limbs rose and fell. They whirled, arms and faces working in pantomime.

I remained in my crouch, worried the witch had caught me unawares. I put my hand to my side, noting the reassuring weight of Rush's pocket watch. It remained still; no ticking, no vibrating.

No witch.

With wards and spells at the ready, I pushed to my feet. The apparitions spun around me, their motions slowed, their panic made graceful. Their movements grew ghastly. Pain. Mute screams. Flailing. And then, the unseen hand of a giant crushed them to the floor.

Impressions of blazing heat, charring, swept over me. I tasted acrid smoke. Felt crushing weight.

I steadied myself.

For a moment, my ears rang with groans, screams, pleading, moaning. The roar of an inferno. The agony of thick beams sundering. Yet beneath all that cried a voice, thin and faint, from which I only caught one word.

"Minister."

As the windmill quaked, I called out, "Gerald?"

The air trembled. A new wildness spun up around me, a surging of energies and power. A strange synchrony of vibration took hold, some dangerous alignment of the forces coursing through the windmill.

I leaned over and spread apart the silver filings, breaking the circle, erasing the pattern.

The deadly currents tore apart, taking with them the concentration of force that had seemed about to split the windmill into two. The sounds, the smells and tastes, the impressions of destruction, all receded like a deadly funnel cloud breaking apart into wisps and curls and tatters, an angry storm retreating.

The beams and boards of the windmill muttered their displeasure at the strains they'd undergone, gradually settling. Dust filled the air, roiling. Yet as I looked, I marked that the sunlight coming in through the high up windows had risen to the top rafters, high in the corner, a deeper molten orange, verging on rust.

How much time had passed?

It felt as though it had been no more than three or four minutes. But to judge by the lowering sun, it looked to be closer to forty-five minutes, or even an hour.

I snatched up the planar compass. The readings showed a spike of energy unlike any I'd ever seen outside of the maelstrom that had swept over Salem on the day Rush and Swaine perished. My pulse raced, the symphony of creaks, bangs, howling winds, and spectral voices replaced by a disconcerting silence filled only by the sound of my own ragged breathing. As I brushed off the dust from my shoulders and elbows, my gaze landed on the floor. My hand stilled.

Scrawled into the silver filings on the floor, two letters that hadn't been there a moment earlier.

H. H.

25

THE SUBTLE CHASE

Ephraim Rush's house stood tucked away on Crooked Lane. The dark, shadowy little home's interior remained locked in time, as if Rush himself might walk in again at any moment, leaving his walking stick next to the door, hanging his jacket on the empty hook next to it. Everything remained neat, arranged just so. The narrow foyer. The cozy sitting room. The den where he'd done his writing. Air rich with the scent of old fabrics, of aged windowsills and century-old resin emanating from the boards. Fifty years' worth of tobacco smoke still redolent, strongest near the doctor's collection of pipes. In his final will and testament, he had given the house to me, a young witch he'd known only for a short time.

I'd felt the best way to honor his memory had been to leave it intact. Members of the Ten Gables staff dusted it once a month. Otherwise, it remained unoccupied—though sometimes I stopped in to consult one section or another of Rush's library. While many of the works had been boxed up and brought to Ten Gables, some of his collection belonged in the house, I felt. Perhaps it gave me an excuse to come by more often than I otherwise would, to reconnect with the faint essence that remained of the man. I found solace in the sense of time frozen.

As I wandered through the drawing room, I lifted the cover protecting the ivory keys of the harpsichord that stood along the back wall. I plinked out a few notes. They broke the silence, slightly out of tune. I went up the narrow staircase, running one hand lightly along the worn banister. The door to the library stood at the top of the stairs. His collection, much like the decorations throughout his house: the map of his lifetime.

A portion of which I suspected held the answer to the strange tangle of events that confounded me.

KNEELING before the lower right section of one wall of books, I ran a fingertip along the spines. Scanning the shelf, I kept up my search until I found the book I'd come for. A middle-sized printing, shorter than most of its neighbors. The title, embossed into the letter of the cover, read: *The Subtle Chase*. Beneath that: *Observations of the Luminous Scaffolding of the Known Planes*.

Virgil Croswell, a disciple of the great Alfred Summerfield, was regarded, in as much as he was regarded at all, as a minor figure in the unseen arts. Something of a gadfly amongst London magicians in the seventeenth century, he'd theorized the existence of a planar lattice: an entanglement of energies providing the scaffolding for the large-scale structure of the universe. That hidden scaffolding consisted of a dark planar essence, made up of subtle currents of force, and a luminous planar essence, composed of the numerous layers of reality, all linked by the shadowy filaments undergirding them.

I sat back on my heels and flipped carefully through the old pages.

There it was: *tenebressence.*

The dark elements, *tenebris essentia*: the occult planar

medium. In Croswell's theory, such substrates created energies of such activity and density that they generated the very planes. He also theorized a special kind of plane known as the *sub-luminous*, which he originally thought to be the result of two normal planes merging, but then took a greater leap to assert grew from cold energy pouring in from neighboring planar webs. Where Croswell deviated most starkly from his contemporaries was in his assertion of what he called the *subtle chase*, infinitesimally small channels through which magic and witchcraft flowed.

Much of Croswell's writings had earned him merit in Swaine's eyes—only to be dashed against the rocks of Croswell's more infamous theory, which Swaine dismissed out of hand.

The ghost realm.

Swaine had been insistent that ghosts were a childish figment of the common mind. Any such talk of aimless souls, passage between the earthly realm and the afterlife, of haunts and polter-geists troubling the living struck him as ridiculous. Demons, or nothing. And when Swaine shut the door on a theory or idea, the door remained closed.

According to Croswell, the ghost realm arose from the subtle chase, the *tenebressence* creating an unconscious imprint of the world as experienced by the living. Within this realm, spirits passed through to reach new layers of planar reality. And of course some spirits remained, too afraid to move on, or confused, or greedy for more life. Trapped by demons, in some cases. In all cases, linked by this dark essence to their corpse, in some fashion designed to direct them where to go, how to move on.

At locations said to be haunted, some seal had been broken between the ghost realm and the physical world. Places where spirits might traverse the barrier.

Croswell's great leap was to hypothesize a direct relationship between the occult planar medium—his hypothetical forms of planar energy, which he referred to as *scalar fields*—and the exis-tence of this ghost realm.

So what interest had I in the writings of an obscure magician regarded by most as an eccentric?

Because Croswell had first recorded the existence of the *summa-praecentio* band of unseen frequencies, frequencies beyond the range of any natural expression of the planar or the infernal.

I TURNED THE PAGES CAREFULLY, coming to a section titled *On a Grand Theory of Planar Unity: Wherein the Reader Might Consent to a More Prodigious Exercise in Speculative Theoretics.*

Swaine would no doubt have rolled his eyes.

I scanned the dense text. A taste:

Thus do we leave behind the stolid comforts of data; rigorous encapsulation of the measurable facets of the firmament; reliable rows of numbers, of degrees, of the mathematical semaphore signaled to us by Nature; the certainty of cartographic boundaries and borders. One must, after all, be willing to cast off from the rocky shore for the far horizon to reach the virgin forests of a new continent of Understanding.

"What do men hope to find as we set off across the gulf of igno-rance, eyes bright, hand firm on the tiller? The Truth: elusive and magisterial, rising in great buttresses and arches, giving symmetry and structure to the universe: precision, grace, purpose, form, and a logic infusing all of reality.

It continued in such a florid fashion, I'm afraid. While I'd developed a taste for the antiquated diction of magicians, I couldn't vanquish the impatience I knew Swaine would have choked on. I practically heard his muttered *The point?*

I read the pages, turning them quickly, certain I was on the right track.

Fragments of the text leapt out at me:

...the substrata of planar formation...scales vast enough to delude

our perceptions...infinitesimal filaments aglow with the heart of all force, mineral, and organism, forever eluding revelation...

Croswell recounted his exploration of a strange realm he'd explored as part of Alfred Summerfield's Secret Doorway Guild: *Flares of a most unusual luminescence, finer than silk, ran through the decrepit stone of the archway beyond which brooded a shadowed hallway receding into darkness of a purity never encountered.*

The readings he taken there strayed well into the *summa-prae-centio* band. He noted detecting 4° *of shadow harmonics, reaching down to an almost unimaginable five Holmstrom cycles.*

Almost precisely what I had measured.

Of course, it could have been no more than a startling coincidence.

He went on to describe the ghost realm as a structure formed by oppositional energies, one opaque, the other of a luminous nature, bound through separate planes, aligned into some greater consistency than might otherwise be expected. I searched through the text, more and more convinced that it all aligned too much to be passed off as mere coincidence. As my gaze danced across the pages, I skimmed an account of an exploration of the alleged ghost realm, stopping at the word *cinder.*

In Croswell's telling, the ghost realm was deadly for the living. He'd conducted a series of experiments that had demonstrated as much. A mouse, a cat, a dog, all coaxed in through a temporary access point instantiated at the site of a haunting. All retrieved, dead. And within moments, they'd turned to solid cinder of a distinct consistency.

I closed the book.

If Gerald had slipped into the ghost realm—as all the signs pointed—did he have any chance whatsoever of returning alive?

DUSK GATHERED OUTSIDE THE WINDOWS. I sat in Rush's rocking

chair. The house gave me comfort. And inspiration. Even into his ninth decade, the gentleman had been unafraid to reconsider his understanding of the unseen realms. Moreover, he'd dared everything to do what he knew was right.

Shadows deepened around me. Would Clara ever hold me in the kind of reverence I held my mentors?

Besides, you're much more like Katie. Overthinking everything. Worrying what everyone thinks. Studious. Happy with a pile of books. Shy.

It seemed unlikely.

I rocked in the chair, engulfed in the silence of the house, torn between the viewpoints of my two dead mentors. Struggling, balanced between doubts.

Gerald's words about his sister came to mind.

I'm not compelled to work around the clock to better run from the ghosts of the past, piously regarding even a moment of relaxation as a sinful indulgence.

The thought stung. Was that what I was doing? Was I mistaking dedication and loyalty for something else? Maybe it *was* just grief. Or self-doubt. Was my searching for some definitive answer just a wish for some measure of posthumous approval?

Because I wasn't August Swaine. I wasn't Ephraim Rush.

I stopped rocking.

No, I was alive, in the midst of my life. And both my mentors had trusted me.

Maybe I should trust myself.

I got up from the chair, Croswell's *The Subtle Chase* tucked under my arm.

I had other ghosts to deal with.

26

CRUDE MAGIC

The builders had yet to fit the small windows into the walls of the new belfry of the First Congregational Church. Each raw opening afforded a magnificent view of the city. The western horizon smoldered, the colors of sunset draining from the sky above. Looking out the eastern opening presented a clear view of the rising moon, a day or two from full, emerging from the harbor to peer between ships and masts. Ample reward for climbing the seventy-four new steps from the ground floor—though I hoped for an even better prize, a more revealing vantage.

An errant lightning strike during a January storm had set the original steeple on fire, nearly taking the whole church with it. I'd always admired the austere interplay of space, form, and light, so I'd been glad to see the belfry and steeple rebuilt better than before. Doubly so to see it constructed by Gilbert Flucker, a builder of immense skill who had worked with me to design and construct Ten Gables. We'd remained on fine terms. So fine, in fact, that he'd allowed me to place one of my witch lanterns in the corner of the First's belfry.

From the window opening facing north, the evening lights of Boston and Cambridge came to life, divided by the darkness of the River Charles. I rested my fingertips on the rock maple sill plate. The scent of new construction—sawdust, wood shavings, pine tar to seal the boards, the aroma of progress—pleased me as I waited.

The lantern tucked into the corner remained unlit.

Above the opening in the unstained planks of the floor, not yet graced with a railing of any kind, a tiny cascade of blue sparks erupted. I stepped from the window and knelt by the lantern, my back to the opening in the floor.

Should I casually whistle? Wonder aloud why the lantern wasn't working properly?

It might have been a bit much.

Seventy-six steps. It wouldn't take long.

"How clever, with these lanterns. Credit for impressing me." The voice floated up from the stairs, melodious and amused.

I remained by the lantern. "I had mixed emotions, to be honest," I replied. "They've an unpleasant history. I'd rather have left them in storage."

"Shame to keep such genius hidden away," the voice suggested. "More interesting than just about anything else in Boston."

"Just about?" I said.

"Well, there's you. And there's me."

"I'm sure I'm not that interesting. You, on the other hand."

Penelope Bayard came into view, a riding cloak over her shoulders, the hood over her hair. She looked as lovely as she had at the governor's dinner. "I am rather fascinating," she agreed. "But you—feted across the colonies. And why not? You elbowed your way to a place at the table. Disarmed all these self-important men. Now that's even more interesting than sixty-two functioning lanterns."

"You count well," I said. "And you didn't seem to have much trouble manipulating them. Even more impressive."

"I know how to have fun."

"And you figured out how to avoid them altogether and disappeared."

"I'd no idea they worked on more than one frequency. Elegant, I adore it. Of course, once I figured *that* out, after your little friend slipped off with that mirror, I realized my mistake. And rectified it."

She'd cloaked herself so well that I hadn't been able to find her, any sign of her, along any of the frequencies to which I tuned the network of lanterns. "Leaving me wondering if I'd had yet another bad lantern."

"I think you're smarter than that," she said. "In fact, I'm starting to wonder if I've just done exactly what you wanted me to do. You know the lanterns all work perfectly well at this point, don't you? Of course you do. Well played."

"I didn't think you could resist," I said.

"I can never resist."

"You could have just come to Ten Gables," I said.

"Could I have?"

"It has several doors. They all work."

"Boring," she said. "And is there any place in Boston better watched? I'm trying to be discreet."

"Ah, discreet. That explains James Breckenridge." I sat back on my heels. "His remains are too dangerous to handle, by the way. That didn't go over very well with your governor, in particular. He's quite upset."

"He wasn't supposed to die." She flicked her hand as though tossing off a comment about a broken taper.

"How inconvenient for him," I said. "Just a taunt, then? If that's what you mean by *interesting*, I'm not sure you've categorized the two of us properly."

"Far more interesting than a tedious letter. And he was

unpleasant. Always prowling around. Staring. Obsessed with what he could never have."

"So why not kill him," I said. "How perfectly sensible."

"Oh, don't tell me you don't trust me now," Penelope said.

"You'll forgive me if I don't."

She pursed her lips and looked around the space. A thick beam crossed beneath the peaked ceiling. "They'll hang the bells from that?"

"I expect so."

"Well you *should* trust me," she said, turning back to me. "More than those others, don't you think? They can't be making life easy for you. Your governor. Those members of the council. The chattering gazetteers. All of them with all their whispers. Their ridiculous expectations. All the time looking askance at you. As if they stand above. Do you ever ask yourself: what have they ever done? Aside from having been born wealthy? With lucrative names and pedigrees? Had their way carved out from them from the day of their first crawl? And look what they've made of it. Really, their chief accomplishment might be having learned how to stab someone in the back with a smile on their face. Please. You're better than that, and they all know it. You know it. I know it. So enough of this not trusting me. Why wouldn't you trust your own blood?"

"That's rather a claim."

"One I think obvious enough."

"Somehow I must've missed you at the Christmas dinners growing up."

"Don't be so literal minded. Smarter to think of us as cousins. Or maybe even long-lost sisters, of a kind. Wouldn't it be nice to have a sibling?" she said.

"I had siblings, thank you."

"I know. But they're all gone. And I'm right here. I don't have any siblings left, either, so there's another area in which we are shockingly alike." She made no move to come any farther up the stairs.

"I trusted my brothers," I said. "They didn't play games. Didn't go sneaking around, spying on me."

"Number one, I'm sure your brothers tormented you. That's what brothers do. And secondly, you accuse me of spying as you kneel before one of sixty-two other working devices you had placed throughout Boston to spy on me. So we might agree that's what siblings do."

"Do you know the one thing that I admire most about you?" I said.

She bit her lip and her eyes twinkled. She clapped her hands together lightly, gleefully. "Do tell. I love where this is going."

"The ghosts. The little bow they took. I have to admit, I'm baffled."

"It's nothing," she said. "Okay, it's not nothing. Should I call it my trademark? I shouldn't get carried away, but I can tell you— sister to sister, I know you're not quite there yet but I trust you shall arrive—I was hoping you'd notice." She looked up to the top of the belfry again, waving her fingers toward her face, as though cooling off her excitement. "That's how it started for me. I don't know how it started for you. But I saw them, all my life. I would sit up in my cradle and see them. Do you know I had no idea they *weren't* seen by everyone else? I just assumed there were two kinds of people in the world: my family, and the other people you could see through. Isn't it strange?"

I might not have trusted her for even a moment, but that much I could relate to. I'd grown up catching glimpses of magic, seeing trails of witchcraft, and thinking nothing of it. Surely everyone else must've seen it, too, I thought. No different than spoons, cats, clouds.

"Why spirits, do you think?" I asked. "I've never seen them." *Until you showed up*, I added silently to myself.

"I'm sure you have," she said. "You probably just didn't realize it. You convinced yourself it wasn't real. I understand. But for me, I have a special rapport with the dead. They seem to enjoy my company, which I can't always say is true of everyone else." She frowned, her eyes still lively.

Had I seen spirits without realizing it? It struck me as absurd—though in a moment of unsettled understanding, I thought back to some of the stranger moments of my time in Salem.

"I find it ever so interesting," she said. "I could show you. Really, I think there's a lot we can show each other. Don't you think?"

"One might assume. But tell me, why here? And now?" I said.

"Well, I'd have come sooner if you hadn't been so furtive about things."

"I prefer to think of it as discreet."

"Now don't be like that. You know what I mean."

"I should have stepped into the public square, draped in flowing black silk, making my entrances and exits through chimneys, traveling from place to place through the air, riding a you-know-what?" I said. "My dear, this is Boston. I'm the subject of ugly enough whispers, as is, thanks very much."

"Of course, I understand," Penelope said. "You have to put all those men at ease. The slightest discomfort and they fall apart. Like babies put down for a nap: tiptoe around them, keep your voice soft and soothing. Play their game by their rules—rules which, by the way, are designed to let them win and keep winning. It's not just Boston, sadly."

"It's not just men," I said.

"Excellent. There you go. I wondered if you'd be more sophisticated than I imagined."

"Lucky me," I said. "But back to these ghosts."

"Ghosts, ghosts, ghosts. What else is there to say?"

"Where is he?" I said.

"He who?" she said.

"I've lost someone whom I shouldn't have lost," I said. "And I've maybe lost him to these ghosts, ghosts, ghosts."

"I told you, that was an accident."

"No, not him. A different one."

"There's another one? I'm afraid it wasn't me. Unless I'm sleepwalking again. And that's always awkward."

"Let me ask you this: if someone living were to slip into the ghost realm, how would one get them back?"

"I have no idea."

"I thought we were being honest with each other," I said. "Like cousins."

"Sisters."

"Not quite there yet. But here's your chance," I said.

"Into the ghost realm?" she said. "Assuming they weren't dead —there would be nothing unusual about that, so why would you even ask—I'm not sure how they could. It's not, well, not like stepping into a closet and appearing in a field. Spirits get very reticent if you try to talk to them about it. So I would say you have a mystery on your hands. But luckily for you, you are related to something of an expert on the subject."

"One who sounds like she just exhausted her knowledge," I said.

"Just because you asked me an impossible question doesn't mean I don't know what I'm talking about," she said. "I've tried. Believe me. What do you think the first thing I attempted was? Once I sussed out that ghosts were ghosts, I wanted to see where they came from. But if there's some trick to it, it's eluded me for almost twenty years."

"What about for a person with no witchcraft?" I asked.

"I can only imagine we go from *might not be possible* straight to *not possible at all*. But this will be intriguing."

"This is my problem to solve. And I work alone," I said.

"Not true. You have that well-dressed friend. And the misbehaving one. And your staff. And that company of beautiful soldiers. You just don't want to work with me. My feelings are hurt."

"Oh, dear," I said.

Penelope waved my comment aside. "Sarcasm doesn't suit you. You have all the support. Influence. Power. Like no other witch has ever had. Yet what do you do with it? Whatever your short little governor tells you to. That's what I don't understand."

"No. You don't understand. The power I have, such as it is, allows me to do what's really important."

"The governor's bidding."

"A small price to pay."

"Exactly what he wants you to think."

"I deal honestly with him. I earn what I have."

"Oh, ho—because I don't?" she said. "Because you think I'm a slattern. I bat my eyes and play my little games. I make the men around me dance as though they were on strings. I amuse myself at their folly, regarding them as disposable when it suits me. Well, maybe. But we could both do more. All this toying with men, all this begging for their approval, all this be good little partners— why should we even bother? Why knock politely at the door when we could blow it off its hinges?"

"I admire your humility," I said. "But all of that is more than I'm interested in."

"Don't tell me you haven't thought about it."

"Thought about it, dismissed it as fanciful. And likely far more problematic than you seem to think, even if I had the slightest interest in what you suggest. Which I don't. What I do have is a problem I was hoping you could help me with. But it doesn't sound like you can."

"The world could be ours, and you want to hear more about ghosts. You depress me."

"The cinders," I said. "I don't understand the cinders."

"What's not to understand? A human goes into the ghost

realm, they come out as cinders. Hence: they shouldn't go into the ghost realm."

"Is there any way around it?"

"See, you need my help after all," she said.

"You seem to be offering."

"Well, I don't think I should just ignore the fact that our paths have finally crossed. And perhaps I've grown bored with causing trouble for my own amusement." She pinched up her face and thought for a moment, eyes closed. "No. There's no way around it. Whoever you lost in the ghost realm is going to have to stay there. Sorry. What's the next case we can work on?"

"I told you, I work alone," I said.

"You know the other thing about siblings?"

"Yes?"

"They can get on your nerves," she said. "Mine did. It's why I killed them."

The massive oak beam designed to support the weight of the bells tore loose from its moorings and swung down at me in a hail of splinters with ferocious speed. I lifted my right hand, releasing a stream of witchcraft strong enough to deflect it. The beam slammed into the wall like a battering ram, the collision deafening in the hollow space of the belfry. Penelope tried to leap into the space, but the special glamour I'd placed on the top steps flared to life, filling the air around her with sizzling sparks.

"Not fair," she grunted.

The lantern behind me skated across the floor, clipping me in the back of my calf. I couldn't catch my balance, and tumbled backward, landing on my hip and elbow. The lantern passed through the sheet of sparks and Penelope grabbed it with both hands.

"Why do I always want to destroy everything in a giant blaze?" she said.

She hurled the lantern at me, accelerating its speed with a

fierce display of witchcraft. It was all I could do to stop it with a burst of my own.

For a moment, the lantern hung between us, both of us putting all we had into it. It tore apart into dozens of sharp fragments of tin, iron, and glass. Shards stung me like angry wasps on my leg and side. My arms and face were spared by witchcraft, sending the pieces ricocheting off into the wall next to me. The spellwork wound into the fractured lantern by Dr. Rush reacted with all the clashing energies in the air, blazing out into every corner of the belfry, snapping, scorching, and stinging.

Penelope cursed from the opening to the stairs. I rolled up to my feet, whispering a spell that would bind her ankles together as if with iron manacles.

She proved just as quick.

The giant beam shot across the floor. I leapt, and it careened through the spot where I'd just been standing. It would have broken both my ankles.

Penelope disappeared down the stairs—but not without loosing more mayhem in the belfry. Boards shook and tore loose. Iron nails and wooden spikes spun through the air like leaves and branches in a hurricane, turned to deadly projectiles. I hunched my shoulders, crouching as I hurried after her, shielding myself with a spell of deflection: *Shimmering Mantlet.*

I jumped down into the stairwell, the pelting of metal and wood deafening behind me.

The stairs to the belfry were narrow, four short flights that hugged the walls, leaving room in the midst for the ropes and pullies of the bells. Across from me and two flights down, Penelope blurred. She somehow neutralized the binding I'd cast on her legs, though she didn't seem to be moving smoothly.

The runners beneath me split apart. "No you don't," I said.

Before Penelope could reach the bottom, I shouted a spell and slammed the belfry door closed, the hollow boom echoing throughout the space.

"Not fair," she spat. "This should be witchcraft against witchcraft. Not boring, crude magic."

She lifted her hands and the wood under my feet collapsed with a great wrenching *crack*. I flailed as I harnessed what forward momentum I'd had, managing to grab hold of the landing in front of me. With a twist, I managed to get one leg onto the steps in front of me. Fifteen feet of empty space yawned beneath me.

I filled the stairwell with a shifting crest of neutralizing magic, an elemental technique that harnessed the grounding qualities of the stone floor at the bottom. As I did, I wrenched myself to the remaining steps. Penelope tried to tear down the entire flight of stairs, but her witchcraft was drawn to the stones.

"You're a horrible sister," she cried. Turning to the door behind her, she found it sealed shut, not giving way. "What did I tell you about doors?" She bunched her shoulders up around her ears, then thrust her chest forward, lifting her hands to the door —which exploded into the transept beyond.

She fled the belfry.

I sprinted after her, taking the steps two and three at a time until I reached the bottom. The air hummed with wild magic and witchcraft. My hair lifted, the linen and cotton of my clothes clinging to my skin. The remains of the door fanned out across the floor, into the pews, and all the way to the pulpit.

I would have to apologize to Gilbert Flucker.

A glimpse of Penelope's cloak vanished through the side door. I skirted chunks of the shattered belfry door, running down the main aisle after her, cutting right to reach the door, only to find it open to the night. I paused in the doorway, my left hand against the door frame. Color drained in the sky to the west, the stars coming in bright.

Gone. No sign of her.

A carriage rattled down the street, a lantern hung by the driver. Gentle winds shook the newly bloomed trees planted along the edge of the church. Shadows and darkness in every direction. I stepped out into the night, searching. When it grew clear she'd fled, my breathing slowed. The shadow of the steeple blocked out the stars behind me.

Penelope Bayard might not care for magic, but magic would do what I needed it to. It wasn't always crude; it could be quite subtle.

So much so she wouldn't even realize I'd marked her.

27

MONSTROSITIES

"You *are* sure you know where we're going?" Mary had fallen behind. Again. She confronted the boughs of a hoary old pine tree as though they were impenetrable.

"It's not much farther," I called over my shoulder.

"You know how much I despise nature." She ducked beneath the heavy branches. "Give me cobbles, streets, plazas. Lovely floors, sturdy walls, sound roofs. A well-kept garden now and then, if the weather is agreeable."

I picked my way through a patch of nettles, withholding comment.

She might not have cared for nature, but she'd made quite an effort to dress the part. A high brimmed tricorn banded with what looked to be a strip of raccoon skin, a trio of hawk feathers angles back beneath the band. Tawny deerskin jacket with a line of fringe along the backs of the arms, over a rustic shirt. Slim wool breeches tucked into brown, calf-high boots. One might have thought her heading out to the western frontier, rather than the deep woods of Andover. Her hair hung down in a long braid over her shoulder.

I led us along a faint trail that looked to have seen more

deer than humans over the past half century. It wound downhill, passing between craggy hillsides that rose twenty and thirty feet, often topped with great weathered prows of granite. The forest canopy teamed with birds: black-and-white chickadees, raucous crows, scarlet cardinals with their sharp chirps, blue jays, starlings, and the occasional glimpse of a larger bird of prey circling in the warm air above. Half-buried boulders dotted the ground, some large as cattle. Those, and the crests and troughs of the ridges, resonated with me, for I often thought stretches of my own heart too rocky and uneven to settle.

"Should be just over here," I announced.

"You said that twenty minutes ago. And twenty minutes before that." She paused to fuss over a thatch of burrs clinging to her sleeve.

I kept going. Soon enough, a flash, bright as jewels, shone through the trees.

"I see it," I said.

The air, rich with the essence of pine and soil, now carried a note of mud and fish. Stretching out from the edge of the forest, the wide expanse of the pond glittered with reflections of the overhead sun. Somewhere in the area of three hundred feet across, roughly circular, the dark water was framed by tall trees. Off to our left, the water opened into a stretch of marsh land, dotted with green tussocks, and the skeletons of dead trees. High up, wide nests of branch and twig were home to a gathering of the great herons—birds who spent much of their days standing motionless in the water on their long legs, ready to bring sudden death to the silver fish beneath the surface. Some days I felt I was the heron: others, the fish.

Mary came up behind me, breathing heavily, a sheen of sweat on her face.

"I think we'll have to swim from here," I said.

"I will kill you."

I shaded my eye with my hand, searching the shoreline to our right. "Over that way."

"I knew you didn't know where it was," she said. "I'm surprised we're within the same mile."

"Oh, ye of little faith."

We set off through the bramble, following the shoreline. Ferns sprouted amongst the gnarled tree roots edging to the water.

"Are you even sure this is the right pond?" Mary said, trudging along after me. "They all look the same to me. Horrible, deep, and smelly."

"Look," I said. "Ducks."

"Unless you can assure me they are roasted, with gravy, and potatoes, I'm not even going to look."

I soon made out the dark shape of a cabin set back twenty-five yards from the water's edge, near a stretch where the trees thinned out. To reach it, we had to cross a six-foot-wide outlet, moving carefully from one stone to another. The bronze water was clear, with silt, stones slick with wavering green beards, and old, dulled branches submerged at the bottom. Mary slipped and cursed as she dunked one boot below the surface. I turned and extended a hand to her, which she gripped tightly with a grimace.

Once on solid ground, she shook her foot. "How I love wet toes."

"You'll find it within yourself to persevere, I'm sure of it," I said.

"Oh, how your words of inspiration keep me going. Truly. You're sure this is the right place?"

"I don't know how many hard-to-reach, haunted ponds there are in the area—but worst case, we can cross this one off our list if I'm wrong."

The path, such as it was, wended between the shore and a short rise. An acquaintance of mine, Corey Lane, had confirmed the rumors surrounding the pond. Something of an expert on such matters, himself living by a similarly isolated lake over in a small village called West Bradford, he knew of several such places dotting the crannies of the landscape, if not the maps generally in circulation. Ranges of forest or marsh. Turns along rivers. Lonesome ponds, deep in the woods. Places unsettled and untraveled, many with reputations that stretched back generations, if not centuries: shunned, unfit for the living. Places where the veil between the living and the dead had torn. Some, like the unnamed pond we tramped alongside, also bore a more recent, but no less unseemly, history. As we neared the remains of the old cabin, I didn't wonder it had made Gerald's list.

Coming to the clearing where the cabin stood, I paused. Mary came up next to me, resting her hand on my shoulder as she balanced herself on one leg, prying off her boot. She dumped a thin stream of water from it with a frown.

"If I find a tadpole wedged between my toes when I take off my stocking, I shall know whom to blame." She set the boot down and jammed her foot back into it, stomping it down until it was all the way on again. Only then did she seem to take in the cabin before us. "Not that I claim to understand the minds of hermits, but I'm confident even hermits would find this too much to bear."

None of the walls of the cabin stood straight, nor did they lean in quite the same direction. The rough-hewn logs wore more moss and bird droppings than bark. One window stared dumbly down to the water. The door gaped wide, a few fallen planks that might have been a door lying across the timber foundation. Instead of a chimney, or even a stovepipe, a mound of sod gathered on one corner of the roof, a hole in its midst. The entire effect was of the cabin having sprung up from the woods and shore themselves, some strange manifestation of the uneasy spirit of desolation that held sway.

"It's worse than that," I said. "Sadder. The man who built this was a former slave. Appeared on his own one winter and settled out here by himself. Whatever he contended with out here on his own, he made it work. For over a decade, according to Corey Lane. But it turned out the spirits weren't the problem."

"No, I don't imagine they were." She wrenched her gaze from the leaden waters. "People are horrible."

The land around the cabin stood barren. Patches of sickly weeds drew what little nutrients they could from the sandy earth. The skin along my shoulders crawled as I neared the cabin.

Mary said, "Do you think Gerald came out here himself?"

"Possibly. He mentioned it in his journal."

"So he might try to communicate to us."

"That's my hope." I paused where the cabin merged with the ground. The rough stone foundation peered from beneath the logs decomposing into some undefined state between timber and soil.

"But why not stay where he'd already made contact? Wouldn't that make more sense?" Mary said.

"It would—unless he couldn't."

"Because of the ghosts."

"Or something else," I said.

"Such as?"

"I'm not sure." The old planks leading up to the doorway compressed beneath my steps, the wood grown soft. The air within the cabin tickled my nose with mildew.

"Yet you don't think it's Penelope Bayard," Mary said. "It seems rather obvious to me. On one hand, Gerald and the ghost realm. On the other, an obnoxious witch who proclaims to specialize in ghosts. But here we are, tramping through streams to investigate the loneliest dwelling I've ever imagined, instead of confronting this Bayard woman directly. We know where she is. There's two of us, and only one of her. To me, that seems the shortest route to getting Gerald back."

"Henrietta's women are watching her now," I said. "And now

that I've marked her, she won't surprise us again. This is more urgent."

The inside of the cabin was dim after the flat light of the shore. The lone window showed as a bright square on the opposite wall, seeming to only make the rest of the interior darker, drawing out the daylight. As my eyes adjusted, I noted the cabin seemed largely untouched, despite having been abandoned for more than half a century. No scattered piles of acorns or their shells, brought in by squirrels and chipmunks. No nests of leaves or twigs in the corners. No thick cobwebs spun into the corners, husks of dead insects littering the floor beneath. No droppings. No bones. Only a few touches of the inanimate kind: swaths of dark mildew, pale mushrooms, a few sickly stalks of plants, their seeds floated in through the doorway.

Mary stood in the doorway behind me, holding the back of her delicate hand to her nose. "I'd arrest her. That'll get the smugness from her."

"Just the thing Governor Reddington needs to wrap up his trade negotiations," I said.

"Trade negotiations on one hand. Murder on the other. I see you've made an interesting weighting of the two."

"I don't think she killed James Breckenridge." I stepped gingerly through the cabin, unsure what I was looking for. The ancient remains of what looked to have been blankets covered thin, half-collapsed struts of branch and sapling that had been a cot. A crate missing several boards squatted beneath a rusted lantern missing its glass. A tin plate, skimmed over with soil and bark that looked to have fallen in from the roof.

"You can hardly say he isn't dead because of her," Mary said. "Not to mention how insulting she was to you."

"Quite rude," I admitted. "Attacking me and whatnot."

"Then why aren't we interrogating her in the relative comfort of the Boston jail instead of making our allergies much worse at this empty cabin?"

"One thing at a time." I shifted the satchel on my shoulder, lifting aside the flap and retrieving several instruments: a planar compass, two ordinary pocket watches, a vial of silver filings. I placed them on the crate.

"H. H. Those were his initials, the man who lived here?" Mary said, her voice rising as she held back a sneeze.

"Corey told me his name was Jupiter," I said.

Mary sneezed, twice. "Then what is the H. H.?"

"I'm not sure yet." I walked the length of the cabin with a planar compass, watching as the dial registered erratic surges of energy. "Take these down." I paced the cabin calling out the readings I registered.

Mary noted them in a small travel book, jotting them down in neat columns in her perfect handwriting. The frequencies were in line with what I detected in the other areas where the ghost realm had intruded. In addition to the notable spikes in these unusual bands, we noted a shifting of the overall planar stability. Having spent the early morning hours comparing readings from the past week against an average of the past three months, the change was readily apparent. Such planar shifts rarely boded well. I put the device down next to my other equipment.

"She's wrong, you know," I said.

Mary capped the small inkwell she carried. "She who, darling?"

"Penelope Bayard. The way she looks askance at me for being part of the establishment."

"Why do you even care what she thinks? She's odious, and just as obviously deranged."

I pulled out a bottle of silver filings. "Look at what's happening. Would I even know about it if I was tucked away in my house somewhere? And if I did, what could I do about it? As it is, I can go where I want, when I want, with whomever I want, and no one stops me."

"Except the governor," Mary said. "And his trade negotiations."

"There is that, I suppose."

Unstopping the bottle, I cleared a space on the warped boards of the floor near the remains of the cot. Pouring carefully, the first circle I made was small, roughly the diameter of a tea saucer. I smoothed out the filings, making sure the circle connected, intact.

The glamour I spoke over it had taken several hours' worth of research and practice the night before. The couplets were tricky, and the diction required—in German, the only language I found reference to—brought me to the limit of my concentration. Such a glamour, of a category known as a mirrored glamour, required both a spoken invocation and a physical enchantment to be performed simultaneously.

Rather like singing an unfamiliar song while at the same time pantomiming the directions to your home.

I'd rehearsed it a dozen times after midnight; my success rate ran somewhere in the range of two out of three. Mary remained quiet as I worked. When I reached the final quartets of the invocation, I reached into my satchel and retrieved one of two ordinary pocket watches I'd brought with us. I placed it within the circle of filings. The second hand ticked evenly. Lifting my hand away, I turned both palms, one up to the ceiling, the other down to the glamour, and sealed both the invocation and the physical enchantment at the same moment. Everything within the small circle blurred: the watch, the word, the air.

"Help me with the other one," I said.

Mary—who'd worked through the night with me, though as ever, looked as though she'd had a luxurious nine hours of sleep —assisted me with the second glamour next to the first one. This one was larger, an advancement on the basic circle of silver I'd observed at the other locations.

It was also quite a bit more dangerous.

Mary handed me everything in the precise order, retrieving the additional ingredients from the satchel she'd carried. Coins, individually magicked with elemental sympathy to the canonical directions: north, east, south, west. A copper band, tied in sixteen spots with twined catgut, each knot tuned to emit a small planar disturbance along the scale that made up the Helmstrom series. She then handed me a tin filled with the ashes of a potpourri of herbs and flowers: hemlock, sage, lavender, cedar leaves, and bitter clove. A small wooden box contained sixteen iron nails, each with a rose-shaped head.

All the ingredients laid out before us, I got to my feet. "Why don't you fire it up?"

"Me?" Mary said.

"You don't think you're ready?"

"The more important question is do *you* think I'm ready?"

"I wouldn't have asked."

"But—won't Gerald's life rather depend on it?"

"Your life might depend on your magic one day. Or mine," I said.

For all her predilections, fancies, and airy cynicism, Mary was as smart as they came. She missed nothing. Once aimed in the right direction, her mind invariably bolted ahead: a thoroughbred who lived to gallop. While Clara might have possessed a deeper natural talent, Mary wasn't far behind, and infinitely better organized. Both simply needed more practice, and more confidence.

"This would be so much easier if my right foot wasn't soaking wet," Mary said.

"Persevere, darling," I said. "And I need to take detailed readings while you're instantiating it. I can't do both."

She looked as though she was about to offer to be the one to take the readings, but recognized what I wanted, so arranged the materials before her. I took down the readings as Mary worked. Each step, correct. She didn't hesitate. Her voice remained steady.

Mary didn't even need the small mallet we'd brought for the nails; the floorboard was so rotted she was able to just press them in with her thumb while reciting the short incantation with each one. The silver, the copper band, the ashes spread evenly. She gathered her focus before the invocation, which she delivered flawlessly. A far cry from the impatient dilettante who'd yelped in surprise when she'd first managed to lift a single coin half an inch into the air after months of halfhearted practice.

"Well done," I said.

The elements of the glamour and the spells entwining it rippled across the area of floor they occupied in unison. Mary got to her feet, and we stood across from each other on opposite sides of the two glamours. I motioned for her to take down the readings, which surged yet again. This time, instead of reading them to her, I handed her the device.

I approached the larger of the two glamours. "Gerald? Gerald Phipps?" I called.

The tail end of my voice took on a strange quality, as though spilling out into a much larger space. Mary and I exchanged a glance. She went back to recording the numbers.

I reached behind me to my satchel and retrieved Gerald's journal. Holding it with both hands, I embraced it with a spill of my witchcraft, letting it swirl around the pages, the cover, the ink within, the essence of Gerald left by his handling. Switching his journal to my left hand I crouched by the glamour.

"Gerald. This way."

I reached down and gently placed my fingertips on the silver boundary of the larger glamour. When I made contact, I kept my hand steady, though I wanted instinctively to pull back: it was as though I had stuck my hand into a powerful torrent of water, one so strong that it wanted to jerk me forward, dragging me off in its ferocious currents. I steadied myself, setting my jaw.

"Gerald."

Mary gave me a look and turned the face of the device toward me. All three needles within the dials quivered, slammed to the highest readings.

The walls, floor, and roof of the cabin creaked, the wood straining. Mary looked past my shoulder, her eyes widening.

Turning, I found myself face-to-face with a tall, hunched figure. The lanky man had a prominent nose, face like a corpse, slack-jawed and hollow eyed. He appeared lit from below as though standing over some spectral fire. A tide of despair flooded the cabin. Mary let out a small noise of surprise.

"Is she—"

"No. She's still in Boston." I ignored the ghost next to me. Difficult to do with such a horrific visage leering at my shoulder. I kept a grip on the journal and called for Gerald again. Sounds from the cabin spilled into the glamour, where the silver blazed, moving in and out of focus, appearing to double, to treble.

As I'd suspected.

Mary kept glancing at the apparition.

"Ignore it," I said.

The figure began stalking the cabin, heaving his left side forward, dragging his right, swinging his head to and fro as though enraged at our presence. I increased my flow of witchcraft into the journal in my hands. Tendrils of glowing filaments extruded from the leather binding, stretching down into the glamour. When they reached the floor, the nail heads began to glow, then one by one flared to brilliant orange before reaching a blazing white.

"Gerald—this way," I said.

The ghost most certainly didn't care for this new development, his face a mask of purest hatred. For a moment, all the forces seen and unseen within the cabin pulled taut: a sail straining at the mast, a string on the violin pulled to full tension. A great exhalation of cold flowed from the glamour. Frigid air coiled around our ankles, our knees, driving the warm air of the cabin up and out until our breath showed in wisps and clouds.

"Listen," Mary said. Her shoulders shivered from the cold.

"Be careful."

The voice came from the glamour, distant and thin.

Mary looked at me.

"This way, Gerald," I said, raising my voice.

I lifted my gaze to Mary. She pulled a small pouch from her satchel and fumbled at the drawstrings for moments. A ferocious wind howled from the glamour. The boards of the roof slammed up and down as though a troop of cavalry raced across them.

Mary slid open the drawstrings. "Now?"

I nodded.

Into the glamour, she dumped the contents of the pouch: a dozen of the coins Gerald had used at the meetinghouse. As soon as the first of the silver coins hit the floor within the glamoured circle, the cabin filled with bloodcurdling screams.

Heads, torsos, limbs burst through the floor all around us. Vague shapes coalesced into contorted figures. A dozen, more. Dressed in antique garb, or more primitive clothing. The ghosts writhed and flailed. Voices erupted in several tongues, cries of despair, screams of fury. Fragments of French, English, Pennacook, other tongues I didn't recognize battered our ears.

To her credit, Mary didn't flinch, keeping her attention on the glamour. The coins floated an inch above the floorboards and glowed brightly, the white-hot seen at the blacksmith's anvil. Magic and heat scorched the wood, smoke rising in twists.

The gathered spirits were not happy with us.

All around me, faces roared. They swarmed me. While their touch was largely immaterial, passing right through me, the sensation was far from pleasant. Each contact, the press of ice. And as their hands, fingers, limbs slipped through my own, a foul sensation filled me, drawing forth unpleasant shudders.

Within the circle, beyond the floorboards, visions of another space formed. The effect was dizzying, as though we were peering down through the ceiling of a large, strange room the interior of which couldn't quite decide what it wanted to be. A stairwell one second, the cabin the next, the forest floor seen from high branches the next. For a moment it turned to a smooth stone floor of even gray, an upright metal chest spouting shiny tin limbs to the side, instantly shifting back to bare ground.

Yet no Gerald.

I opened the journal and read aloud, gripped by some instinct I hadn't anticipated: *"And while one might surmise, through some form of spectral acquiescence, that the dead are desirous of reenacting their demise, I should think it more likely they might surrender their secrets through respectful communication instead."*

Gerald's ruminations on the behavior of spirits were immaterial, but the effect on the apparitions was instantaneous. Spirits shrank from me, fleeing the light streaming from the glamour.

As I continued to read Gerald's entries aloud, the spaces appearing within the glamoured circle stabilized into a corridor of some sort.

The distant voice spoke again: "Look...out...he'll..."

The demon caught me unawares.

LIKE SOME HIDEOUS AMPHIBIAN, trailing fin and tendril, the fiend slid through the wall of the cabin from the outside, trailing curls of darkness.

Eyes—five? seven?—blazed a vile yellow as it hit my right side. The journal slipped from my hand to land inside the glamour.

I whipped around, letting fly a potent stream of energy, similar to a ward, yet faster. The fiend drew back like a wounded serpent, taking up half the interior of the cabin.

Mary didn't hesitate. She raised her hand and shouted Hume's Ninth Ward. For a moment, I almost felt bad for the demon. Whatever it had expected to find in the sudden well-spring of ghosts, two women well armed with magic and witch-craft clearly hadn't crossed its mind. The thing shrieked. Coiling, twisting.

"Hold it off!" I shouted to Mary.

While she advanced on the demon, I knelt before the glamour. Gerald's journal floated above the floor, turning slowly in the air. "Come on, Gerald. This way," I said.

The air snapped with energy. Tremors welled up through the floorboards. A potent energy coursed through the cabin, as an uneasy intersection of planes threatened to grow into a much more dangerous collision.

The wall behind me buckled.

Chunks of the roof tore off, spiraling hundreds of feet up into the air. The nails in the glamour started to dissolve. The copper band ignited, strangely colored flames carrying away flecks of metal in every direction, causing the entire circle to warp and burn.

I reached in to grab the journal, horrified at how much energy coursed through the opening, even as it broke apart.

Around me, the cabin, the demon, Mary all flickered.

Not a good sign.

Kneeling, I closed my eye, putting the fingertips of my left hand to my forehead as I recited the dissolution convocation. What should have felt no more difficult than snuffing a taper nearly slipped from my control. Still, I continued, plodding my way through the phrases, the words grown stubborn, enunciation almost impossible. In the end, I drew on my witchcraft to complete the phrases by opening up the air around me to give me more space.

With a gut-wrenching quake, the channel closed.

The illumination snapped off.

The coins, the journal fell to the floorboards. Nail heads faded to red dots as they cooled.

I looked up. The monstrosity had backed Mary into the

corner. Hume's Eleventh Ward flew from her tongue. I could have jumped in. I didn't.

She formed the correct movements with her hands and fingers as she let fly the closing line. The demon didn't even have time to shriek as it tore apart into long strips of darkness, spiraling up and whipping through the walls of the cabin. Gone. Mary looked around, eyes wide, breathing hard. Her chest rose and fell. After a few moments of silence, she looked at me. "A little help might've been nice."

I stood from where I knelt by the glamour. "I might not always be around. You have to be able to do it on your own, flawlessly."

"Well, I wasn't alone. And I did do it flawlessly. But even still." She smoothed down the front of her jacket with trembling fingers.

"You did well," I said.

"We still don't have Gerald," she said. "I can't help but note."

I walked over to the first glamour, the smaller one. I waved my hand over it and said, "*Steppen.*"

The magic released. The blur dissolved, revealing the pocket watch sitting on the floor within the silver filings. I picked it up.

"Not quite yet we don't," I said. "But we're getting there." I walked over to the crate where I'd left the rest of my supplies. The second watch I'd brought sat undisturbed in my satchel. I pulled it out with my other hand. "And we may have something just as important."

28

A MIND FILLED WITH GEARS

We followed a well-tended lane on the far side of Andover. The meadow beyond a wall of field stones swayed on the warm breeze, alive with bees, gliding butterflies, and the song of crickets. The house and barn before us nestled up against the wooded hillside. On the far side of the meadow rose the bones of a new home: hewn maple beams, studs, and wooden scaffolding. Meticulous. The sight of it warmed my heart.

As we neared the existing house, signs of the same thorough attention to detail leapt out at me. Two boulders placed at the end of the lane, whitewashed. A new wooden fence built around a paddock. Neat stacks of lumber beneath an overhang extending out from an addition to the barn. The house itself wore a fresh coat of brown paint. A porch that hadn't been there before wrapped the front and side. A wagon wheel hung above the front door. Along the other side of the house, the vegetable garden I'd once tended now offered a profusion of bounty, row after row. Small trellises draped with peas. Late spring stretches of squash coiled and spread their vines. Rows of corn stood knee-high.

Greens, carrots, and radishes poked their heads. At the far end, broadleaved grapevines coiled across another set of trellises.

"They rather made themselves at home, haven't they," Mary said. "How rustic."

Once I'd moved to Ten Gables, I'd lent the Andover property that Swain had left me to Robert Twelves and his new bride, Anna. The house on the far side of the meadow was to be theirs, going up bit by bit as Robert found the time.

"I love it," I said.

"Of course you do, with your dreams of total isolation."

We trotted up to the front of the house. Robert stood on the porch. He lifted the hat from his head in greeting as we drew near. He'd grown thicker after three years of marriage, a trimmed beard filling out his rounded chin. I urged my horse forward and dismounted with something of a flourish in front of the porch. When he stepped down, I caught him in a tight embrace, glad to rest my head on his sturdy chest for a moment. "I love the new house. How is it coming?"

"Everything I could ask for," he said. "The best lumber, a perfect view, a beautiful wife spurring me on—and no time to do any of it."

"How is she?"

"You'll see," he said.

Mary rode up then, having kept her horse at a slower pace. "Mr. Twelves. How very wonderful to see you. Busy as ever, I see."

Twelves inclined his head. "Miss Whitelocke. You're going to make me spend more money, aren't you? Every time Anna sees you, the local tailor is busy for a month."

"You're welcome, Mr. Twelves." As she got off her horse, Robert lent her his hand.

The front door to the house opened and Anna Twelves stepped out.

"Have her wait a month or so," Mary said. "You'll save money on fabric."

"When is she due?" I said, getting a good look at her.

"A week ago, as far as she's concerned."

"Katie," Anna said. "I owe you."

"For what?" I said, walking over to give her a hug. Over six feet tall and nearly nine months pregnant, Anna Twelves looked set to burst. She was even more fun to hug than Robert. Her golden hair hung loose, and she had good color to her cheeks.

She held my hand after our hug, her grip warm. "He's been getting on my every last nerve. Fretting, checking on me, telling me to sit down. Asking me if I want more water, more tea, a bath for my feet. Your letter gave me the first good break I've had in a month. So thank you."

From the open doorway burst three-year-old Abigail Twelves, the spitting image of her mother. She crashed into me, wrapping her arms around my leg and pressing her face against my hip. "Auntie Katie."

I rested my hand on her head for a moment, her hair softer than cornsilk—then she was off, leaping from the porch step like a baby goat and dashing over to Mary.

"Mary, pretty Mary," she sang.

Mary reacted to children in much the same way she reacted to slobbering hounds, drunken soldiers, and minor demons. That is to say: with a touch of concern around her eyes and one hand extended in a keep-away gesture. Abigail raised her arms.

"She wants you to pick her up," Robert said.

Mary lifted the child as though she were small dog who had just crashed through a puddle. Abigail had none of that, grabbing at the shoulder of Mary's jacket and pulling herself tight, clinging to Mary's neck, a bright smile on her face.

I put my hand to my mouth to stifle the laughter.

"You wouldn't believe how much she talks about you," Anna said. "The two of you have all kinds of adventures together."

"I am absolutely devouring the look on your face right now," I said to Mary.

"Yes, I can see you're all enjoying this a little too much," Mary said.

THE TWO NEW devices Robert constructed for me sat on a table in the half of the barn he'd converted into a workshop. Identical, they had maple bases in the approximate dimension of bricks, one side hinged and latched for access to the interior. The elaborate gearing within connected to a steel post rising from the center of the top, the peak of which split into three separate arms, each bearing a concave half sphere. While each half sphere faced the same direction, they were made of three separate grades of silver. Inset along each front was a watch face. As with all of Robert's work, the craftsmanship was impeccable, bearing true angles, fixed with brass accents, and honed to a fine polish.

I shrugged my satchel from over my shoulder and put it on the table next to the devices. "They look amazing."

"It's a new gearing pattern I'm trying. It's been in my head for a while."

"The advantage?"

"More efficient use of energy."

"You're a genius, I adore it." Going through my satchel, I pulled out a small brass box. "The cylinders?"

"Here." He opened the side of the first device, unlatching it with fingers as dexterous as the gearing he'd devised. The autumn before, I'd watched him pluck a minuscule thorn from his young Abby's shin with a single, graceful roll of his index finger and wide thumb.

The interiors of the devices contained a trio of narrow cylinders an inch in length, each no wider than a goose quill. A dimpled steel cover twisted off the ends, revealing the hollows within.

"And which is which?" I asked.

"Tiny nibs on the sides will tell you. One, two, and three correspond to the grades, highest to lowest."

"Excellent."

Using the nibs for guidance, I inserted the strips of tightly rolled paper I'd carried in the box. Each bore a spell written in fine script, the ink made from an enchanted tincture of disrupted silver filings held in a liquid state courtesy of a technique known as *denatured entrancement*. Each spell differed, uniquely designed to sensitize the particular grade of silver at the end of each arm. As I slipped the rolled papers into the tubes, I whispered the phrases needed to activate the connection to the target silver. A glimmer of light, pale like the moon reflecting off the surface of a lake, ran along the tubes into the gearing when I did. Once I finished, I replaced the end caps, twisting them carefully onto the fine threading in the metal.

"All you have to do is wind them now," Robert said.

He produced a small steel key and handed it to me. I prepared the second device with its spells. When I was done I looked at both. "And to activate them?"

"Flip up that little slider on the ends," Robert said.

The metal clicked smoothly into place. As it did, the arms began turning, soon reaching the proper speed of thirty-three-and-one-third rotations per minute. The half spheres of silver spun, emanating the slight pressure of the spells—not that anyone else would have felt a thing.

"Very nice," I said. "Hardly makes a sound."

"I could've made it silent—I didn't know that mattered."

"It doesn't. I was just noticing." I crossed my arms, watching. "I'm glad I could keep you busy."

"Oh, I'm driving her crazy," he said. "I can't help it. I just want her to slow down a little. She's still out there gardening, pulling stones out of the ground, washing clothes. I'm happy to do all of it."

"And construct groundbreaking devices for me. And build a

house at the same time."

"There's twenty-four hours in every day."

"You are a good husband."

Both devices spun in synchrony. By using three separate grades of silver, I'd be able to triangulate with precision between the relevant frequencies. The spells imbued the metal with delicate indicators, for lack of a better word, sensitive enough to react to even the faintest discrepancies in planar stability. In doing so, they could provide me with a connection to the energies associated with the ghost realm—and a way to manipulate them. It was good I'd had Twelves make two devices. If my growing suspicions held true, they held the key to rescuing Gerald.

"Gears," Robert said.

I looked up at him. "Beg pardon?"

"Your mind. It's filled with gears. Finer than any I can put together. I see them working right now. How do you think of all this?"

"As any good Minister of Magickal Sciences would: hunched over books, wearing my sight down to nothing while all others are outside enjoying magnificent spring weather. That's how."

"He'd be proud." He glanced at me. "Swaine."

"Or he'd have rolled his eyes at me for stupidly ignoring the shortcut obvious to him but utterly obscure to me."

"I doubt it. I mean—look at this. This design is yours. Easily as elegant as anything he had me build." He looked at me more closely. "You doing all right?"

"I haven't started murdering people yet."

"That's a start," he said. "What you need is a nice supper. Abby's been excited since she sprang out of bed this morning. She's fascinated by you. You're like some kind of Greek hero to her."

I watched the devices spin.

The problem, I knew, with Greek heroes: the gods always had their knives out for them.

29

DOWN TO EMBERS

Wind in the trees, cricket song in the darkness, landscape softened by moonlight. Mary and I followed the silvered lane into the center of western Andover. After spending the afternoon with the Twelves family, we'd decided to wait until morning to ride back to Boston. The lane bent to the right, leading us through a small cluster of homes near the intersection of two roads. At the crossroads stood a two-story tavern, the cheerful coat of yellow paint adorning its sides lovely in the moonlight. A pair of lanterns burned on either side of the door. The sign on the post out front read *Nagel's Tavern*. Few places felt more like home to me.

Mary had fallen into an expressive silence. I refrained from intruding on her thoughts as we reached the tavern and tended to the horses. Afterward, she passed ahead of me through the tavern's door without comment. Inside the large public room, the air smelled of roasted chicken, thyme, ale, and tobacco smoke. A few locals gathered at one of the tables. Craftsmen by the look of them.

Bertram Nagel, his red hair grown out and tied back, an apron around his slender waist, lit up when he saw us. He put down the tin mug he'd been drying with a towel and tossed the towel over his shoulder. The conversation of the locals continued, though they'd noted our arrival. I wasn't an altogether unfamiliar sight to them. As for Mary, she drew the lion's share of glances. She ignored them.

"Mary, you look lovely," Bertram said. "And you also look —hungry?"

Behind Mary's shoulder, I shook my head, warning him off.

"I've already had one child climbing into and out of my lap for hours," she said. "I don't need another."

"And it's very nice to see you, Bertram," I added.

Mary raised her hand in a dismissive wave.

Bertram required no further edification. I gave him a quick kiss on the cheek and a tight hug.

"If it's not the Governor's Witch," he said quietly.

"Don't believe everything you read in the gazettes," I said. "You look good."

"I could sleep for five days," Bertram said as he offered to take our satchels from us. I told him I was fine. Mary handed him hers with a crinkling of her eyes.

"We're hoping you have a room for us for the night," I said.

Bertram shouldered Mary's satchel. "You can have your pick of rooms. One fellow down from Maine, but that's it. This lot will be out of here soon enough. They've been arguing about who's going to pay me for twenty minutes already. I keep reminding them doesn't matter who pays what, as long as all the coin ends up in my hands."

Mary walked farther into the room, taking a seat at a small table near the main hearth. She treated the table of locals as though they were invisible—which only made them more interested. I joined her.

Bertram helped me with my chair and began, "Would you—"

"Some of those little cakes you make," Mary said. "I trust you have some?"

"I baked a few this morning. Almost as if I knew you—"

"Four or five will do," Mary said.

"Katie?" he said.

"Just tea, please."

As we waited, the other party pushed back their chairs and readied to leave. A few of the men gave me a tip of the hat. I raised my hand in return, recognizing the local cooper, and a few of the others. Bertram bustled back in a moment later, a kettle in one hand, a tray of small round cakes in the other. He called a good evening to the men as they left and set the items down on the table. Next to the cakes were two shallow dishes of preserves. "Now those are warmed up perfect. If you spread a little—"

"I can't stand warm fruit," Mary said.

"The dark one is blackberry and currant, the other is strawberry. I'll get you to change your mind."

"Is it warm?"

"Yes."

"And is it fruit?"

"Indeed. It is fruit."

"Then, no."

"Go ahead and try it when I'm not looking. You'll see," Bertram said. He poured me a tall cup of tea. "The things they write about you. Though to be sure, it might help my business for you to show up every now and then and spark people's curiosity. But as I read it, I wondered: what does Katie think of this? I landed on furious. How close am I?"

"She's flattered." Mary nibbled at one of the cakes. "And more than a little intimidated."

"I doubt that," Bertram said. He started clearing the plates and mugs from the other table.

"It's true," Mary said. "You should see her around Mrs. James Spenser. She cares more about that woman's opinion than the governor's."

"She makes me feel insecure," I said. "The way she judges me."

Bertram stacked the plates. "Now you know how the rest of us feel when we're around you."

"Not comparable in the slightest," Mary said. "Katie judges from a place of accomplishment—with just a touch of moral superiority. Mrs. Spenser judges from a place of jealousy."

"She's hardly jealous of me."

"She seethes with jealousy. You're the new flavor of feminine success. Which makes you a threat to her. She's a woman who abandoned all else—any sense of fashion, any hope of romance, clearly—in favor of carrying on her husband's gazette. That loyalty and dedication has transmuted into what she believes is her mission. And so there she stands, smeared in ink, burning the midnight oil, waiting for some applause that isn't forthcoming. It's only natural that such self-loathing would turn into venomous jealousy."

"Quite a theory," I said.

"Don't fall for her little ploy, darling. Meeting her once was more than enough to prove she thrives on making the people around her feel stupid, especially when she wants to get her way."

"She's not dimwitted by any stretch."

"I didn't say she was." Mary examined her nails. "She's quite smart. She may even be five percent smarter than you or me. Possibly. But in her own mind, she's five to ten times smarter than you or me, and likely everyone else she meets, as well. That's not a matter of intellect. That's a character flaw. Trust me."

"You sound certain."

"And worse, she congratulates herself on her own aloof isolation. Her dedication, unimpeachable. Her utter lack of fashion, proof of moral superiority."

"My, aren't we prickly today?"

Mary undid the top button of her vest and adjusted the silken cravat protruding above it. "You saw that dress she wore. It's as though she wants to drive any prospective man away."

"And romance is all she needs?" I said. "To be complete, that is."

Mary finished off a second cake, eyeing the fruit preserves warily. "I'll admit to having this conversation with exactly the wrong audience. I don't mind telling you both how much you exasperate me."

"We might both be rather busy," I said.

"Yes. That is one of the stories you both tell yourselves. But as stunning as this news might be to both of you, there is more to life."

Bertram reemerged from the kitchen, wiping his hands on his apron. He said, "More to life? Perhaps you've confused me with someone who doesn't have a tavern to run, begging your pardon."

"Now, now," Mary said. "That's precisely the kind of thinking which will lead you both into old age by yourselves. And then you'll eventually live together. Like brother and sister spinsters. And I will have to feel sad for the both of you every time I come to visit you. And your cats."

Bertram wiped the table where the party had left. "That will be kind of you."

"Never fear," Mary said. "I'm on the case for everyone I care for. The both of you, hard cases though you are. Even young Clara Dod won't escape my charity. I loaned her a lovely dress just last week. To try to civilize her. If I can tame that wild thing, it will be an ample display of my expertise. After all, just look at my brother. I've poked, prodded, and steered his idiotic instincts unceasingly in the proper direction. Now he's writing love letters. Staring moodily out the window. Sniffing things."

"Unlike me," Bertram said, "Katie can get her pick of the crop."

"You'll do well enough," Mary said, eyeing him as though scrutinizing a jacket of middling interest. "And as for Katie, she will have to get her nose out of the books. She will also have to stop being so picky. There's a match out there for her somewhere." She turned back to me. "I've often thought if I were a man, we'd be perfect together. We do get along, darling."

I put my tea down. "Now you see why I spend so much time with my nose in my books."

When Bertram had his back to us, Mary dipped a finger in the dark fruit preserves, took a taste, and frowned. "Yes, and look how successful your romances are when you always put the work ahead of everything else. Poor Francis Knox tried for almost two years. And after running headlong into that brick wall enough times, he left for New York."

"That's not why he left," I said.

"It most certainly is."

Bertram said, "She's right."

Mary spread some of the preserve on a cake. The bite she took of it clearly dazzled her. "Listen to Bertram, if you won't listen to me."

Bertram, seeing what Mary had done, looked at her with a raised eyebrow. She gave him no more than a reluctant half smile.

"I didn't realize the two of you had gotten so chummy, with your gossip," I said. "Perhaps there's a future of romance for the two of you."

It was hard to judge which of them shuddered more.

THE FIRE in the kitchen grate was down to embers. Brushing aside Bertram's protests, I helped him tidy up.

"How are you really doing?" he asked.

"Confused. Paranoid. Worried. Exhausted."

"I can't imagine," he said. "I have enough trouble keeping stock of ale and coffee."

I leaned against the big oak table in the center of the room.

Rows of fresh herbs hung from the beam in front of the windows, drying. "Just like Iris used to do."

"Aye. Seems I miss her more and more lately," Bertram said.

"I know the feeling." Starlight fell in through the window. "There are days when I wish I could take all the memories and shove them in a box. Only open it when I want to. And then there are other days when I start worrying I'm forgetting everything about them. They're just slipping farther and farther away."

Bertram leaned on his broom. "I talk to her. As if she were still here. When no one's around, of course."

"Do you?"

"Don't tell Mary, or no one. It just—I don't know, makes me feel like she's still around. Like they're all still around."

"I think I'm afraid to," I said. "Ashamed to. Maybe I don't want to hear what they'd say back to me."

"You're too hard on yourself."

"I don't think I'm hard enough on myself."

"Now you're just looking for pity," he said. "Which is probably the one thing you won't get from me. Problem is, you get yourself too twisted up. Thinking you should've done this, you should've done that. This one did everything, and then some. The other wouldn't have doubted himself. But listen: ghosts aren't going to scold you for doing the best you can. Or for anything, really."

"You've got the medallion?"

He slid aside the collar of his shirt to show me the small silver pendant hung on a thin chain around his neck. "I never take it off. Not even to bathe. Probably another reason the lasses stay away."

The tavern itself, as well as the stable, were also well glamoured. While such efforts didn't keep the women away, they certainly kept demons away. For the year or so after Swaine and Rush had died, after Bertram's sister Iris and her family died, I'd barely let him out of my sight. I'd spent two out of every three nights in one of the tavern's spare rooms; Clara in a room across the hall, dealing with her own confusion and displacement. It hadn't been an easy time.

"Though I can't wait to see who Mary arranges my marriage to," Bertram said. "As long as she meets with your approval, of course."

"She really needs to stop worrying about me," I said.

"She cares about you. She even cares about me, not that she would ever admit it." He paused. "And she's not wrong about how hard you push yourself."

"I know. But everything takes time. Everything takes work. Research. Study. Practice. Running a ministry. You can't just wish these things into being."

"Is that what it's really about?"

"It's exactly what it's about." I crossed my arms and watched him. "Go on. Spit it out. I see it welling up behind your lips."

He stared at his hands on the broom handle, then looked up. "Well, you can take it or leave it, as you see fit. I'm just a fellow who found himself owning a tavern where he'd once thought he'd be lucky enough to earn a few pence mucking out the stables. But I do know you. And you *do* want to do a good job. It's your nature."

"But?"

"But, the way you push yourself isn't always about that," he said. "It's more like—well, you think if you drive yourself hard enough, all the time, and never let up, you'll succeed where Swaine and Rush both failed."

Before the protests escaped my mouth, he raised his hand to me. I closed my mouth.

"You're not being careful, either. You take chances, sometimes crazy chances—maybe you think they did the same thing, but I don't think they did. Doing more now isn't going to change what happened in the past. You were just an apprentice then. So you couldn't save them, as much as you tried. You couldn't save everyone you wanted to. But look at who you did save. You don't give yourself enough credit for that, do you? Instead, you've let what you couldn't have done haunt you."

I said nothing.

"I'm not saying it to be like that," he said. "I just worry. What with you taking that same path Mr. Swaine took. All work. Everything regulated, nothing messy. Everything precise, a pattern. I'm just saying you could let up every once in a while, that's all. It won't kill you."

I looked him in the eye, thinking of what he'd just said.

"You're furious with me," he said.

Everything precise, a pattern.

A pattern.

Pattern.

I pushed away from the table. "I'm going to Ten Gables. Now."

Bertram's face fell. "I didn't mean to—"

I stepped over, put my hands on his shoulders, and kissed his cheek. "You're my best friend in the world, and I love you dearly. Thank you."

"But it's half past ten."

I headed back out to the public room to fetch my satchel. Mary had already gone up to bed. "And one other thing. Don't even try talking with her until she's had at least one cup of coffee in the morning. The two of you will be fine. Tell her to hurry along when she can. But tell her gently."

I pushed out the front door and headed for the stable, the night sky thick with stars.

30

THE SORCERER'S KEY

Maps.

My world was maps, three of them tacked to the wall of my workshop. I stared at them as though the very force of my frustration might wring an answer from them.

The answers remained unwrung.

The one map that behaved properly stood on an easel off to my side. A small white spark danced above the surface of the paper: Penelope Bayard. It remained in one spot, hovering over the markings of a small lane two streets over from King Street—Milk Street—where the visiting New York delegation was staying. It hadn't moved in the two hours I'd been back at Ten Gables. I lifted my hand and held it half a foot from the center of the map. A faint golden trail lit up, the record of every movement Bayard had made in the past twenty-four hours. She hadn't wandered far, two excursions into various spots in the city, one into Cambridge, another to the governor's manse, and then mostly back near King Street. The trail of light danced before me, re-creating her movements.

I turned to the other maps.

Pattern.

I'd tried putting everything on a single map at first: the confirmed entrances into the ghost realm; the locations of rumors of strange activity reported across the city; the places mentioned in Gerald's journal.

Nothing had stood out.

Separating them out onto three separate maps was my current effort. *Like with like*: an old principle of the magical sciences. In separating them, I could better discern their differences. And there were differences—but I had no idea why, or what they meant.

I paced the workshop, coming to pause at one of the windows. Night held Boston. Did the top floor of Ten Gables shine like a beacon, the only windows illuminated in these hours past midnight? I rested my forehead against the glass. If I could see all the way to Cambridge, to Mount Auburn Street, would I see a light burning in the *Provincial Gazette* building even then? The burning midnight oil of another soul tormented by all she'd lost?

What had Gerald said of his sister?

I'm not compelled to work around the clock to better run from the ghosts of the past, piously regarding even a moment of relaxation as a sinful indulgence.

I turned from the window. A touch of panic gripped my heart as I looked about me. The rows of books—those on the shelves, those that had separated out from the flock, wherever they may have wandered. The shelves. The workbenches, stacked with half-finished projects, new investigations, lesson plans for Mary and Clara. The tools, the ingredients, the bottles and their labels, the tins, tinctures, all of it. The entire enterprise seemed suddenly less noble.

And more pathetic.

Robert Twelves could pursue his craft and raise a family, finding time for all of it.

Clara, wild and untamed, eked out an unexpected success in the unseen arts while at the same time living her life, however confused, self-righteous, and adolescent it might be.

Mary studied, she took her job seriously, yet she had a life outside of Ten Gables: fashion, friends, gossip.

Grayson, with his escapades.

Bertram, an open book for the world to read, and he'd lost just as much as I had.

They all found balance.

I had none. The midnight stillness of Ten Gables revealed my emptiness for what it was: my heart a map with all the important locations struck through and scratched out.

Maybe Penelope Bayard saw me more clearly than the rest, after all. Maybe we did stand apart from everyone else.

"What's your game?" I whispered, staring at the easel.

Once again, I held my hand out above the map, illuminating her travels. The lines refracted, flowing across where she'd been during the course of the day. I stared at the shape made by her passage. I paused. Turned my head to the other maps. Put down my tea.

It didn't take me long to enchant three small bottles of ink. I used a trio of spells, harnessing a touch of elemental magic through a channel of transferent energies. I gave each bottle a different *flavor*, as it were. When I was satisfied the spells had taken hold, I took the first bottle and walked over to the map on the left, the one marking the known entrances to the ghost realm. Using a yardstick, I traced straight connections between the spots. I made quick work of it, for that map had the fewest locations marked.

I did the same using a different bottle of ink for each of the other two maps. By the time I was done, each map was overlaid with a series of dots and lines. I put down the ink and the straight edge. In front of the first map, I held my hand out and whispered the invocation. The lines lit up above the map. As the current passed through them, the lines shimmered and moved, not unlike the tracking map for Penelope Bayard, dancing with a faint red hue.

I activated the second map, the lines holding a bright green. A more complex pattern arose. Likewise on the third map, which when activated shone with gold lines stretching across the paper.

All three patterns hung in the air, vibrant and alive. I stepped back.

With a motion of my hands, I overlaid the illuminations over the center map. The intuition I'd had clicked like the tumblers in a lock springing open: all three patterns connected.

Red, green, gold portions in different arrangements, yet connected.

I knew the shape.

But what was it? How did I recognize it?

As I got closer, it grew harder to discern the pattern, so I stepped back. And then back again. The lines intertwined. A shape like an X, intersected by three horizontal lines. Around that, a crescent. The patterns were incomplete, yet I recognized their shapes in general.

As I stared, the tickle of recognition grew.

The first symbol resembled the arcane symbol for *copper*. The partial crescent pattern, *silver*.

My breathing stopped. I checked myself, convinced for a moment I was imagining it. But no, it was a pattern I had seen once before. A passing reference. An offhand comment.

The *Zaubererschlüssel*: a centuries-old emblem, known as the *sorcerer's key*.

I raced to the library, tore through the shelves. Pulling out

Helmut von Brücke's *Der Schattige Weg,* I flipped my way through the pages as though they were on fire. When I found the illustration I'd recalled, I jammed a quill to mark the page and sprinted with it back to my workshop.

Holding the book open, looking at the precise pattern, I noted the addition of the symbol for iron as part of the emblem. I studied the pattern hovering in the air before the center map. Some of the lines could correspond with the iron symbol—but not all of them.

I put the book down.

Standing before the illuminated pattern I lifted my hand and spoke the words that forced it backward until it lay atop the paper itself. Grabbing up a pencil lead, I connected the missing points, drawing them onto the map itself. The symbol for iron resembled a stylized arrow extending up into the right.

The three symbols overlapped at one point: the center of Salem.

The tip of the crescent. The right arm of the X. The point of the arrow.

My heart pounded so hard in my chest that I didn't at first register the footsteps coming up to my workshop. The knock on the door wrenched me from my thoughts. Before I shouted at whoever it was to go away, I glanced at the clock on the mantel: 3:10 in the morning. No one would disturb me at this time if it wasn't urgent.

"Yes?" I called out.

"Sorry, Minister—it's Henrietta."

With a glance at the map, my mind spinning, I crossed to the back of the workshop and stood at the top of the stairs.

"What is it?" I said.

The door opened and Henrietta looked up at me. "The governor sent a messenger. He needs you over on Milk Street. One of the New York delegation has been found dead."

"Dead?" I said. "What happened?"

Milk Street.

"It doesn't sound good."

The governor wouldn't summon me if it wasn't dire, I knew. I snatched a coat and shrugged it on. "Who is it, the one who died?"

"A woman, Minister," Brookshire said. "Penelope Bayard."

31

REACH OF THE GHOST REALM

A small retinue of the Minister's Own, five soldiers led by Henrietta, escorted me to Milk Street. The women were not to be trifled with. Uniforms crisp, muskets well oiled, eyes as sharp as their bayonets. The house was already contained by a contingent of the Governor's Own, the premier regiment in the city. Whatever the true nature of the relationship between the regiments was—and rumors to such effect were an ever-popular pastime in Boston—they eyed each other warily as we headed inside and up the stairs.

"The rest of the New Yorkers?" I said. The stairs creaked as we wound our way up around the sharp bends to the top floor.

"Word has gotten to them," Henrietta said. "Most of them are staying down the street, at Benjamin Abbot's house."

"Not here?"

"She wasn't officially part of the delegation."

At a doorway leading up to the garret, a pair of Governor's Own stepped aside for us. Henrietta ordered two of her soldiers to wait at the bottom of the stairs, while the others followed us up. The suite of rooms, though small, commended itself with fine, tasteful furnishings. Tightly woven rug to keep the chill from early morning feet. A polished cherry sideboard, stocked with liquors. Couch, chairs, settee of recent vintage, all in immaculate condition. The impression of wealth and fine taste was broken only by the torso of Penelope Bayard, protruding halfway out of the whitewashed bricks above the hearth.

I lifted my hand. "Everyone stay back."

The bricks remained intact, no sign of having been pried or hammered apart. No blood ran or pooled. The effect was rather of an illusion: a parlor trick gone wrong. Penelope's arms hung as though she were reaching for something on the floor. Her hair hung loose around her face.

Before I got much closer, I retrieved two of my detection devices and took a set of readings. The first thing to check for, of course: the presence of any coiled witchcraft, a trap ready to spring. I certainly took nothing on face value.

Nothing registered of that nature.

I made a quick tour of all three rooms. A drawing room, decorated with a few books, needlepoint materials, cards, a small writing desk, high-back chair, and a cushioned window seat. The bedchamber lay beyond. A featherbed, lost beneath rumpled sheets and blankets, occupied most of the side of the room where the ceilings slanted down to the wainscoting. Two dormer windows, one to either side of the bed, showed views of the streets below. A bed warmer leaned against a cedar chest at the eaves. I opened the chest to the clear scent of the unfinished cedar within. A week's worth or so of clothing lay folded neatly within. Nice dresses, and one finer outfit I recognized from the governor's dinner in the Indigo Room. Silk shifts, petticoats, stockings. Next to it, a pair of riding boots, and a pair of dress shoes.

The readings I took in the bedchamber and drawing room indicated no magic. Nor did I feel any of the strange energy I'd picked up from her witchcraft, as I'd felt in the First Congregational Church.

Back in the main room, Henrietta and the soldiers waited as I continued to take readings. Near the hearth itself, I picked up strong currents of unseen energy. Adjusting the device, I wasn't altogether surprised to see that it registered the frequencies of the Helmstrom series. The closer I got to Penelope, the stronger it got.

I turned to Henrietta. "Search everything. But keep away from this particular area."

The women spread out, beginning a careful investigation under Henrietta's direction. I turned my attention back to Penelope.

No magic. No witchcraft.

Just the unmistakable reach of the ghost realm.

Her skin was cold to the touch. Her hands and face were mottled, dark blood had pooled at her lower extremities after her heart stopped beating; the change of state between life and death was sharp, as ever. Startlingly so.

She came through the bricks roughly at her waist. Running my hands along the fabric of her dress, I sensed an instability not visible to my eye. I double-checked the readings again. While distinct, they didn't appear to be as strong as at the cabin, or the meetinghouse. More akin to what I'd noticed at the Phipps household.

Extending my witchcraft, I sensed nothing active. Nor anything residual. I frowned.

"How are we going to get her out of there?" Henrietta said quietly next to me.

"Good question." I ducked beneath Penelope's outstretched hands, pushing aside the iron screen before the fireplace. I poked my head inside, placing my hands on the sooty bricks, and craned my neck. "*Ignis*," I whispered. A heatless flame fluttered along the inside of the chimney above me. Brick and stone extended upward to a small rectangle of gray that indicated the coming dawn. What I didn't see: any sign of Penelope Bayard. Her corpse was half in the ghost realm, half out of it.

I wouldn't have thought it likely. Then again, nothing about the situation particularly fell under the auspices of *likely*. I wiped the soot from my hands and approached the body again. Lifting my palms, I activated the tracking spell I'd put on her as she'd fled the belfry. Such a minuscule spell—as I'd intended—had eluded her notice.

Yet it shouldn't have eluded mine when I set it to reactivate in my presence.

No sign of the spell illuminated—but I sensed it.

Turning from the body I gazed about the room. Something through the wall drew me. I stepped to the doorway leading to the bedchamber. There, draped across the footboard of the bed frame: the blue cloak she'd worn. Two soldiers who searched the room paused as I stepped forward to pick up the cloak. The fabric glinted with my tracking spell—but it shouldn't have glinted there alone. I snatched up the cloak and went back to the main room, bringing it closer to the body. No magic shone. Nothing.

I threw the cloak to the floor; I'd been played for a fool.

Penelope Bayard hadn't been in the belfry at all.

Just her cloak.

The actual witch had used it to disguise her identity: generating the appearance of Bayard, mimicking her voice and mannerisms. All a performance, a deflection. The bonus had been to render all the tracking I'd done had been of Penelope, going about whatever business she did, useless. If she'd not somehow fallen victim to the ghost realm, I might not have figured it out at all. Or at least not until the witch took advantage of my distraction to flank my defenses without warning.

"Minister," one of the soldiers said. She brought over a small piece of folded paper, a letter. "This was beneath the petticoats in the chest."

I took the letter. The stationery was a pale blue. I unfolded it, immediately recognizing the handwriting.

You've got me right where you want me, don't you? Thinking about you all the time. Counting the minutes till I see you next. Making lists after lists of things I want to share with you, observations, quips I know you'll enjoy. You would think I might know a thing or two about magic, but yours defies my understanding. I must see you tonight. G.

I read the note again, then lowered my head and closed my eye.

Grayson.

The pitter-pattering of my heart providing me with a lovely melody.

Penelope Bayard—despite his denials—was the woman he'd suddenly been in love with.

AFTER THE GUARDS searched every nook and cranny of the rooms, coming up with nothing else of importance, I sent them out to wait at the bottom of the stairs.

Fine.

I may not have had balance in my life. Relaxation eluded me. Maybe I was hiding, running, contorting myself as I wrestled the ghosts of the past. But it was not for nothing that I was good at what I did. I might have been an imperfect tool, but I was without question the most effective tool for unraveling the infernal. I would chase every thread of this mystery. I unfolded a map, quickly plotting out the pattern I discovered back at Ten Gables. But when I took out a quill and made a small X at the location on Milk Street where I knelt, I couldn't see how it fit the pattern. Was it a mistake? The ghost realm certainly intruded—so was my theory wrong?

Or was it merely incomplete?

What had the witch done?

Time to find out. I approached Penelope's body, getting my shoulder beneath her arm. I lifted her weight and pulled. She came loose more easily than I had anticipated. I almost staggered, having braced for her entire weight, but as I pulled her from the bricks, a spill of cinders cascaded down to the floor.

She didn't come out alone, either.

Behind her, grasping her legs, was a second person. Everything below Penelope's waist that had extended into the ghost realm had turned to cinder: her legs, and the body of the second person.

James Breckenridge.

I placed what remained of them on the floor. Even in death, Penelope retained her austere beauty. I closed her eyes. Breckenridge collapsed into ash, along with her legs. I thought back to the way he'd stared at her at the governor's dinner; his unwelcome presence amongst the delegation. What had happened?

The pieces didn't fit together—not at first. So I took them in order.

Penelope: oblivious to having had her identity co-opted by the actual witch, she'd had her trip to Boston disturbed by the appearance of a spurned lover, Breckenridge. Said lover soon after died under mysterious circumstances. Was she relieved? Saddened? Both? Whatever her genuine feelings, she'd not expected to see him again. And in the meantime, she'd begun an affair with Grayson.

Breckenridge: his strange behavior had caught my eye at the governor's dinner, as perhaps it had caught the other witch's attention. To taunt or confound me—or both—she'd lured him to the remains of the tavern where he'd seemingly met his end. But had he? Or might the ghost realm have yet again done something to the time stream? I'd seen him turned to ash—as I'd seen

Grace Stoughton turned to ash. Yet Grace had also been alive, still in this world.

I looked back and forth between the two bodies before me.

Had a different version of Breckenridge found himself on the other side of a time split—caught on the ghost realm side of it? And had he somehow—driven by his obsession with Penelope—stalked her from the ghost realm?

With fates intertwined, they'd both met their ultimate ends that very evening.

Was that what I was looking at: the climax of a tragedy; a tale of passion, scorn, and revenge, staged in part in the ghost realm?

I TURNED BACK to the hearth. Strange energies gathered where she'd been, even as the bricks themselves remained intact. Strangely, the bricks where she'd been felt warm, a good ten degrees hotter than the bricks next to them. I knelt, using an iron poker to stab at the ashes and embers piled in the grate. The barest hint of residual warmth remained, graying embers cooling in the heart of the ashes. Some bricks warm. Some bricks cool. I couldn't see why.

A tinkling sound drew my attention. Something fell down the chimney, ricocheting off the iron grate, hitting the stones, and rolling to a stop next to my boot.

A silver coin.

Nothing else handy, I lifted the coin—of similar styling to those I'd seen at the Phipps house, and the meetinghouse—with the love note from Grayson and placed it carefully next to my satchel.

Time. I didn't have enough time.

I looked at the coin. I looked at the letter. I glanced at the body.

I grabbed my things and stood. Henrietta looked at me.

"Lock it all up," I said. "No one comes in or out. No one touches the body."

"What am I going to tell the governor's men?" Henrietta asked. "The governor will want to know."

I headed for the stairs. "Anything you like. I have to see someone, and I don't care how upset the governor gets."

32

ANOTHER CRUEL JEST

Dawn set the sky alight. The eastern horizon, the knife edge where the Atlantic met the sky, grew clear and bright with sunrise as I hurried to Mackeral Lane. The last of the morning's fishing boats set out into the harbor. Down the length of the Long Wharf, the business of the day was already in motion: bells ringing, thick ropes being coiled, wagons working through the crowds of wharf hands. The scent of brine and seaweed hung in the cool air. Grayson's house stood at the corner, a narrow three-story affair of brick beneath a slate roof, slabs of gray granite below each windowsill. I held on to the iron railing and paused for a moment, steeling myself before I bounded up the four steps to his front door. I rapped the brass knocker loudly, three times. After the count of ten, I did it again. And so on.

A shape moved past the small half window of glass set in the top of the door, and the door unlatched. "Good God, do you know what time it is?" Grayson stood before me in a long night shirt, his feet bare, his hair tousled, a day's worth of beard decorating his cheeks and chin.

"I need to talk," I said.

"Yes, I would assume so, the way you're raising a racket on my door like an invading barbarian." He stepped aside and motioned me in.

The front room glowed with light filtering in through the thin curtains drawn across the windows. "I didn't mean to wake you," I said.

"Then you might have tried a more reasonable hour." He pushed his hair back from his face. "But since you're here and sleep is gone, coffee. Come."

He kept his home neat, sparse. Tasteful pieces hung on the walls. Unusual acquisitions occupied shelf or mantel: a gilt-handled sword; the skull of a curious horned animal; a pair of foot-long curved tobacco pipes. I followed him past the stairs and into the small kitchen at the back of the house. Grayson stabbed at the embers in the grate, threw on some kindling, started a fire to snapping. "If you could be a love and start the coffee. I'm sure you're no more thrilled to be looking at my bare legs and feet than I am to have you looking at my bare legs and feet. Back in a minute."

He left the kitchen. I should have stopped him, told him right then—but instead I busied myself setting a kettle to boil, fixing the coffee. I crushed the beans—as I was about to crush his heart—with a motion second nature to me from my spellcraft.

Footsteps passed by overhead. Then down the hall, disappearing for a few minutes. And soon enough heading back down the stairs. Grayson reentered the kitchen, his hair tied back with a dark green ribbon. Loose muslin shirt in the process of being buttoned, a dark pair of breeches over plain stockings and brown leather shoes. By then the water was boiling. Taking a kitchen towel from the hook on the wall, I lifted the kettle and poured the boiling water into the coffee pot, then rehung it in the hearth.

"I'd offer you a bite," he said, "but I'm afraid you've caught me unawares. You're welcome to come over and make coffee for me any morning, say—at a more respectable hour, such as nine, or if you are a dear, ten."

While the coffee brewed, I gripped the counter board. "Listen. I have some terrible news."

"Those are not kind words." He watched me.

"It's Penelope Bayard. She's dead."

Grayson straightened. "Oh, no. That's terrible."

I gave him a moment for the news to sink in, ready to rush over and embrace him.

"God damn awful timing, too." He frowned. "And the sugar's over in that jar. It's from Barbados, you'll adore it."

"You did hear what I said?" I said softly.

"Miss Bayard, dead. Did I miss something?"

"Grayson."

"Throws something of a spanner into the works." He chewed the side of his lip, his eyes tracing a quick pattern across the surface of the table in front of him. "What happened to her?"

"Are you—weren't the two of you?" I fumbled. "I wanted to be the one to tell you."

"I appreciate the consideration. Always putting my interest first and all. I quite encourage it—but normal business hours would suffice, if I'm being honest."

"You're not exactly taking this news the way I thought you would. Why?"

He looked up at me. "Is there some other way I should be taking this news?"

"You're in love with her. Your heart pitter-pattering. Wanting to tell her the news first. Your quips." I took the letter on the blue stationery out for my coat pocket. "This."

His eyes widened. "Where did you get that?"

"She had it," I said. "That's your handwriting."

Grayson stood and took the letter. He unfolded it, scanned it for half a second, refolded it, and put it on the table in front of him. "I'm not in love with Penelope Bayard. Nor have I been.

Nor would I be, her undisputed attractiveness notwithstanding."

"But the letter."

"I didn't write this for her," Grayson said. "And I don't know how she might have gotten it."

One hand on my hip, I said: "So you're not romantically—"

"No. Not at all." He drummed his fingers on the folded letter. "Miss Bayard is—*was*—delightful, in fact, but, no. Not to sound crass, but this was a business opportunity. I wasn't looking for romance from her. I was looking for a deal. And if you had listened properly, she's Giles Walcott's mistress. Amongst other gentlemen, as well. Including that Breckenridge character, who'd harassed her ever since she'd lost whatever momentary interest she'd had in him."

"What did she tell you about him?"

"They'd apparently dallied at some point last year. He hadn't gotten over how quickly she'd dropped him. She confessed to me not two days back her relief at his...misfortune. I suppose we can at least give her credit for being honest." He poured us each a cup of coffee. He slid the sugar jar in my direction, taking his own coffee black.

I added a spoonful of the white sugar into my coffee, stirring it in. It dissolved at about the same speed as my previous understanding of the situation. I told him how Penelope appeared to have died. He watched me closely, not flinching at the description of her body and Breckenridge's. When I told him how I'd found the letter, he lifted his gaze to the ceiling.

"I see it now," he said. "She'd been worried, you know."

"How worried had she been?"

"Apparently his presence at the governor's dinner had quite unnerved her. To be honest, I mostly just tried to shepherd the conversation back to Giles Walcott."

My gaze fell on the letter on the table. He rested his fingers on it. "Then who was that for?"

Grayson closed his eyes and rubbed his brows. "Who can say where the human heart will carry us, don't you think?"

"Don't tell me it's Mr. Hastings's cousin," I said. "The maid."

He moved his hand away and opened his eyes. "No need to make it sound so terrible."

"Grayson. I asked you to help me—"

"Find a witch, yes. I remember. And she spilled wine on me. And seemed both frightened, and devious, and witty, and ridiculous. Trust me, I had no intention of any kind—until she showed up at my door the next day, with a new set of stockings for me, and an offer to polish my shoes."

"Your shoes?"

"I don't know how these things happen," he said. "She's odd. Interesting. Forward. And there's just some...current that runs between us. One thing led to another. And that thing led to my bed."

"And now you want to tell her all your best quips," I said.

"Smirk all you want."

"I'm not smirking."

"Oh, no?"

"Tell me this is just another of your Grayson adventures," I said.

"Do you know what I've decided?" he said, sitting back. "All those, as you say, *Grayson adventures*, were nothing at all. They were like glasses of brandy. Designed to make the ordinary more interesting, but eventually leaving me with little more than a headache in the morning, and a conscience full of regret. But with Kizzie, I finally understand I didn't even know what it was I had been hoping to find."

"Kizzie?"

"Yes. She has a name. And that's it." He looked up at me. "With her, it's not as though she's doing me a favor. Nor engaged in a negotiation. Nor checking off a box. She isn't wrapped up in a story about herself, where I have the potential of playing a walk-on role, or even a leading role, should I prove worthy, or wealthy, enough. She isn't patiently waiting for me to say my proper lines. In fact, she argues with me. And the more we argue, the more attracted we are. To tell you the truth, I think any hint of normal romance would drive her away. Which is why I hesitated to even write this note. I was sure it was going to end in my humiliation, though I couldn't help myself. In fact the minute I dropped it off I was convinced I'd seen the last of her."

"And have you?"

Grayson rubbed his hand over his face. "No. In fact she came right over. She was here all night. At least so I thought. Until someone's pounding on my door knocker wrenched me from the most satisfied and comfortable sleep I've had in years."

"Oh, no. No, no, no. You're in love with her."

"More than I've ever been with anyone."

He wasn't joking. Since maybe the first time I'd known him, he wasn't joking. My heart sank. I heard it in his voice, read it in his face.

"Grayson." What would I say next? The woman you're in love with is a homicidal witch? One who's tampering with ghosts, the ghost realm, and me? A woman who seems notably less than perfectly sane? Please, let me ruin the one thing you've just found, the thing you didn't know you were looking for—because that's what good friends do. As soon as I told him, the look in his eye would change, how he thought of me would change, and might not ever go back to the way it was in that very moment. And what did I have, if not a handful of friendships that meant everything to me? For a moment I couldn't get any words out at all. He watched me.

"She's the witch."

We stared at each other.

Grayson sat back and laughed.

When he saw that I didn't join him in laughter at the joke, he drew himself up with a sniff. "And here I'd thought we'd agreed

Rose Donlon was the witch." He took a deliberate sip of his coffee. "And thank you, Katie. Thank you ever so much."

BY THE TIME I finished telling him everything that had happened, he held his face in his hands. "Of course. What other kind of luck should I ever expect besides the utterly miserable kind."

"She's using you to get to me," I said.

"And that's supposed to make me feel better?"

"I don't know what to tell you."

"You could try telling me you're wrong. That this witch—whomever she may be—is even more of a genius at deception than you're already giving her credit for. That she took this note and slipped it into Miss Bayard's cloak to stir the pot. To throw you further off her scent. No less plausible than your theory."

There was a hardness in his voice I wasn't familiar with.

"You say she was here overnight," I said.

"You are implying she fled because of you?"

"No. Or, not necessarily. But what I'm saying is that if she were here, there might be a way for me to know she'd been here."

"You're the expert."

"This is awkward," I said.

"So sorry to hear that. After all, it's only *me* who finally found a woman who changes everything for me, only to be told by his best friend that precisely none of it is real." He leaned back and stared at me. "What? You'd like to go and take a sniff of my bedsheets?"

I said nothing. He pushed himself away from the table and stood up, heading for the stairs without a word.

GRAYSON'S BEDROOM had a lovely view out across a short strip of the harbor alongside Long Wharf. I'd rather have admired the view, but I tore my gaze away to take in the rest of the scene. The decor was flawless. Carved wooden bed frame and headboard. Attractive seascapes from two of the city's best painters on the wall. A stylish armoire, matching chest of drawers. A lovely rug from the looms of Boston's finest weavers. On the bed, a wild sea of storm-tossed sheets and blankets. I wasn't sure which one of us wanted to disappear the most.

"You don't know when she left?" I asked.

"We got back here sometime around midnight," he said. "And then we—" He motioned to the bed. "I rather lost track of time at that point."

A flush rose up my throat, burning my cheeks, even as I willed it away. "And after you—"

"Really, it went on like that for some time."

My cheeks burned no less. "Did you get any sleep at all?"

"You know how these things are, don't you?" he said, crossing his arms in front of his chest. "Bit of a blur. Some resting. Some more, you know. I suppose I drifted off eventually after she wore me out. I don't know. Three o'clock? Three thirty?"

I took a planar compass out of my pocket, giving him an apologetic glance as I did so. I walked around the room, observing no unusual readings.

"I can't help feeling that the device is judging me nearly as cruelly as you are," he said, arms still crossed.

"I'm not judging."

"You most certainly are."

I put the compass away. "You don't have to be here while I do this. If it's uncomfortable."

"I shall bear the abject humiliation. Stiff spine, and whatnot."

I stopped myself from ordering him out of his own room just to spare myself a further ounce of discomfort. I stepped to the bed and lifted my hands. With a slight release of witchcraft cascading down across the sheets and blankets, I detected hints of the same unusual energy I'd felt in the belfry of the First Congregational Church. Where Kizzie had arrived with Penelope Bayard's cloak, copying her facial features, manifesting them in some sort of illusion I'd never encountered before. But even though she disguised herself, she couldn't entirely obscure her own energy, energy she had needed to use to maintain the illusion. The same energy lingered over the bed. I lowered my hands to my hips. "That's her."

"Well thank God you don't have to hold your hands out over any part of me," he said.

"She must've known I was coming," I said.

"Not necessarily. She's a minx. The last thing I would expect out of her would be for her to do anything normal. If she'd thought I expected her to stay, she would most certainly have left. Rebuff all my advances, then ambush me. Laugh when there is no joke, leave my perfectly targeted quips cold. So she might well have slipped out on her own. Because maybe not everything is about you."

He left the room, leaving me standing in front of the silken battlefield of the night before. My thoughts weren't kind. As I examined Grayson's bedroom, embers of fury in my chest sprouted greedy flames. This Kizzie knew what she was doing.

We might have both been witches, but only one of us was an arsehole.

Finding nothing else noteworthy in the bedroom, I needed no further excuse to flee it. Stopping at the top of the stairs, I extended my witchcraft again, struck by the possibility that Kizzie was still in the house somewhere.

Though, to be clear, it wasn't the time to be anywhere near me, if she knew what was good for her.

When I extended my senses throughout the house, I didn't pick up anything. Still, she was clever. Before I headed back downstairs I peeked into each of the rooms on the top floor.

Wardrobe, through the guestroom, even the attic, which I had to press up a small square to peek into. She wasn't anywhere.

Grayson stood in the kitchen, fiddling with a decorative quill, iridescent green peacock feather extending out, seeming to practically float. "Satisfied that you are the better person? Better still —that you are the better witch? Or is it the better friend?"

"Please don't."

"My sentiments exactly for the past quarter hour." He regarded the peacock feather. "Even this. Now I have to wonder if this was all further mockery. She bought me this at Nathan Winslow's shop. Back yesterday, when I thought I was in love. Perhaps I had been strutting. Taking her here, taking her there, buying her things." He placed the decorative quill on top of the note still in front of him and pushed them both off to the side.

"It may not be like that."

"Oh, it's most definitely like that. I couldn't see it more clearly. She could have at least gotten some jewelry out of it, do you know? She didn't want any. Made me feel a fool for even offering. Which of course only served to drive me mad with desire."

I stepped over to him and put my hand on his shoulder, which he shrugged off.

"All she wanted was an ivory handled hand mirror," he said. "And the way she'd smiled when I looked at myself in it now makes me think it was another cruel jest. A self-admiring peacock. Do you see the hilarity? Because I suddenly do."

"Hand mirror?"

"It wasn't cheap, either. Well, I suppose Winslow has done enough favors for me over the years, in spite of my slowly but surely encroaching on his territory. At least if I have to be humiliated, it's benefiting someone I admire."

Hand mirror.

Clara.

33

APPRENTICE OF THE APPRENTICE

I burst into Ten Gables like a whirlwind. Even though it was early, activity had started for the day, with staff getting their morning assignments from Anne Moreland. When she saw me storm through, it took only a glance from me for her to hand off the list to one of her assistants. She peeled off from the morning huddle and hurried after me as I made my way to the residence.

"They've collected the body," she said. "What's left of it. And I directed—"

"Where is she? Clara?" I hurried up the stairs, my hand tracing the railing.

"She left half an hour ago. She said you'd approved it."

"No. Where?"

"Helping her friend Mena. Something about her relocating her room. She claimed you were fine with her taking part of the morning to help."

"Did she have anything with her?"

"What has she done?" Moorland said.

"Send someone over to find her," I said. "Check at Mena's, though I doubt that's where she actually is. Lean hard on Mena.

The girl will melt under the slightest question. Find out everything she knows about where Clara is, and who Clara has been talking to."

"Of course. I'll ask Henrietta to have some of her women check elsewhere. We'll find her."

"Keep an eye out for anyone suspicious: in particular a woman, young, lurking about anywhere."

I went straight to Clara's rooms, throwing open the door. Impossible to find anything in the chaos. I pushed aside, kicked aside, nudged aside anything and everything in all the likely places, looking for an unfamiliar hand mirror.

"Do you need—"

"A mirror." I used my witchcraft. And came up empty. But did I detect a hint of Kizzie's energy? I couldn't tell. I was so paranoid I wouldn't have been surprised to toss back a blanket and find her sneering up at me from beneath. Or maybe I'd carried her scent with me from Grayson's bedroom. I felt like I needed to take a bath.

"Hopeless," I said. "She probably has it with her. Put off anything on my schedule for today. Even the governor. Make some excuse. If his men ask, tell them I'm working on it."

"You did get a letter, just run over half an hour ago. From Mrs. James Spenser. The messenger said it was urgent."

She followed me through the door and up the stairs to my workshop.

"Wonderful. Put her off, as well. I don't have her bloody brother yet." I took off my coat, hung it on the back of a chair.

"The messenger insisted you read it," she said.

I sighed and held out my hand. Anne retrieved the letter from her coat pocket.

Esteemed Minister of Magickal Sciences Finch, the salutation on the outside read.

Lovely.

I broke the wax seal and unfolded the page. The note read:

Minister Finch,

I've just received word of strange goings-on up in Reading, in the cemetery near Baldpate Pond. I believe my brother referenced it in his journal. I will be there at 10 o'clock this morning. I suggest you meet me there.

I'm not sure why I'm doing all your work for you, Minister—but here we are.

M. Spenser

"Dammit." Folding the note, I walked over to the maps I'd set up. The magic still shone, illuminated. "Do you know of a cemetery in Reading? Near Baldpate Pond?"

Anne stepped up next to me. "I've passed it by. It's right next to the pond. I know it."

"Where?"

She ignored the magic, leaning in to look at the map. She traced her finger up from Boston into the town's north. After a few moments, she put her finger down at a spot near the indication of a small pond. "There."

"Hold your finger right there, don't lift it." I backed off and lined myself up with a front view of the map. The tip of her finger sat directly beneath two glowing nodes of light. The pattern overlapped exactly there.

Exactly where Madeleine Spenser should not go alone.

I pressed my fingertips against my left temple. It was nearly eight o'clock. If I hurried, I could probably get there a little after nine.

But what about Clara? As I wrestled with the choice, the map off to my left flickered: the tracking that had been on Penelope Bayard's cloak. Except now the pattern changed. In place of a series of straight lines resembling a scattershot trail made by a determined mouse, the shape had transformed into an oblong spiral. With a handle.

A hand mirror.

"Everybody looks for Clara," I said. "Staff, soldiers—everyone.

Get her back here. And get my horse ready. I'm leaving for Reading."

Clara would have to take care of herself for a while. The girl absolutely trailed mayhem—but she had a knack for staying one step ahead of it. The apprentice of the apprentice of August Swaine ought to be capable of no less.

34

THE ENEMY PART

The sun burned away the last of the morning fog which huddled in the shadows of the cemetery. Damp grass and headstones steamed in the growing warmth, putting me in mind of spirits of the dead, rising from the earth. Madeleine Spenser's horse—the only horse in sight—stood tied to the branches of a tall lilac tree. I rode over next to it and checked my watch: I was three-quarters of an hour late. Silence wrapped the burial yard.

Have you heard the song of bones? the ghost at the meeting-house had murmured. *It's so lovely.*

Madeleine Spenser was nowhere to be seen. I dismounted and tied my horse next to hers. As I did, my senses reacted to an unexpected energy—the sort of planar fluctuation I'd felt at the meetinghouse, and the cabin.

I called for Spenser and got no response.

Closing my eye for a moment, I centered my concentration and whispered the incantation for a spell of tracking I'd devised two years earlier: a combination of Gordon McLaren's *Persistent Paths of the Footpad* and a more traditional locating spell from the Germanic *Höllenhund* school of tracking. It required nothing specific to an individual, rather revealing the passage of any person within a recent window of time of up to twelve hours. Infused with my own witchcraft, the magic flowed from my outstretched palms, extending out across the cemetery. As expected, a set of footprints grew clear, dazzling a bright gold, starting from just beside the horse and proceeding to wind amongst the headstones.

The footprints ended halfway across, with nary a hint of Spenser to be seen at that location. At the site of a fallen headstone, the footsteps ended, one ahead of the other. I found a partial print, as though she'd perhaps crouched in that spot.

And then apparently vanished.

The spring grass showed no signs of struggle. No droplets of blood. Not a stray thread evincing violence or mishap. There should have been some signs beyond that point, but there weren't. Looking closely, the spot had a strange air about it. When I released a flow of witchcraft, a small gasp escaped me.

A touch of frigid air rose from the earth.

Also concerning, I detected the unmistakable presence of a demon.

With a glance around the burial yard, I reached into my satchel and took out a small planar clock: a device designed to catch demons. Between that and my own vigilance, I didn't worry overly much about being ambushed by a fiend.

Next, I retrieved a delicately calibrated instrument that stored the precise indices of the major planes across a series of springs and gears. Using a planar compass, I registered and then entered the findings detected from each of six canonical planes. A small window in the upper right hand of the top displayed six concentric circles, each face etched with a series of numerals and symbols. The circles turned individually depending on which reading I entered, the final vertical combination in the center giving a precise cartography of the intersecting planes and the time.

Once I put in all the readings and let it run for a minute, the faces filled with numerals. I recorded the index.

A solid reading at hand, I pushed back the cuffs of my coat sleeves.

Time to look for the ghost realm.

AUGUST SWAINE HAD WRITTEN EXTENSIVELY on the sorcerous principle of *infernal incitement*, a technique for attracting short bursts of attention from demons. By creating a localized atmosphere that might interest any nearby fiends, one could gauge the proximity of such entities. Of course, as it had the potential to draw in demons of unknown strength, it was not a technique to be used casually; certainly not one I typically favored, my general mission being to rid the colony of demons, not entice more into it.

My recent research had pointed me toward another facet of demons: they took energy from ghosts. Feeding on them, after a fashion. And after what I'd witnessed at the meetinghouse, in Madeleine Spenser's root cellar, and in the cabin in Andover, there certainly seemed to be a connection between these entrances and exits of the ghost realm and nearby demons.

Coincidence?

I was about to find out.

The first spells rolled off my tongue with ease. Then I relaxed the constant cloaking of my natural energies, which immediately exposed me to demonic attention, for demons sought out witches.

For the second spell, I whispered into my hand, trapping the words within a localized aura of silence I generated. As soon as I finished the final couplet, the exposure swept across not only the cemetery itself, but into the nearby planes. Enough to draw the attention of any fiends, the cycles were short and set in a pattern that would partially obscure my exact location.

Now, if I had done my job as Minister of Magickal Sciences well enough—which I had—no swarm of infernal entities would sweep down upon me.

A touch of attention disturbed my awareness. Like any good sorcerer—and every capable witch—I recognized the sensation immediately. The raising of the hackles, akin to the sudden sensation of being watched, along with the shifting atmosphere, as if something large and dangerous had moved in my direction.

I kept my attention focused on the fiend, ready to bat it away should it grow too curious. It didn't feel too dangerous—though any demon, given the right moment, could be deadly. A shadow rolled over the nearby headstones. The demon circled warily.

I let the incitement continue for another half minute, then released the spell, raising my cloak back up. The demon moved on after it lost my scent, not having fully entered our world directly. My temples tingled from the exertion of the spells.

But as I looked up, I froze. Four figures—no, five—surrounded me. Indistinct and shadowed. Two women, one in some sort of funeral garb, the other more plain. Three men, one with a distended abdomen, one missing a leg. They stared at me, eyes glimmering darkly.

A ward at the ready, I reached down and lifted my planar compass, stealing glances at the dials. I approached the nearest figure, the woman in the veils. She floated back, keeping her distance.

Getting as near as I could, I said, "How did you get here?"

The woman didn't change expression. Details about her person flickered. Old strands of lace. A wooden button. Pale skin. Her features went in and out of focus, reminding me in their ephemeral quality of sunlight in mists.

"Can you speak?"

Still no change, no attempt at communicating.

Trying a different tactic, I lifted my hands and lowered my cloak, extending my witchcraft, letting it flare.

That got a reaction.

With a look of terror, the woman before me shrank back, lifting her arms before her face—then she slipped into the ground, disappearing like a fog.

Had she not liked that I was a witch? Perhaps if I'd explained I was the Governor's Witch, they might have shown the proper respect and stood around for questioning.

The other ghosts vanished.

I wandered the cemetery, wiping dead leaves from a cracked headstone here, reading an engraved name there. The wind sent a glimmering curtain of raindrops loose from the nearest pine boughs. My hair lifted on the breeze, as did the edge of my coat.

A chill grabbed at my ankles. From the earth came faint sounds, along with a deeper rumble. Cautious, I pressed my palms into the ground, leaning my weight into them. While the soil itself remained in place, something else gave way and my hands lowered below the surface, wrapped in a whirling chill.

It was the strangest thing.

Almost—but not quite—like slipping into an adjacent plane. What it lacked was the sharp pull, the gravitational insistence, the physics of crossing from one plane into another, a process with its own momentum. Hard to initiate, hard to stop once initiated.

"I think it's your curiosity I admire the most."

The maid Kizzie McCormick stood three paces behind me. Gray cloak, black mop of hair framing her narrow face and dark eyes. I lifted my hands from the strange planar position they found themselves in. "Care to tell me what you did to Mrs. Spenser?"

She cocked her head quizzically. "Sorry, who?"

"Drop the games," I said.

"Games? Do you mean the way I've led you around by your nose ever since we first met? I suppose I can respect that you keep coming back for more."

"Where is she?"

"Oh. Her. She stumbled in on her own. I just watched."

"I doubt that."

"Well, it's true. I'm not quite as homicidal as you seem to think. As long as no one is mean to me."

"You killed Penelope Bayard."

"Killed her? I stole her cloak."

"She's dead. She was stuck half inside the ghost realm."

She pursed her lips. "Strange, but it wasn't me. I shouldn't wonder if it was that sweaty little boy, though. He'd been following her, spying on her. Maybe he hasn't given up."

"Hasn't given up? He's dead."

"Not if he slipped into the ghost realm he's not. He's never coming back here, but he's not dead. And who cares? They're stupid humans. Jealous, and vain. Petty—and did I already say stupid? Chasing after their own obsessions without even realizing they're doing it." She made a gagging sound.

"Tell me what happened to Mrs. Spenser," I said.

Kizzie's skin was pale, paler than even Mary's. Her eyes were sharp, though red, with dark circles around them, as though she hadn't slept in days. "She went right in, didn't even see it coming —you're really not doing your job very well at all, are you? It might almost make me think twice about working with you once they drive you from Boston."

"I'm not going anywhere," I said.

"But your friends are. That little ward of yours—she's burning with curiosity, don't you think? I talked with her, you know. Showed her a little tip on fire spells, no offense. Not too hard to win that one over, desperate for approval as she is. Wouldn't it be funny if everyone you care about disappeared into the ghost realm?"

That was it.

She must've sensed I was about to launch a spell at her, for she raised a skinny hand and tutted. "I wouldn't."

"Oh, I absolutely would," I said, right before I loosed a spell to drive her into the headstones behind her.

With a whispering flick of her fingers, she raised an invisible wall that deflected my spell and instead flung me backward. I only had a moment to manipulate the granite and marble of the headstones, allowing me to crash through a row of them, shattering them as I plowed into the earth. I came up spitting dirt.

"Told you," she said. "We can play this game all day if you'd like."

Whipping myself around, I leapt toward her—only to grunt as I was hurled to the ground at her feet.

She sighed, "But it's boring." With another whisper, a sudden weight pressed me down, locking me in place. I'd never encountered anything like it, not even from the more worthy demons I'd tangled with over the years.

Kizzie came over to stand just beyond my reach. "Here's what I think should happen," she said. "Because I can't stand the thought of digging up half of this sad little graveyard by using you like an angry shovel this way. Though I could, mind you."

I was so furious I lost the ability to talk.

"Listen carefully," Kizzie said. "We're going to be friends, or you're going to go away to a place you won't like. And to be very clear: it's not here. No more Minister of Magickal Sciences. No more doing everyone else's bidding. I forbid it."

"You're insane," I spat out.

"So they tell me. But look who's still here. Me." She reached up and pushed aside a strand of her hair. "I'm giving you a chance, you sad, friendless sister. Make your threats all you like— but you're either my friend, or my enemy."

She lifted her hands above my back and the pressure on me grew crushing, grinding me into the earth. "You really don't know who you're dealing with. I'll hurt you. Unless you can show me that you will listen."

I didn't like the energy coursing through me. I struggled to breathe. "Fine, I'll listen."

"Promise," she said with an amused lilt to her voice.

The pain became unbearable. "I promise," my voice crawled out, a crushed whisper.

"One chance," she said. "I'm giving you one chance."

Just when I thought she was lying, that she would somehow kill me, the pressure relented. The relief: exquisite. She sighed. With a raised eyebrow and a flicking motion of her hands, she—oh, the gall—motioned for me to get up.

Able to breathe, my own energy flooding through me again, I backed off, crawling away from her. I dragged myself up, humiliated.

"Just one," she reminded me. "Your single chance."

That time, I gave her no warning. Slipping into the shadowy eaves of the planes, I could move fast when I wanted to. Faster than a musket ball. Faster than a streak of lightning cutting a line in the summer sky. So that's what I did, whipping back around to appear directly in back of her. She didn't see me coming.

Or so I thought.

Blackness. Spinning. Torn and stretched as I rotated, around and around and around. I couldn't tell up from down, each rotation growing more powerful, wanting to rip me limb from limb. I didn't know how she managed it, but she thrust me into some kind of planer whirlpool, a ferocious current locked in place by tremendous forces.

And in an instant, it stopped. For my body, at least. My mind still spun, leaving me disoriented and wanting to die. I hung upside down before her, my arms limp, my feet locked together.

She shook her head. "Pitifully predictable. But good on me. And sad for you."

She raised three fingers. A jolt of agony cut through my dizziness, the hottest fire I'd ever imagined searing the space above my eye. She pulled her hand back, opening and curling her fingers.

"Now here comes the enemy part," she said with a frown.

My cry was cut off as the unbelievable planar current took me, twisting me in a thousand rotations before cannonballing me off into who-knew-where.

35

CONVERGING

How to describe the planes as I experienced them?

There's no easy analog, I'm afraid. Unless you've done it, it's difficult to conceive of slipping the coils of the material world. It's not like passing from one room to another. Or shifting from wake to sleep, sleep to wake. It's more like remembering a world you've forgotten. Stepping through a mirror to find a brand-new world. Realizing you don't need your eyes to see.

One can glide from one point to another, with practice. There are passages. Currents. Spots where the edges of the planes twine. Doorways, if you know where to find them. And I wasn't the Minister of Magickal Sciences for nothing. I knew how to cross through the edges of planes known as the planar eaves. A specialty of my predecessor, Dr. Ephraim Rush.

Normally, a graceful endeavor.

Not this time. I hurled myself into the planar eave with all the force I could muster. Imagine leaping headlong through the window closest to you with all your speed.

Not pleasant.

And worse, Kizzie's witchcraft tore at me like hundreds of

cruel barbs. My bones shuddered as I penetrated the membrane of the plane, a groan of agony grating in my throat.

But then the cemetery was behind me.

And I was safe, sprawled out on the cool ground of the woods perhaps half a mile away. I picked myself up, and then dusted myself off, quaking, weakened—altogether amazed at what I'd pulled off.

Oh, and also: my fury runneth over.

AFTER A FURTIVE RETURN to the cemetery—where I found my horse untouched and no sign of Kizzie—I raced back to Boston. Bursting in through the front door of the ministry, I found Mary and Anne deep in conversation.

"Have you found her? Clara?" I said, not breaking my stride.

"Not yet, Minister." Anne kept up with me. "But they found Mena, who claims she hasn't seen her in two days."

"Perfect," I said. "Have them keep looking."

As I headed toward the stairs, Mary hurried to catch up with me. "Oh, no you're not," she said. "Leaving me behind like that. If there is a more awkward human being in all of the province—no, there isn't. It's Bertram. He practically had a stroke when I asked him for a washbasin, and that was just the start of my morning. You can't just gallop off without me."

"I don't have time for this right now," I said.

"Then make time, darling. I can't help you if I don't know what's going on. And I'm your secretary."

As we turned the corners and went up the flights of stairs to the workshop, I told her what had happened.

"Have her arrested," Mary said.

"Too dangerous. She's not going to let herself be taken." The left side of my face tingled, still numb from her witchcraft. I shed my jacket. On my main workbench, both of the new devices from

Robert Twelves spun their gearing, activated. I leaned down in front of the one on the left, noted the recorded levels of energy, and scrawled them onto a piece of paper. The energies had doubled, as I'd expected. The watch face inset in the lower left corner read 12:35. Turning to the other device, I noted the time it displayed: 12:41.

A six minute shift.

I looked back and forth between the minute hands.

"Why are they different?" Mary asked.

"Because this first one is entrained to the device I brought along to the cemetery. And that's it, don't you see? *Time.* Something has happened with the flow of time in these instances where the ghost realm has burst through. It explains why Gerald and Grace each had a different experience at the meetinghouse."

"I don't understand."

As I compared the sets of readings, I explained, "There's something more going on here, and there has been from the very beginning. Some kind of split in the stream of time where the ghost realm emerges. It's why there were two Grace Stoughtons. It's why there were two James Breckenridges."

"Two?"

"The one who touched the ghost realm and then turned to cinder, and the one who'd remained inside the ghost realm and went on to stalk Penelope Bayard."

I brought my calculations over to the maps.

"I first noticed something of a small shift in time at Windmill Point. No more than a few minutes, but it was suggestive." I uncorked a bottle of magicked ink and found the approximate location of the house on Milk Street where Penelope Bayard had met her end. Mary stood beside me, her gaze casting over the maps in front of us. I did the calculations, accounting for the shifting time. "See these three patterns. It's the same pattern: known as the key of sorcery, but it's repeated three times, and if you look at the points"—I tapped the maps at the spots where there had been documented ghost realm phenomena—"and compare the readings, the ratios match precisely with the Helmstrom series."

Mary traced the patterns. "But they don't line up."

"Not yet they don't. That's where *time* comes in. The reading I just took is the most precise available, but if I extrapolate what I detected at the grain mill, I think I can see what's going on."

"The patterns are hinged," Mary said, standing back and staring at the maps. "Connected at the top, spread out at the bottom. Like—I don't know, like keys on a key ring."

"Exactly." I jammed my finger on Salem. "This is where the ring is. The readings all align here. The farther south and west you go, however, the more they diverge, each pattern less potent. But as they swing into full alignment, the energies are growing exponentially. The points are converging." Manipulating the shining patterns, I aligned the fanned-out edges together. "The next major convergence will be here." I put my finger on the map where three nodes aligned.

"Where's that?" Mary said.

"It's in Andover. Holt Hill, according to the map."

Mary looked at me. "H. H."

"Gerald knows. He figured it out before we did and has been trying to tell us. All these locations—places where there were hauntings, rumors, stories, and all the places he had a connection to—somehow, they're all connected to the ghost realm. They form a pattern." As I finished my calculations, I frowned. "Which might align as soon as midnight."

"Meaning?"

"Meaning that will be our only chance to rescue him and Madeleine Spenser." I pointed to the pair of devices. "With both of these activated, sending properly tuned energies to all six bands of the Helmstrom series, we can stabilize the connection between this world and the ghost realm. Create a passage of sorts, one where the discrepancies in the streams of time work in our favor—and where we can get Gerald and Madeleine through without turning them to cinder. It will work. I'm sure of it."

My gaze returned to the name written in small print on the map: Holt Hill.

I knew that name from somewhere else, not just from Gerald's journal. Swaine had mentioned it to me when we lived in Andover. In fact, if I recalled, it was part of the reason he'd first settled there after he'd come over from London. I put a hand to my brow.

"What is it?" Mary said.

I crossed to the back of the workshop, to the shelves containing my journals—and Swaine's. I ran my finger along the spines of his journals until I came to the smallest of them all, a short diary he had kept during his crossing of the Atlantic in 1734.

I'd read the account more than once since he died.

I slipped the slender volume out and opened it up, flipping through the pages. I remembered roughly where in the journal it was. It took me only a few minutes to locate the entry from December 28, 1734.

Another interesting tale from Turner. Not quite demons I think. The nut of it is this: the grandfather of Turner's closest childhood companion claimed the ability to track the dead as they made their way from this world. Rather like the practice of "bee lining," that peculiar technique for tracking a honeybee to a wild hive, as I understand it.

I scanned through Swaine's handwriting.

...departed spirits. Tracking them. Watching them wander, fated, shades. According to Turner, the old man insisted that the technique only works in certain parts of the province.

I found the part I'd recalled:

Might these specters be something along the lines of a temporal echo? The residual energy left by the passage of the person in question when they'd been alive? A collision of planes is certainly more than capable of such phenomena: temporal displacement, prismatic reflections, textures and motions retained as impressions in the planar boundaries. A warping, a redirecting of the currents of time, albeit faint. Turner mentioned a location by the name of Holt Hill in the town of Andover as a particular destination of such spirits, according to the old man. I shall investigate when we finally arrived. Take a set of readings. The thought gives me a certain thrill—to document the first hard evidence of the untapped energies predicted by my theories. My mind raced through the possibilities in lieu of actual sleep last night. Could the vein of planar energy be indicative of what lies in Salem itself? Can my theories of harnessing it be confirmed?

I closed the journal. "A temporal echo. Where the ghost realm openings align."

"How much does she know about it, this Kizzie?" Mary said.

I put the journal down. "I have no idea. I think she's insane, and a genius, both at the same time. She has some connection to ghosts and the ghost realm I don't understand." I started gathering ingredients. "But I think as far as she's concerned, she thinks she somehow sent me into the ghost realm back at the cemetery. Which should buy us some time." I looked up at the clock. "Because we're going to need all of it that we can get. We have work to do."

36

A THOUSAND LITTLE AVENUES OF LIGHT

The spellwork took hours. As did preparing the devices. Readying the materials for the glamours we would need. Gathering the other equipment. It felt like great progress, yet every time I looked at the clock another hour had sped by—and we didn't have many more to spare. Worse, the incantations had brought on an episode of *accursus vomica*, the summoner's bane. The relentless headache crushed my skull, blurring the vision in the corner of my eye, setting my temple to tingling as though with buzzing lightning. Not the time to falter.

The sun neared the horizon, flooding in through the workshop windows. I double-checked everything. Mary, to her great credit, had borne more of the work than I'd hoped, putting the entirety of her focus on laying down the base glamours, and imbuing the materials with the proper spells. She'd tied her hair back, kicked off her boots, and rolled up her sleeves.

"We'll need lanterns," she said.

"Use the ones in the storage room," I said. We loaded everything into two medium-sized trunks, wrapping the more delicate items in sections of old wool blankets I kept for that purpose.

"Two, maybe two and a half hours to get us there, forty-five minutes to set everything up—this might work."

Mary looked at me. "It bloody will work."

In spite of the pulverizing headache, I went to one of the workbenches and gathered up three small wooden boxes.

"You're sure about those?" Mary asked.

"Better to have them and not need them than the opposite." I shoved the boxes into the pocket of my coat, which hung on the rack at the top of the stairs. I lifted the coat and put it on. A knock came from the door below me, and I called down, "Yes?"

The door opened and Anne Moorland leaned in. "Sorry, Minister. The governor is here to see you."

Mary and I exchanged a look. I turned to Anne. "I'll be right there."

"What do you need me to do?" Mary slipped her feet back into her boots.

"Finish loading everything up, then have some of the women help get it in the carriage. If I'm not back by the time it's done, head off to Holt Hill without me."

"Without you?"

"I can get there faster on my own if I need to," I said. "But the equipment has to be there. Don't stop for anything. Take Henrietta with you. And some of her soldiers. But I'll do what I can to get back on time."

I buttoned my coat and set off down the stairs, trying to iron out the worry wrinkles around my eye.

Governor Reddington waited for me in my private audience chamber. Council members Endecott and DeWitt were with him, looking rather pleased. Seeing those two in my private audience chamber was akin to finding a spider in my porridge, albeit less palatable.

"They are about to leave," Reddington said, not even giving me time to close the door. "Governor Jansen. His entire retinue. So fix this. Now."

I didn't shrink away. "I need to get a situation—"

"Everything else waits." He walked over to my writing desk, pulled back the chair, turned it, and sat on it.

"But I—"

"They're frightened out of their wits, the rumors are flying, and *you* have sent it all right back to square one. One more time: fix this."

Endecott and DeWitt watched me with barely concealed glee. If I handled this poorly, I'd be dismissed for good. And if they had their way—jailed.

I clasped my hands behind my back. "Yes, sir. I'll speak to him now. I'll take care of this. I'm sorry you had to come over here."

Reddington stared at the musket above the mantelpiece. He didn't turn to look at me. "Hurry."

I turned on my heel and left them in my room, keeping the cursing as far down and away from my lips as I could.

Sunset washed over Boston, a thousand little avenues of light tracing over cobble, slate, and brick. Reddington hadn't been wrong: a line of carriages were being loaded, taking up half of the top of Milk Street. Servants, footmen, butlers, busy with loading and readying the carriages. Various members of the New York delegation stood by the doorways, waiting to set off. I hitched my horse and hurried over, pushing my way through the currents of departure, uncertain if I had any chance of stemming the flood.

The glances I got weren't encouraging.

In the foyer of the house, I stopped one of the New York council members I'd met. "I need to see Governor Jansen. Tell him it's worth his time."

I thought the fellow might flinch and beg off, but as he had been one of the few members of the delegation to actually have shown me some warmth, he headed off into a side room. He reappeared two minutes later, waving for me to come with him. I followed him through a formal dining room and into a parlor beyond. Jansen stood at the window, bundling a handful of correspondence. He wore a coal black jacket, his hat on the table before him. He gave me a quick glance, then put his attention back on the correspondence. "Your governor must be desperate, sending you here."

"Governor," I said, "this isn't the time to flee."

"Flee, is it? You think me that gullible? This is not for us."

"There's a reason I hold the office I do," I said, "and it's to control situations such as this."

"Control?" he said, turning to me. "That woman is dead. My people are shaken. One devastated. And you are fine with, as you say, situations like this? I see now how very different things are in here in Boston."

Two of the governor's staff hurried in. One took the correspondence from Jansen. The other took him aside, with a sidelong glance toward me, and held up a hand whispering something to Jansen, huddled by the fireplace.

Beside me, a silver tray held a pitcher of water and two tall glasses. The surface of the water vibrated. In both glasses and in the pitcher itself, concentric circles rose and shook.

Magic.

I looked at the governor and his man, then interposed myself between them and the vibrating water. Thin voices came from the glasses and pitcher, along with hints of motion, an out-of-focus view, indistinct and blurry. The voices were no louder than the buzz of a fly—but I recognized them immediately.

"Just think how pleased she'll be. You can help her. She will love it. She will adore it. If you are the one to rescue Mrs. Spenser, just think of it. And I think it will be quite an adventure."

The second voice, Clara's: "Is it another plane?"

"That's a perfect way to think of it, dear. It's safe as could be."

"I love Andover," Clara's voice buzzed. The sound of it trailed off and the surface of the water stilled.

I didn't know how she'd done it, but the message was clear.

Jansen's man turned and left with the other messenger.

Jansen himself picked up his hat and set it on his wide head. "I see no reason to stay in Boston a minute longer, Minister Finch."

I had no idea what he wanted to hear. Nor did I have any idea what Reddington expected me to say.

So I said, "Maybe you shouldn't."

He tilted his head back. He hadn't expected that answer, whatever else he'd expected. He waited for me to go on.

"Do you recall the first night of your visit?" I continued. "When the wife of one of our council blurted out the word *witch*? I think you noticed."

"You spared her a rather painful humiliation," Jansen said.

"Then maybe I can spare you one. Because I could try to appease you. Flatter you. Beseech you. Cut a deal, in your interest —or to some degree in my own." I looked him straight in the eye. "But you're going to make up your own mind about us. And, no— we're not like everyone else. Or anyone else. This province comes with complications. You know your business better than I. But at the moment, I don't have any time for flattery, or whatever other tricks seasoned diplomats might offer—someone I care for is in great danger."

"I think Reddington has chosen poorly in which envoy to salvage our talks."

"In that, I believe we're in agreement, sir." With that, I threw away the last hope of a trade deal, and along with it any possibility of retaining my position as Minister of Magickal Sciences. I turned and left, not willing to waste another moment on governors and their demands. Or niceties. Or conniving council members and their smirks.

None of it mattered to me any longer.

37

SHADOWS ALL AROUND

I raced my horse north as fast as she could gallop, ghosts behind me, ghosts ahead. The moon breached the tree line to the east, shaded a coppery red. Pacing me. Judging me.

"Oh, shut up," I said.

I'd made my choice and I wasn't much interested in hearing about all I'd thrown away.

Because I knew what I was *not* willing to let go of.

I couldn't save much. Not the trade deal. Not my office. Maybe not my most vociferous critic. As much as I drove myself, as much as I pretended otherwise, I couldn't save the world every time. I could only do what I could do, save who I could save. The moon offered no comments. She stayed at my side as I raced through towns, villages, stretches of farmland, meadow, and thick woods, faster, faster.

I slowed my horse to a trot at a stone bridge. At the other side, the lane intersected with a narrower path. I swung down from the saddle and let the horse drink from the stream for a moment, my hand stroking her flank. While she drank deeply, I retrieved a mirror from my satchel—the main reason I'd gone back to Ten Gables.

It was the original mirror Clara had stolen from Mary; the one I'd taken from her. I moved my hand across the glass. As before, only blackness showed. My guess was that Clara had the companion mirror shoved into one of her pockets, possibly the rucksack she often pounded about town with. I couldn't see—but I could hear.

The voices were muffled, nowhere near as clear as what I'd heard in the room with Governor Jansen. My theory: Clara had found an opportunity to transmit clearly to me, somehow. However she had done it, the technique had involved water magic, and an understanding of mirror magic. It was impressive, I would give her that. And better still, she'd known not only *how* to do it, but *when*, somehow trusting I would understand what was happening. As my horse lifted her muzzle from the river, dripping strands of water, I listened to the prattling of Kizzie's voice. Over the sound, the creak of wagon wheels, the steady clip of horse hooves. Clara made some remark or other, her voice louder than the rest of the sounds. I couldn't make out the words, but I recognized the tone: agreeable, cloying, her tone rising up into a question.

Good for her.

She was doing her level best to buy herself time. And me, as well.

I didn't risk revealing myself in trying to communicate directly with her. I didn't know how loud it would be. I didn't know how Kizzie would react to the activation of incoming magic. So far, Clara had gotten away with transmitting what was going on without alerting that maniac.

That would have to be enough.

Ninety minutes later, I reached Andover. The back roads and forest paths were as familiar to me as any in the province. I crossed over the main road heading south to Boston, taking a trail that skirted a wide, boggy stretch of land, reaching back into thick woods cut with swaths of boulder-strewn gullies. The lone farmstead nestled against the edge of the deep woods, fronted with a rolling expanse of farmland. Crickets sang, spring frogs peeped, their calls as plentiful as the stars overhead.

I picked my way along the narrow trail, ducking low branches. I'd been that way once before, on an autumn afternoon with Bertram before I'd moved down to Boston. The top of the hill, as I recalled, offered a clear view all the way to Boston, twenty miles or so as the crow flew. A watchtower of stout lumber and logs rose near the peak.

Where the trail grew steep, I stopped. I climbed down and tied my horse to a nearby sapling, hefted my satchel, took what I needed from the saddlebags, and set off on foot. Shadows all around, sliced with chinks of bright moonlight. I stumbled a few times, my boot catching on root or stone. The trail snaked up a steep hillside. Birch trees shone bone white amidst the darker skirts of pine and hemlock. The path grew so difficult to follow that I abandoned it altogether; the crown of the hill was easy enough to steer toward. I pushed my way through undergrowth, grabbing hold of branch or trunk here and there, steadying myself.

Finally cresting to the hilltop, I paused at the tree line. The peak of Holt Hill extended across a rounded expanse of open grass no more than an eighth of a mile across. After the murk of the woods, the moonlit scene beneath the stars was as clear as day. I looked off to my right, where a wider lane reached the top. Empty. I might have been the only person in the world.

The landscape fell away beyond the hilltop, furrows and gentle curves stretching into the dark. I could make out distant lights marking the night all the way to Boston. To my left rose the watchtower, adorned with two platforms: one at fifteen feet, the other at thirty, wooden ladders connecting them. And somewhere before me, the opening to the ghost realm, bare hours from its greatest alignment.

I STAYED JUST within the edge of the tree line and began organizing my equipment.

I checked the mirror first: the sound of wheels, as before. But while I didn't risk communicating, the mirror was useful in other ways because of its entrainment. I knelt and placed it on the ground before me, speaking a spell of proximity. Once I finished the casting, a series of firefly lights extended out from the center of the glass. Two blue dots near one another: the mirror, myself. A yellow dot, like the flame of a taper, hovered off in the air to the right, slowly nearing. Extrapolating the scale, I guessed they were less than a mile away. I could've taken a more precise reading, plotting it out on a map, but I had no time.

I released the spell and took a set of readings with the planar compass and my other devices, zeroing in on the strongest currents, which would lead me to the opening of the ghost realm. As I set off on foot, I came across a level portion of the hill just down from the watchtower. A series of flat rocks was set in the ground, the stone partially obscured by long grass. One of the stones had a straight line carved into its surface, running east-west. My devices vibrated, a massive river of planar energy rising up from the spot. I poked and prodded at the ground near the stones, finding the same unnerving instability I'd discovered at the cemetery where Madeleine Spenser had disappeared.

A movement off to the side drew my eye. A carriage drawn behind a four-horse team raced around the curve of the main road, two riders just ahead of it. I got to my feet and waved, motioning for them to steer the carriage off to the side. The riders spotted me: two of the Minister's Own.

Technically, I was still the Minister of Magickal Sciences—if only until word got around.

38

THE HELMSTROM SERIES

The carriage rolled to a stop on a level stretch of ground. I hurried over to meet them, even as the doors of the carriage flew open. Henrietta got out first, her shadow pooling at her feet in the moonlight.

"There's another wagon or carriage not too far behind," I said. "You need to stop them. Do whatever you can—but be careful, one of them is a witch."

She didn't surprise easily, but her brow came down at the word. "And the other?"

"Is Clara," I said. "So be careful. But you can't let them get anywhere near the top of the hill."

"The witch won't know what hit her. This will be fun." Henrietta gathered up her soldiers, not wasting a moment. In a flurry of orders, snapping reins, and the taut muscles of the horses as they turned, the mounted soldiers raced back the way they came, their muskets tipped with steel bayonets glinting in the moonlight. Henrietta herself climbed on the driver's bench of the carriage, getting ready to turn that around, as well.

Mary climbed down from the carriage, adjusting the hem of

her jacket. "You sure you don't want me to go handle that trollop? I'd be more than happy to teach her she's not the only one around here with a temper. No one plays with the heart of my baby brother."

"No," I said. "You need to help me set everything up. I found the location. Let's get the trunks, we don't have much time."

We carried the trunks to a flat spot of ground by the stones. In the light of a lantern, I checked the calibration of the devices. Mary took out a heavy canvas roll containing the spikes we'd prepared, undid the hemp ties keeping it closed, and rolled it open. Keeping them all in the proper order, she worked them into the ground one at a time, measuring the intervals with a thin chain we had sized for that purpose.

"Once we get into the window of alignment, we'll have to work fast." I hefted a wooden box from one of the trunks, putting it down just outside the circle of spikes Mary was placing. I flipped the lid open, checking that the bottles of ingredients were all undamaged, and in the right order. "The glamour will span both instances of the ghost realm. Somewhere in the area of twenty-two minutes' worth of stability. When we light up the signal lamp, the illumination will pass through, into the ghost realm, and be a strong enough signal that Gerald and Madeleine will see it. And with both of these devices reaching up into the Helmstrom series at the same time, the two time streams will link together. Entrained. Locked. They'll be able to get out."

"If either one of them is anywhere near here." Mary knelt in the grass, leaning all of her weight onto the spike as she drove it into the ground. "And they do it within the next twenty-two minutes."

"Gerald will see it. He told us so."

"And Spenser?"

"I don't know. Let's hope she figured it out."

"Or if she hasn't yet, let's hope she does it fast." Mary sat back on her heels for a moment and ran the back of her hand across her forehead.

I placed each of the two devices into a separate glamour, mirroring each other across the larger glamour Mary assembled. Both were lined with silver filings: that restless metal. Within each, I also lined up a small circle of connecting silver coins: further signal to Gerald.

Cold seeped from the ground. The grass and the stones within the main glamour took on a frosty sheen.

"Katie." Mary paused after getting the last spike into the ground. A bead of sweat clung to the tip of her nose.

"I see it," I said. As the glamours activated and the magic within flared, thin silver strands of light and leaping sparks stretched across the stones. I lifted the lamp and held it over the first device. The readings were stronger than I had anticipated. I checked my pocket watch. "This isn't good."

Mary looked at me.

"They're already aligned," I said. "And we're not ready."

"How long have they been—"

"No telling."

We worked in silence, moving through every step as we'd rehearsed it throughout the afternoon. Spell after spell, enchantment after enchantment. Mary laying the foundations for the main glamour, while I braided the energies connecting the two devices together. As they fell into synchronous entrainment, they framed the energies of the ghost realm, creating a doorway, one capable of creating a safe escape from the realm that would otherwise prove fatal, as we'd seen in the bodies turned to cinder. The energies in question, according to my calculations and research, were enormous. I wasn't fully confident that the opening we were creating could withstand that amount of pressure for the entire length of the convergence.

Mary stood on the northern side of the large glamour, her arms outstretched as she completed the spells of binding. Her diction, perfect. Her concentration, unbroken. The temperature dropped around us. Glints of frost clawed their way out across the grass. The air above the glamour trembled.

Just then, the inside pocket of my coat came alive.

The mirror knocked against my ribs, banging and banging. I reached inside and pulled it out to see the glass flash: silver, white, silver, white. Then, darkness, broken by what looked like scraps of mist. The glass shattered.

"It's Clara," I said. "She's in trouble."

Even as I said it, the doorway created by our spellwork opened before us, activated. Both devices in the side glamours vibrated, quickly turning to disorienting blurs. The filings and coins outshone the moon, bright as silver fire.

The grass and stones in the center of the main glamour vanished. In their place, an identical scene appeared six feet below the surface of the opening. The effect was disorienting, as though a hole had been ripped in the fabric of the world, only to reveal a second world beneath it: just as real, just as solid. The moonlight within, however, shone from a different angle, indicating a time shift.

"Dammit," I said. "Take this." I tossed the mirror to Mary.

She caught it with one hand. "What exactly do you think you're doing?"

"Clara just told us what's happening. I don't know if she got dragged, pushed, or dove in herself—but she's in the ghost realm. Dammit." I knelt at the edge of the large glamour, the doorway. "I'm going in. She's not going to know how to find her way out. And neither will the others. If they haven't seen the lights at the doorway yet, I need to find a way to get them here. Get them all out."

"Oh, no you don't," Mary said. "This isn't time for you to work out your August Swaine issues. Nor am I about to spend the next half decade of my life reliving this moment over and over again, trying to work out how I might have saved you. Think of some other plan."

"There is no other plan," I said. "Make sure the doorway holds as long as possible."

Mary made some exasperated reply, which cut off the moment I lowered myself into the ghost realm.

39
<hr>

FOG AND FAINT MOONLIGHT

Passing through the doorway felt like falling through a layer of ice water: the shock of it took my breath away as I dropped to the turf below, landing hard. I pressed myself up. The scene felt wrong. Air, still. Color faded from grass, soil, stones. Neither crickets nor frogs disturbed the soundless night. A place drained of life.

I shuddered.

The doorway we'd created hung in the air, a blazing constellation leaping down from the heavens. It shone like a beacon—though one considerably higher than the six feet it had seemed when I'd dropped into it. I could just make out the vague shape of Mary, her outline wavering and indistinct. The edges of the doorway tore and feathered out like the heatless flame of pale starlight. I wasn't sure how I'd get back up—but other worries eclipsed that in the moment.

Nothing else quite matched the scene I'd left. The woods encroaching on the open meadow towered up with unfamiliar trees. Some gnarled and twisted, others stretching up to blot out strange stars. I moved out from under the doorway.

"Clara?" I called. "Gerald! Madeleine!"

My voice didn't go far, muffled, sticking, and slow: a wool scarf pulled through the folds of a thick blanket. Before I called out again, I stopped. A line of figures crossed the hillside, twenty-five paces from me. A dozen or more men, dressed in an unfamiliar garb, grim faces, moving with the gait of warriors. They glanced over at me, eyes glittering. I recoiled from the yawning gap of centuries, the unbridgeable eternity between lives in the past and my own. The sensation unnerved me.

They appeared unconcerned with me.

I called for the others again, and again, but my voice remained muffled and indistinct. Shouting for them wasn't going to work.

What would Gerald do?

He was smart. So was Spenser. If they'd made it to this alternate Holt Hill, then what?

They weren't alone, as they would likely have discovered. And they wouldn't have known where or if the doorway would appear.

I searched my memories of Gerald's journal.

Tower.

He'd made note of the watchtower.

I roughly aligned the location of the watchtower back in the real world with where it would be in this strange landscape. He would've kept his eye on that. Used it as a landmark—but he would've stayed out of sight. I hurried from the doorway to where I guessed the tower to be, hoping they might be watching from the cover of the trees, breaking into a sprint.

I nearly tumbled headlong into another planar opening.

Windmilling my arms, I fought to save my balance, my right foot out over the lip of an irregularly shaped hole in the ground. Once steady, I peered down into it. My stomach sank. A dozen feet below me extended another version of Holt Hill, this one half-lost in fog and faint moonlight.

40

ALREADY LOST

For several long moments, my mind refused to accept what I saw, what it meant.

Another instance of the ghost realm? Another ghost realm entirely? The temporal displacement of the ghost realm? Any, all, neither?

No way to tell. And, worse—if my calculations were off, there was no way I would ever find any of them again. It wasn't just looking for a needle in a haystack, it was looking for a needle in an unknown and possibly infinite number of haystacks. I glanced back over my shoulder. The doorway Mary and I had created still shone brightly. I knelt at the edge of the new opening. Leaning down to the lower realm, I called for them again: "Clara, Gerald, Madeleine!" This time, my voice echoed out as though into a mountain pass—and no one replied.

Something landed next to me.

A curiously dark pine cone, in the grass. A figure stood at the edge of the trees, waving his arms.

Gerald Phipps Jr.

I sprang to my feet. "Throwing pine cones at the Minister of

Magickal Science, are we?" I shouted, relief nearly lifting me from the ground.

"I knew you'd come!" he called out. Turning back toward the eaves of the woods, he added, "I told you she would come—I told you!"

Madeleine Spenser stepped from the woods beside him. The look on her face suggested she had yet to share the same degree of relief I had.

No matter, I'd found them. Now all I had to do was get them out.

Within minutes.

Gerald looked the worse for wear. His hair, matted and askew. Rips in his clothing. Smudges of soot and dirt decorated his clothing, his skin. Yet for all that, he looked a changed man. Gone were the furtive little glances, the wariness in his eye, the defensiveness, self-pity, and adolescent bravado that had lurked just under the surface of his every word and glance. Instead, he strode toward me and said, "Thank you, Minister."

Madeleine Spenser, for her part, didn't look quite so sure of herself, some significant portion of her mind perhaps suspecting it all to be some sort of bad dream. While her hair was tussled, she looked otherwise unharmed. "How do we return?" she said.

"We don't have much time," I said. At least I had two of them —now I just had to find Clara. "This way."

They made sure to stay with me as I hurried them back to the doorway hung bright in the air.

"We're not the only ones here, you know," Gerald said. "Not by a long shot. Utterly fascinating. And, to be clear, terrifying. Most of them fled just before you arrived. The dead. Centuries' worth of them. Millennia. I've seen things with my own eyes I'd never imagined. And yet it's here. It's real. Unbelievable."

I gave a wide berth to the opening in the ground.

"Something is happening," Spenser said. "To the ground. To the air."

"I know," I said. "We're in the midst of a convergence. One instance of time overlapping another. Possibly more than that. Keep your eyes open for anyone else—my ward is in here somewhere."

The ground shook beneath our feet. The air trembled. Off to our right, a patch of earth vanished in a sudden flare of light. I didn't take the time, but I knew if I ran over there and looked down, I would likely see yet another expression of the ghost realm. More concerning, the edges of the hillside seemed to be draining of color, everything fading to the dull gray of cinder.

That couldn't be good.

"Some of the spirits have trailed me ever since I got here," Gerald said. "Quite disconcerting. They haven't harmed me yet—well, save for nearly stopping my heart a few times. I don't think they can. But they're fascinated by me, as far as I can tell."

"Altogether too much fascination, in both directions. Let's just get out of here," Spenser said.

"I'm beyond your sniping now," Gerald said to his sister. "Think what you will. Everything I've seen here, all of it, fills me with joy unlike anything I've ever known, horrifying as it is. Don't you see?"

"You can pontificate about what it means, and how it's changed you, once we're out of here," Spenser said.

"Yes, I know how difficult it is for you to fathom any display of confidence or utility on my part. Forgive my sister, Minister Finch —she's struggling to put her gratitude fully into words. Yet all the same, I knew where to find her, and I've made sure she stayed safe. One almost wonders what the more trying experience has been for her: making our way here, or seeing me at last comfortable in my own skin. But I should think my actions speak loudly enough."

As we neared the doorway, my alarm grew. Outlines of silver in the air had dimmed and displaced. Instead of one solid opening, there now appeared to be two: one overlaid atop the other, separating, both moving in opposite directions, leaving a smaller portion in the center that remained accessible. "This way, hurry."

Madeleine saw it first, as she reached out and grabbed my arm, pulling me to a stop. A twisting, roiling, sparking current of energy tore through the air in front of me.

"No fair, she helped you."

The voice reached me first, like a bad memory. Then Kizzie unfolded herself from a scrap of shadow, standing between us and the doorway. "I'm disappointed at how easy all of this is. I thought you could be more of a challenge."

"Where's Clara?" I said.

"Now there's one with potential," Kizzie said. "Thinks for herself and isn't particularly encumbered by conscience. I love seeing someone who's only concern is to please herself—that's the mark of a clever mind, when you pare all else aside. In fact, I'd say she's clever enough to almost be a witch. Almost. Sometimes fate is so unfair, don't you think?"

"What did you do to her?"

"Oh, that? I'm not really sure. I just kicked her into a hole. And then another. Then I couldn't find her. And sadly, neither will you."

The air around us crew charged. Clumps of ground shook and fell away, dropping into further realms. Cracks took root in the sky.

"Look at you," Kizzie said. "So afraid to lose, but you've already lost."

A violent tremor rattled the hillside. A deep, low note grew in volume, shaking the air. The planar energies coursed through everything as the convergence accelerated.

At least if we were all going to die, we were in the right place to become ghosts.

41

GLOWING WEB OF WITCHCRAFT

Kizzie drove me back with a punishing expulsion of witchcraft. It felt as though an invisible stallion had reared up and crashed down upon me. Before I could right myself, her witchcraft locked around my ankles, dragging me back toward the woods, furrowing the soil with my boots. I barely missed tumbling into yet another planar opening where the ground fell away.

I squeezed my eye shut and released a pulse of my own witchcraft, strong enough to break her grip on me.

Before I even stopped moving, I leapt to my feet, and hit her back with as much force as I could muster.

She cried out, driven back on her heels. I pummeled her with hit after hit, combining my witchcraft with a pair of modified wards I'd practiced, intensifying the impact. I rushed at her, creating a space for Gerald and Madeleine to pass by so they could get underneath the doorway, which had by then shrunk down to half its width.

Kizzie writhed on the ground, the wind driven from her. I whispered a spell of restraint, which she effectively countered, deflecting the magic to skitter off across the grass, turning it all to smoldering embers. Drifts of fog lit up as the sky crackled with forked lines of lightning.

Not a good sign: the instability had doubled, or more, since she'd appeared.

I jammed a hand into my coat pocket and pulled out a bottle of silver filings. I clenched the cork between my teeth and yanked, flinging the contents of the bottle into the air between Kizzie and me. For a moment, every single filing flared a blinding blue. Energy coursed in from not just the other openings, but from dozens of other points in the ground, in the air, in the sky. More than one version of Kizzie appeared: she trebled, quadrupled. For myself, I experienced the almost indescribable sensation of being in more than one place at the same instant, in more than one stream of time.

Massive chunks of the ground fell away.

Spirits flooded in to surround us. Men, women, children. All driven to madness, seemingly—but as Gerald had said, their touch insubstantial. Gerald didn't hesitate, for he knew I was buying him time. He dragged his sister past us, cutting his way through the horde of ghosts, pale limbs, glaring eyes, fixed on the entrance hanging in the air.

Kizzie hit me with a wrenching tug, one that drew me off balance and sent me heels over head to crash into the ground. I threw up a shield of energy which deflected her follow-up blow. I drew her away from the doorway. Behind her, Gerald laced his fingers together, getting Madeleine to step into his hands and brace herself on his shoulder as he lifted her higher and higher, shouting at her to step on his shoulders. She reached up and grabbed hold of the doorway. Gerald shoved his arms overhead, heaving his sister up and through the doorway.

As my witchcraft twined, battered, and clashed with Kizzie's, the spilled silver filings connected in needle-thin strands extending up to the doorway—but also up into the sky and through the ground, in a profusion that stunned me.

The air between us warped.

All her strength cracked into mine.

We both cried out at the same instant, but she hurled me up and over her in a dizzying flight. I spun so quickly, I didn't know up from down. My face sizzled, along with my left shoulder and arm. A searing, razor pain sank into my essence, burning my flesh. I slammed to the ground. A glowing web of witchcraft shone, lines crisscrossing one another across my arms. She entangled me in unforgiving wraps of witchcraft, choking off my air, immobilizing me on the ground. She dragged herself to her feet and sauntered over to me, a quizzical look on her face. She smoothed down her unkempt hair.

"You picked the wrong place to fight me, darling," she said. "I didn't fight you in the middle of your precious Ten Gables, you might have noticed. But you came right in here, as I knew you would." She tutted. "Honestly, I think we both know who the better witch is. And in a few moments, when I'm the only witch left, everyone else is going to know it, too." She stepped closer, and said, "But I'm not going to be so civilized about it. All your waiting, pleasing, hiding, kowtowing, surveilling, always waiting for everyone's approval—no. Ridiculous. Things will be different from now on. Unlike you, I'm nobody's witch."

She came closer, hand outstretched. She coiled her fingers, and my throat closed completely. I felt my face swelling. The last of the air squeezed out of my lungs, seizing them up.

I couldn't speak to cast the spell.

I couldn't move a hand to release a ward.

I had nothing behind my witchcraft, nothing to hold her back.

She'd won.

All around, fine lines of silver extended like a thousand webs of a thousand demented spiders connecting ground and sky. My last grip gave way.

Blackness descended.

42

WITH IT CAME SILENCE

From beyond an eyelid that had closed for the last time—I thought—a warm light flared.

Was this death? Some new ghost realm I was entering as an official resident?

I experienced none of the satisfaction Gerald had claimed.

And then came a shriek. I pried my eye open as though lifting a shovelful of soil from my own grave.

Kizzie staggered before me, arrayed in flames.

In that instant, her witchcraft released me, and I heaved in the biggest lungful of air I've ever taken. My entire body gasped. Kizzie's hair, dress, limbs, danced with fire. I propped myself onto my elbow, fighting back the dizziness and air-starved confusion. Clara stood twelve paces behind Kizzie, her left hand held before her chest, index and pinky finger extended: *Clawing Reach*—and this time she used it to full effect.

Kizzie—though taken by surprise—didn't just stand there, burning. With a cry of fury, she extinguished the flames, filigrees of soot and burnt hair spinning up around her as she did. She lifted her hands and sent Clara flying. She didn't let up, following

Clara, battering her across the field even as it shook itself to pieces. Clara was no match for her.

But I was.

And she was trying to kill my family. And, of course, I wasn't just a witch: I was also a sorcerer.

I reached into the inside pocket of my coat and pulled out the two small wooden boxes I'd put there as a last resort. With the proper word, I threw them to the ground. When they hit, I released the bindings.

Two demons, newly released from their bindings.

And they weren't happy.

But they couldn't get me, not with the medallion I wore. And they couldn't get Clara, for she had an identical medallion. As for Gerald, well, I assumed they would let him go in favor of the witch standing before them.

And so they did.

The rage in their newfound freedom unleashed a rending wave of claw, tooth, and fury at Kizzie. The ghosts all fled.

More dark shapes, strange demons, slithered out of the planes.

God love Gerald, he didn't hesitate.

He ran to Clara, helping her to her feet. Beneath the doorway, he lifted her as he had done with his sister. By then, the doorway was a bare eight inches across—and closing fast. Half of the hilltop was gone, revealing beneath the shattered crust another hilltop, and another below that: a massive collision of ghost realms stacked one atop the other, one inside of another. Everything fractured.

Kizzie wasn't strong enough to hold off both demons—not when she was taken by complete surprise, whatever her natural precautions against such fiends might have been. They drove her back and enveloped her. At the last moment, she somehow scrabbled her way through some kind of opening, vanishing even as the demons trailed after her.

I looked up in time to see Clara's feet disappearing in the air, slipping into the doorway. I staggered over to Gerald.

He turned to me, his eyes wide and alive. "Up you go, Minister." He interlaced his fingers and held them down for me to step into.

"What about you?" I shouted.

"Throw me down a rope," he said.

We both knew there wouldn't be time for that.

"And look after my sister, if you would. Generally insufferable, yes—blind spots galore—but her heart is true, deep down."

The strands of silver flared, glaring. The crashing of the ghost realms shook our skulls. Everything around us disintegrated. I tried to lift Gerald with my witchcraft, but nothing worked. The maelstrom of energies swept away my witchcraft and magic in a current too strong to control.

"Now!" he shouted. "Please."

"You can't do this!"

"Someone has to—and who knows, maybe I'll find my way home somehow. Now, please—step into my hands, Minister!"

I placed my hand on Gerald's shoulder, giving it a wordless squeeze. He grunted, practically tossing me up. I reached my hands up into the sliver of doorway remaining, using his shoulder like the rung of a ladder. I groped blindly upward, barely balancing. Gerald shook, pressing my foot higher and higher. My hands found the opening, and were grabbed by other hands, which hauled me up. My chest and hips barely squeezed through.

I climbed out through the other side, Mary and Clara gripping my arms, Spenser pulling on the collar of my jacket, as well.

"Get the ropes!" I cried. "Now!"

But the doorway between the glamours slammed shut and vanished. One after another, the devices in the side glamours burst asunder, unable to withstand the sudden change in planar energy.

The light of the silver faded, and with it came silence.

43

THE REMAINS OF THE GLAMOURS

The ground was solid earth, through and through.

We searched, we dug, we poked and prodded, both inside of the glamoured circles and without—but the ghost realm had withdrawn. Little by little, the sound of crickets returned to fill the darkness. The wetlands down the hillside sang with frogs. Life continued in profusion, even as the ghost realm receded.

As ever.

Henrietta and her women searched the hilltop and woods, looking for any hint of Gerald, or Kizzie. I held little in the way of hope we would find either. Worse still were the readings: it might have been any hillside in the province. Signs of the *summa-praecento* band, readings from the Helmstrom series, nothing. For such an overflow of planar force to have receded so quickly— well, I needed a bigger theory. Had my two temporal devices withstood the pressures, I might have had more to go on, but as I knelt by their remains, wondering if there were some way I could salvage them, it seemed unlikely.

"That was his one chance, wasn't it?" Spenser said.

"I think he knew it."

"And?"

I could have told her we would keep looking. Of course we would. We would search here, there, and everywhere for him. That some other plausible exit from the ghost realm would surely manifest soon enough. I could have eased her mind, or—if you prefer—allowed her to keep some hope alive.

"I believe him to be gone for good," I said quietly. "I'm sorry."

She looked as though she'd been etched into silver: still, draped in moonlight. Her dark eyes didn't look away.

"He saved us," I added.

Spenser blinked and looked up to the stars, opening her mouth as if to speak, but then said nothing. She wrapped her arms in front of her chest.

"At least that horrible little wretch will know not to mess with a bunch of women with their dander up," Mary said, hands on her hips.

The soldiers found no signs of Kizzie. The wagon she'd ridden in with Clara was where they'd left it, half a mile down along the back lane, untouched.

"I suppose we don't really make it easy on anyone, do we?" I said. Myself, I wasn't quite as cavalier as Mary; it had been a close thing.

Well, I don't think I should just ignore the fact that our paths are finally crossed. Perhaps I've grown bored with causing trouble for my own amusement.

"She's out there somewhere," I said, recalling Kizzie's words from the belfry of the First Congregation Church. "And I'm sure she's not done with us."

Smarter to think of us as cousins. Or maybe even sisters, of a kind.

"I'll make sure she takes the hint the next time she shows her macabre little face around here," Mary sniffed.

"I set demons loose on her. We might be past hints."

"Katie," Clara said. She stood on the far side of the glamour, lantern in her hand. "You'd better come see this."

The silver filings that formed the barrier of the glamour had been smeared into the circle. There wasn't much, so it didn't go far. But within the disturbed filings: writing. As though someone had scrawled a message with their fingertip into the dusting of filings.

Clara looked at me. "What does it mean?"

I looked carefully. Just three letters: *HOZ*. Trailing off, a few more scrawls I couldn't decipher.

"I have no idea," I said.

While I puzzled it out, Clara crossed over to the companion glamour on the other side. "It's the same here—but backward."

The letters and scrawl weren't just backward—*ZOH*—they were the mirror image of the letters in the other glamour.

"*Hoz*?" Mary said. "Who or what is a *hoz*?"

I shook my head. I looked over to Madeleine. "Is that something Gerald ever mentioned?"

She came over to stand beside me, looking down at the letters wiped into the silver. "I have no idea. It doesn't mean anything to me. Maybe something in his journals?"

We stared at the remains of the glamours. The moon offered no comment, and neither did the vast night around the hilltop.

44

TEMPTING

The Council Hall at Ten Gables stood empty: the stage between performances.

Floorboards waxed, seats dusted, strong sunlight slanting through the many windows, the blue skies over Boston beyond the panes. I looked the hall over, with the critical eye of the actor. How easy it was to slip into the role at the mere sight of the stage. But when the performance is over, when the run of the play is finished—then what?

A quiet library? Solitude? Focus, research, time to rest?

Possibly. But would I still have my ghosts? How might I outrun them then, left to my own devices?

Another thought to haunt me: maybe I hadn't been running *from* something, but *toward* something, all along. Maybe I hadn't even known the difference.

The main door to the hall opened, stirring me from my thoughts. Governor Thomas Reddington pushed his way in, dressed in a riding outfit of dark blue. Dress sword at his side, black tricorn on his head, he looked every bit the part of a leader worthy of respect; if he struggled with the gap between performance and his true self, if such a gap even existed, he showed no sign of it.

"There you are," he said. "My favorite minister."

I turned to him. "Am I still your minister?"

"I'm not letting you go that easily." He took off his hat.

"I'm nobody's witch, sir. Not even yours."

"I've never claimed you were." His voice reverberated through the empty hall. "That was Mrs. James Spenser. Who has apparently changed her tune. You saw her latest gazette?"

"I try to avoid punches to my face when I can."

"She noted that the Ministry of Magickal Sciences under my guidance has achieved a small measure of utility. Which we must of course take as a full throated endorsement."

"Utility?"

"We've practically won her over." He walked over and leaned against my desk. The light through the stained glass window proved as dramatic on him as it did upon me when I sat there. He looked around approvingly. "We make a nice team, in point of fact. Productive."

"You wouldn't know it from the unthankful murmuring of men like DeWitt and Endecott."

"Take their jealousy and relentless insecurity as a compliment. Believe it or not, they have their uses, from time to time. Just not as often as you." He looked at his hat from the front. "Whatever you said to Governor Jansen worked. We've agreed on terms."

In other words, I truly had no understanding of the way governors' minds worked. I glanced at the door he'd come through: it stood open. Strong, straight-angled, carved, and imposing. I could walk through it, and out into the rest of my life.

Tempting.

Instead, I turned to the governor and said, "Why, it's almost as if we know what we're doing, sir."

"These New Yorkers will be onto us if we don't stay clever," he said. "And of course London won't be happy about it. They expect us to play nice with one another, but not that nice. They will overreach."

"I expect they will, sir."

"Then I shall count on you. As ever."

Ten Gables had a magic to it. From the intricate windows, to the black oak beams and the whitewashed plaster, to the endless possibilities.

"Of course you can," I said.

45
____

PATTERNS WITHIN THE PATTERNS

The clock on the mantel indicated eleven minutes past the hour. *Tick, tick, tick.* So goes the flow of time, one moment after another. Was it no more puzzling than that? In fact, I'd come to have my doubts.

Mary leaned delicately against the edge of my writing desk, resplendent in a trim-fit scarlet jacket over a white silk shirt. She tapped her nails in rhythm with the clock.

"Give her time," I said. "She did well."

"Yes, yes. Every now and then even a reckless arsonist can come in handy."

Henrietta chuckled. "Sometimes it helps if you don't stop and think things through."

"Clara frustrates you both just as much as she does me," I said. "I've always known it."

"No you haven't," Mary said. "But while we're on the topic, you'd think she has nothing but plain black breeches and long, loose shirts. As if I haven't gotten her the second most impressive wardrobe in Boston. She may run around setting this, that, and the other on fire. She may steal, omit, and dissemble. And yes, Henrietta, not pausing to think might buy her a future in the

Minister's Own. While we're at it, she might even end up better at magic than anyone in Boston one day. Including us. But when it comes to civilizing that savage, let's just be honest: I have the most daunting challenge of the three of us."

The door to my private audience chamber opened, and Clara hurried in. "I made it," she said.

"Ten o'clock means ten o'clock," Mary offered. "Not twelve minutes past ten o'clock."

Clara twitched her nose. She placed a book on my writing desk. "It's basically ten o'clock. And I found this in the kitchen."

Benjamin Hawkins's *The Inner Coils of Temporal Manipulation*. So that's where I'd left it.

"You all did extremely well," I said. "So you will be pleased to know that all three of you will be getting more duties."

Clara, her head cocked, her posture terrible, raised her left hand. "I'll take the fire magic."

"And probably anything else that isn't nailed down, as well," Mary said.

"I'll also take care of any other witches about to murder any of you three," Clara said.

I walked over to the window. "Let's not get carried away with ourselves. We still have something to prove. We will *always* have something to prove. But I think that together, we can handle it."

"We handled that odious little witch," Mary said, "though so much for feminine solidarity."

"I'm afraid we'll have to deal with her sooner or later," I said. "She's clearly crawled off to lick her wounds for a while. I can't find her. Not anywhere. Not using any tool or technique I can think of. She may be a lunatic, but she's a clever lunatic."

"Poor Gerald was clever, too," Mary said, "yet I doubt we're likely to run into either of them again on this side of the ghost realm again. That having been the point of our ridiculous gamble all along, need I remind you."

Outside, pennants snapped on the harbor breeze. Women

and men, going about their business on a warm day, another in a seemingly endless line of days in Boston. Yet I knew that beneath all the life, hidden but never far off, lay the ghost realm. Waiting.

"You think there's more to it, don't you?" Henrietta said.

I turned from the window. "Time. This is what bothers me most. I've gone through all the readings, looked at all the patterns, and I keep coming back to *time*. The multiple instances of the ghost realm didn't just happen in more than one place, but in more than one time, offset by a small degree. There are patterns within the patterns."

"You think Kizzie did that?" Mary said.

"No, I don't. Time magic is the most difficult and demanding of the unseen arts. History is clear on that score. And as clever and as strong as she is, she's neither that clever, nor that strong."

Clara fiddled with a quill from one of my shelves. "What about Gerald's journals? Anything about *Hoz*?"

"Nothing."

"Then what did he mean?"

"I'm not actually sure it was him," I said. "And for the word to be reversed with each of the temporal devices. It's curious."

"How very tight-lipped you're being," Mary said. "I can't help but notice."

Clara looked up at me, as well. As did Henrietta. Three strong women, waiting for my clarifying wisdom.

"It's because I don't know, that's why," I said. "Honestly. I trust you all can handle my honesty?"

I went to my writing desk and picked up a piece of correspondence, handing it to Clara. "Have this posted. And I may need you to travel with me in the next month or so."

The letter was addressed to Georgina Rush, of Philadelphia.

"How many trunks should I pack?" Mary said.

"Zero, for you," I said. "Someone will need to stay here and hold down the fort. Someone who knows what she's doing. As you did back at Holt Hill."

Feathers ruffled, feathers soothed. She looked pleased.

"How is Grayson?" I asked.

Mary flicked her fingers dismissively. "Sulking. His ridiculous pride bruised. His tender heart poked and aching, and how could this not be a tragedy worthy of the ages? You know: a man."

"Yet another score to settle with Kizzie McCormick," I said. "I don't like it when people hurt my friends."

A soft rap on the door a moment before it opened. Anne Moorland leaned in and said, "They'll be opening the Council Hall in ten minutes, Minister."

I checked my collar and cuffs, ready for the performance.

"I'll be there in five," I said. "And have them make sure my tea is boiling."

46

LONG INTO THE NIGHT

That evening, I walked—though maybe not as aimlessly as I told myself. The windows of the *Provincial Gazette* glowed dimly with lantern light. All around, Cambridge was quiet. I hesitated, then went to the door and pushed it open. Madeleine Spenser sat hunched over a bench, setting type by herself. She looked up at me, startled, then sat back, waiting for me to say something.

"May I?"

"Of course."

The smell of ink enveloped me as I closed the door behind me. A lone lantern burned at the bench where she worked.

"I heard about your father this afternoon," I said. "I'm very sorry."

"Thank you. You're kind to say so."

"You've lost a lot," I said. "It's a wretched thing to go through."

She looked at the work before her. "Do you know, it's funny. This was all I could think to do. Another essay. More thoughts, more opinions, more words. One letter at a time. It keeps my mind occupied."

"I understand. Believe me."

"The risk you took to save Gerald and me was quite, well, insane," she said.

"Possibly. But it had a certain *utility* to it, wouldn't you say?"

She inclined her head. "Tell me: did your losses make you do it?"

"Jump into the ghost realm?"

"That. And all the rest of it. Everything you've built. Everything you've done. Is that what you can turn heartache into?"

"I suppose you just make of it what you can. Or what you have to."

She motioned to the stool on the next bench. "You can sit if you'd like."

I did, running my gaze over the ink-stained cubbies full of type. So much potential, so much that could be expressed. Made real. It was another form of enchantment, really. "It reminds me of my workshop."

"What was he like—August Swaine?"

"Madeleine, you're the one grieving," I said. "Tell me about your father."

She held my eye. "Only if you tell me about Swaine afterward."

Sometimes the greatest magic one can achieve is simply to be present, and to listen. And so I listened long into the night. The moon rolled across the sky, silvering the river, and eventually arcing to the dawn.

We each get a few nights in our lives—do we not?—which will stay with us long after they've passed.

47

IN THE HANDS OF A MASTER PRACTITIONER

The woods bordering Salem stretched away beyond the other side of the river. A mist softened the air where water crashed down a noisy falls. I got off my horse. The foundations of the mill nudged the river. Beams of raw lumber reached skyward, crossed with thick joists.

"It's coming along," I called out. "It will be lovely when it's finished."

The miller paused his work at a pair of sawhorses, squinting his eyes against the bright morning sunshine. "Minister Finch." He turned to admire the sight. "Aye, she'll be wonderful when she's done, ma'am."

"It looks like you're ready to raise a building that will stand for a century. Or longer. All the pieces in place. You're a man with a vision." I picked my way between piles of beams, timber, foundation stones. "Though I didn't realize a sawmill could be a *she*."

He walked me through the site, explaining his plans, laying out his vision. Surrounded by his own handiwork, outside of the pressures of the Council Hall of Ten Gables, the hesitation in his voice was gone. I found it encouraging. Beyond us, the river swirled down amongst the boulders, riotous currents spilling, braiding, curling. I admired how the water split, wound, folded in on itself—like time.

Time was on my mind. How it flowed. How it divided.

How it might—in the hands of a master practitioner—be manipulated.

I glanced at the woods across the flowing river. "You're getting on well? Not troubled by spirits?"

"It can get a little lonesome after sunset. But I try to not let my imagination get the better of me." He pushed back the floppy hat from his head. "Why—should I be worried?"

"No," I said. "You'll be fine. I'm just glad to see your sawmill is coming together so well. As you say, she'll be lovely."

He'd be safe, I'd see to it: I was the Governor's Witch, after all.

Would you like to read the letter Finch had Clara post to Georgina Rush? Join my Readers Club and I'll send you a link to it.

It's easy, just sign up here: **Join Newsletter**

The Readers Club is my private monthly newsletter. It's a great way to keep up to date on my upcoming books and novellas, and exclusive offers and content.

As a welcome, I'll also send you the free ebook of Sorcery of the Stony Heart *(the prequel novella to* The Books of Conjury*), along with* A Spark of Will: The Trans-Atlantic Diary of August Swaine, *an exclusive novelette you can't get anywhere else.*

ALSO BY KEVAN DALE

The Books of Conjury:

The Magic of Unkindness

The Grave Raven

The Halls of Midnight

Sorcery of the Stony Heart

The Books of Conjury: The Complete Trilogy

Other novels:

Ghost at Dusk

Revolutionary Dead

The Devil's Key

Shades of the Grave: A Horror Collection

Find out more at www.kevandale.com